SHARON FIFFER

DEAD GUY'S STUFF

St. Martin's Paperbacks

DEAD GUY'S STUFF

Copyright © 2002 by Sharon Fiffer.

Cover photograph by Herman Estévez.

Library of Congress Catalog Card Number: 2002021368

ISBN: 0-312-98680-7
EAN: 80312-98680-3

Printed in the United States of America

St. Martin's Press hardcover edition / October 2002
St. Martin's Paperbacks edition / October 2003

St. Martin's Paperbacks are published by St. Martin's Press, 175 Fifth Avenue, New York, NY 10010.

10 9 8 7 6 5 4 3 2

YOU'VE GOT MAIL . . .

In the moment in which the backroom went dark, they heard a thud, breaking of glass, and another thud in the front of the EZ Way Inn. Nellie, then Jane, then Don ran into the barroom and saw the front window broken, jagged glass now framing the neon DON AND NELLIE'S that hung independently in the window. A brick lay on the floor, and Jane picked it up, untaping the paper wrapped around it.

I know what you did. I know where the
bodies are buried. Same money.
Same time. Same place.

PRAISE FOR SHARON FIFFER'S
KILLER STUFF

For Steve, always
For Nellie, finally

ACKNOWLEDGMENTS

Thanks to my husband and favorite writer, Steve Fiffer, and our children, Kate, Nora, and Rob, who provide creative inspiration, artistic stimulation, and suffer take-out food and messy clutter like true stoics. I am lucky enough to have friends who are willing to share their expertise—thank you, Judy Groothuis and Dr. Dennis Groothuis. Thanks to Cas Rooney, who offers unfailing friendship along with unbeatable research. Thanks to Thom Bishop for encouragement and a fine working title. Thank you, Gail Hochman, Kelley Ragland, and Ben Sevier for everything—cover to cover.

The EZ Way Inn, Bishop McNamara High School, and Kankakee, Illinois, are all quite real and have enriched my life in countless ways. Although some names and places in *Dead Guy's Stuff* might sound familiar, Jane Wheel's friends and family are, alas, fictional. The true exploits of the real Don and Nellie would never be believed—even as fiction.

1

How do you know, Jane Wheel wondered, not for the first time, whether or not your rituals, your own little signature gestures, are celebrations of your individuality and part of your own quirky charm or if they are neurotic tics, proof positive that you suffer from obsessive-compulsive disorder?

For example, at estate sales, as Jane warmed up once inside the house, immersed in the possessions of another, she began humming, sometimes quite loudly, as she thumbed through books, rifled drawers, ran her fingers around the edges of bowls and rims of glassware. Humming seemed innocent enough.

What about the constant checking for car keys in one pocket, checkbook and identification in another, and cold cash in a third? Her fourth pocket, upper left, held a small notebook and tiny mechanical pencil that advertised: GOOSEY UPHOLSTERY—TAKE A GANDER AT OUR FABRICS. Under the slogan was the telephone number WELLS 2-5206. Natural enough to check your pockets in a crowd. She did pat them in a special order, but that was probably something to do with muscle memory or neurological instinct. Right, left on the bottom; right, left on the top. Perhaps left-handed people who checked their pockets moved left to right, top to bottom. She would keep an eye on her friend Tim. He was a lefty.

It was 9:00 A.M. and Jane had just received her number for the sale. Doors would open at nine-thirty, so she had some time for her presale voodoo in the car. She patted her pockets, swallowed a sip of her now lukewarm coffee—after all, it had been sitting there as long as she had, two and a half hours, waiting for the numbers.

Pulling out her little notebook, she checked her list. She had a small sketch of a Depression glass pattern that a friend had asked her to look for and several children's book titles that Miriam, her dealer friend in Ohio, was currently searching for. God, she didn't want to have to fight the book people, but Miriam had said condition didn't matter on these. Miriam had a customer who was after illustrations and would remove them from damaged books that the real book hunters would cast aside. Both Jane and Miriam had shuddered at that. They were both strongly against the adulteration of almost any object, unless of course it was already in tatters and one could feel noble about the salvage. A thoroughly moth-eaten coat from the thirties could have its Bakelite buttons removed. Bakelite buckles and clips that had already been damaged and jewelry already broken or deeply cracked could be refashioned, but by god, Martha Stewart, keep your glue gun away from intact buttons and beads.

Jane's list had the other usual suspects. Flowerpots, vintage sewing notions, crocheted pot holders, bark cloth, all her favorites. She was also hunting old Western objects—linens, blankets, lampshades with cowboys and

Indians, horse-head coat hooks. Tim's sister had just had a baby boy, and Tim was already planning the upgrade from nursery to toddler's room and had settled on turning this small corner of a suburban colonial into a set from *Spin and Marty*, the dude ranch serial from the original—the one that mattered—*Mickey Mouse Club*.

"Not so politically correct, sweetie, but we'll morph into an Adirondack fishing camp if the whole cowboy-Indie thing gets too Village People for the bro-in-law," Tim had said when she'd talked to him earlier in the week.

Jane had only five minutes to write down her Lucky Five. At every house sale, to pass the interminable waiting time, Jane tried to guess by looking at the outside of the house what the inside would hold. She wrote down five objects, and if they were all in the house, she allowed herself an extra fifty dollars to spend for the day. The game didn't exactly make sense, she knew, since if she won, she lost: fifty dollars. But playing the Lucky Five was so satisfying.

She studied the compact Chicago brick bungalow, located a few blocks from Saint Ita's Church. The front side-walk had cracked, and the brickwork on the front steps was in disrepair. The classified ad had said "a lifetime of possessions," "a clean sale, a full basement," and the most delightful tease of all, "we haven't even unpacked all the boxes."

Jane listed the Lucky Five: Ice-O-Matic ice crusher (with red handle); a volume of *Reader's Digest Condensed Books*, including a title by Pearl S. Buck; a Bakelite rosary; pink Coates and Clarke seam binding wrapped around a 1931 "spool pet" card.

Jane looked at her watch. She needed another item fast, and she was blank. She punched at her cellular phone.

"Yeah? Talk loud."

Jane could hear a lot of people in the background. Tim must already be inside some sale or at least scrambling for a place in line.

"I need one last thing for my list!" Jane screamed.

"An advertising key ring with a five-digit telephone number!" Tim screamed back.

"Good."

"Green," he added.

"What?" Jane asked.

"Got to be green. When are you coming down here?"

The phone cut out and Jane unplugged it from the lighter and locked it in the glove compartment. It was almost time. She patted her pockets and drained her coffee. Parked just ahead of her was that nasty woman who had once sent her on a wild goose chase, told her about a great sale, and when Jane got to the address it was a vacant lot. Donna, Jane had named her, for no particular reason other than the fact that she liked her enemies to have names.

Did Donna have a lower number? Would she beat Jane through the front door? *So what if she does,* Jane told herself. She would race through the house with blinders on, allow no distractions, and beat Donna and everyone else to the treasures.

She would make a beeline down the stairs of this sweet brick bungalow on Chicago's northwest side and be drawn magnetically to the current object of her desire— whatever it was. She would know it when she saw it. Maybe a '40s brown leather Hartmann vanity case with intact mirror and clean, sky blue, watered silk lining. Jane would snap the sharp locks that would fly open with a clear pop and find the case filled to the brim with . . .

With what? This was the good part, the gut-wrenching, heart pounding, nerve-racking question. The speculation. The suspense. The mystery of it all. It was why, whenever she went to house sales, flea markets, garage sales, or rummage sales, she tried to come home with at least one box, suitcase, basket, or container filled with unknown stuff. Buttons, pins, broken jewelry, office supplies, fabric scraps, photos, maps, a junk drawer with a handle was what she wanted to carry home and sort through at her own kitchen table.

When a friend once asked her why she bought so many locked metal boxes, so many jammed suitcases, containers that required crowbars, chisels, screwdrivers, picks, and brute force to open, she shrugged. What kind of a person resists a grab bag? Especially when it costs only a dollar or two? Who doesn't want to own a secret?

Charley, her-not-nearly-estranged-enough-but-nevertheless-maybe-soon-to-be-ex-husband, likened her sifting to his own methods in the field searching for fossils.

"We not only collect the bones, we collect the earth around them. We need to know about the plants, the insects, everything that provides us with clues as to how the creature, whatever the particular creature we're excavating, lived," he said, explaining to their son, Nick, the vials of soil that lined the crowded desk in the den where he often worked weekends, despite the fact that he no longer officially lived in the house.

"Like what Mom does with her buttons and stuff,

but . . ." Nicky stopped himself from even forming the whole thought. He might be only a middle-schooler, but he possessed the cautious wisdom of the child hoping for the reconciliation of his parents. He was savvy enough to stop any remark that might smack of a value judgment on their respective work. He certainly didn't want his mother's relatively new "professional picker" status to be put under his father's microscope.

"But what?" asked Jane, who had been eyeing the bottles of soil herself, thinking that the caps looked like they might be black Bakelite.

Nick shrugged his shoulders and looked at Charley.

"When we're in the field, we're looking for answers to big questions about life on earth, and when Mom is in the field, at an estate sale . . ."

"Yes, Professor?" asked Jane, coming to full attention. "What is *she* doing?"

"She's observing how one person or one family operated during their day-to-day lives," Charley said smoothly. "She's gathering the debris of popular culture of the thirties, the forties, whatever. She's keeping field notes on what people saved, what they deemed usable or beautiful. She observes what is still held by our society to be valuable and cycles those objects into the world as artifacts on display at the contemporary extension of the living museum . . . the flea market tables and antique malls of the Midwest."

"Nicely done, Charley," Jane said, ruffling his uncombed hair.

Nick felt his heart rise, attached to a small, hope-filled balloon. His father would give up the tiny apartment five blocks away from their house and move back home full-time. Nick would not need the doubles on shin guards, basketball shoes, and school clothes that so many of his friends kept in their two separate bedrooms. So far, he had not needed a bedroom at all in his father's shoebox studio. Charley just came over three or four times a week and most weekends to work, eat, sleep, hang out. Nick's friends assured him it wouldn't stay that way, all loose and friendly. Pretty soon, they warned him, things would get ugly, doors would be slammed, locks would be changed, and suitcases would be packed. Furniture would most definitely be rearranged.

No, thought Nick. He might only be an adolescent, but he saw how his father looked at his mother while she was watering her plants or dusting her old books or spooning coffee into the pot. He watched Jane follow Charley with her eyes as he crossed back and forth to the large reference books on the dictionary stand in the den. Sure, Nick was only a sixth grader, but he watched television, read books, played video games. His parents were still in love.

Jane hadn't thought much about whether or not she and Charley should make their separation official. In fact, she wasn't sure they were separated enough to give their situation a name. Neither had turned their back on the marriage exactly. Each had turned their shoulders slightly away from the other, picked up a foot to walk, but had not really let it touch the ground, fall into a step.

Yes, Jane had started the slow turn away when she kissed a neighbor last spring and another neighbor had spread it through the block like the plague. But Jane hadn't kissed Jack Balance because she was dissatisfied with

Charley or her marriage. She had kissed Jack because she was dissatisfied with herself, with her own predictable life.

Had she wanted things to grow quite as unpredictable as they had? When she found Sandy, Jack's wife, murdered, her new life as a picker drew her deeper and deeper into a world of crime and suspicion. Concentrating on finding the murderer and discovering clues as well as estate sale treasures had prevented her from thinking much about her marriage gone wrong, especially with Charley off on a dig for the summer in South Dakota.

But since he and Nick, now a well-trained and enthusiastic field assistant, had returned from their exploration, the September routine of teaching classes for Charley, school and soccer for Nick, and fall rummage and flea markets for her had lulled all of them into their old routines. Charley still did much of his work at their house. When Jane brought him a cup of tea with lemon while he graded papers in the den, it was the continuation of a long and comfortable habit. Neither saw any compelling reason to alter the current arrangement. Since she was now keeping the irregular hours of a picker rather than the corporate hours of an advertising executive, Jane counted on Charley to cover for her on weekends when she left the house at 4:00 A.M. to line up at estate and rummage sales, flea markets, and auction previews.

Earlier that very morning, she had left Charley sleeping peacefully on the couch in the den when she tiptoed out the front door into the still darkness. Now, sitting in her car, she read over her "wants" lists, both her own and the ones she kept for Miriam in Ohio and Tim in Kankakee, and reviewed the Lucky Five. Tucking the notebook back into its proper pocket, she let her mind wander. She watched the latecomers scurrying out of their vans and trucks to snag a numbered ticket from the roll on the porch of the house, whose contents would soon enough be scavenged and scattered to the four winds, and pondered her "separation" from Charley.

A marriage, she thought, trying to open an old-but-new-to-her Bonnie Raitt CD she had found, still sealed, at a garage sale just last week and stashed in the glove compartment, is a lot like this packaging. Even if you manage to open the wrapping, get a fingernail under a corner fold and make a start, the transparent wrap clings so tenaciously to the plastic cover that it's nearly impossible to get to the music inside. If she and Charley did manage to separate and listen to what played beneath, around, and under their marriage, would they run back to the comfortable togetherness they had shared for fifteen years or move on to a new and unsteady beat?

Enough pondering. Hearing the sound of car doors slamming, Jane dropped the still-unopened CD on the seat. Down the street, one door had opened and, as if they were all connected by an invisible wire, each early bird had followed the leader. Dealers, pickers, and bargain hunters opened their trucks and vans and stretched, making their way to the porch, where the busybodies who always bossed everyone around were already checking numbers, lining everybody up.

Jane remembered her first estate sale three years ago all too well. The ad in the paper had said that numbers would be given out at 8:30 A.M. for a 9:00 A.M. opening. Jane had allowed extra time, thinking maybe she should get there around eight-fifteen in order to get a good number. By the time she made it up to the door to receive her ticket, she was number 181. Listening to those around her and making sure she loitered close enough to the door to hear what the low numbers were discussing, she heard one ponytailed man say he had gotten there at five-thirty because he had overslept and that the Speller sisters had beaten him again. He had gestured to two gaunt, gray women who were chain-smoking Marlboro Reds under a tree, staring into space.

It was a complicated stare that Jane had begun to notice on almost all of the regular sale goers. She was still trying to decipher it and, at the same time, mimic it. One part conjuring—let the items we want be inside that house—as if by sheer mental force one could make that china be the correct pattern of Spode, make that lampshade bear the Tiffany signature—and one part dead-eye focus—let the route into and through the house be without distraction. It was the look of an animal wearing blinders, with only the path ahead visible. Jane now practiced her own version of the stare. It might not make the carved Bakelite bracelet appear in the bottom of a basket of cheap junk jewelry, but it kept people from making idle chatter, distracting one from the true and straight path, the purpose of the hunt.

Donna was two numbers ahead of her. Seven to Jane's nine. How had Jane let that happen? She didn't really know her, this small, speedy woman with a crooked mouth and pinball eyes that darted from your face to your purse to whatever object you were holding in your hand, this woman who sent you off to phantom sales.

"What do you do with those buttons?" she had yelled at Jane once at a rummage sale, and Jane had been so taken aback, both by being spoken to at all and by being asked a direct question about the functional value of what she was buying, that she had simply shaken her head and shrugged. Being questioned about a purchase could ruin the moment so thoroughly that it never even occurred to Jane that it would be fun to shop with a partner. To have to discuss why the fabric squares and rickrack looked so appealing, to have to explain why one salt-and-pepper shaker appealed, but not the other, to have to convince someone that people really collected mechanical advertising pencils and that a shoebox full of them marked two dollars made perfect sense? The horror. The Donna of it all.

The doors opened and the first fifteen were admitted, handing over their tickets and entering the house like a greedy pack of dogs. Jane heard a man's voice behind her, angry about the number system. She turned to look at the source.

"Nine o'clock the paper says and nine o'clock we're here. What's the deal? Who you gotta . . . ?" Jane turned around and tuned out the voice. *Another new guy,* Jane thought, *Where do they come from? Aren't there enough dealers and pickers now? Can't we just close the tunnel and say, Sorry, full up?*

Jane paused in the small tiled entry and tried to take in everything at once. The living room on her right held the tables with plates, glasses, stemware, and some pottery figures. A case next to the all-business card table with calculator and newspapers for wrapping the more fragile objects held finer jewelry, pocket knives, and small artifacts of eighty years on earth, sixty years in one house. Hat pins, tape measures in Bakelite cases that advertised insurance companies, their four-digit phone numbers recalling a time when one phone line was all anyone ever needed and the possibility of running out of numbers, creating new exchanges and area codes, would have been a joke pulled from a bad science fiction novel. Inside the case were several sterling silver thimbles, which gave Jane hope that there would be buttons. A seamstress hoarded buttons and rickrack and old zippers, tucked them away into basement drawers, and stuffed plastic bags full of them into guest-room closets. That Coates and Clarke seam binding might be right around the bend. In the corner of the cabinet were three gold initial pins from the 1940s. Jane stretched to read them, then realized she would not have to make up a name and fit it to the initials, "RN." *A nurse,* Jane thought. *Perfect. Clean, well organized, good linens.*

All this information and conjecture took no more than five to seven seconds to gather, while Jane got the lay of the land from the tiny foyer. She shook herself out of her reverie on the house's owner and took off in search of stuff.

The kitchen. Jane grabbed a seven-inch Texasware pink-marbled plastic bowl from a box under the table and held it up to the worker standing at attention, pencil in one hand, receipt book in the other. "Fifty cents?" she answered to Jane's wordless question. Jane nodded, and the woman scribbled it down, starting Jane's tab.

Jane filled the bowl with a Bakelite-handled bottle opener, a wooden-handled ice pick, and four small advertising calendars illustrated with watercolors of dogs. The calendars were from the twenties and the picture, POODLE WITH BOBBED HAIR, touched Jane's heart. They were also in perfect condition, taken from a kitchen drawer filled with Chicago city street guides from the thirties and forties, old phone directories, worn address books, some stray S&H Green stamps. Jane's heart filled with appreciation and desire as she realized just how much and how carefully this woman had saved.

Before she left the kitchen, Jane snatched up the oversized oak recipe file. She collected the wooden boxes sized for 3 × 5 cards, sorting buttons and gumball machine charms into them, but this box was more than twice that size and it was overflowing with handwritten cards, yellowing newspaper clippings, and stained cardboard recipes that had been cut from Jell-O and cracker and cereal boxes.

"Six?" asked the worker, barely looking up.

Jane thought the tag on the box said ten, but it was hard to see, and she didn't have two free hands to fiddle with it, so she nodded. Six was probably too much, but if the tag said ten, it was a bargain, wasn't it? The kitchen was so satisfying, filled with the kind of well-maintained but used and loved vintage items that spoke so convincingly to Jane's soul. Take me home, they all said, loud and clear. At least that's what Jane thought she heard them say as she hustled through the kitchen. A souvenir of Florida spoon rest, hand-crocheted pot holders, tiled trivets that some child had labored over in the crafts room of summer camp.

An ice crusher! Not an Ice-O-Matic, though, and Jane never cheated on the Lucky Five.

This was a forties to fifties household where the mother probably stayed home with the kids, baked cookies, and packed healthy sack lunches. Jane's thoughts lingered on the sack lunches, remembering back to elementary school meals in Saint Patrick's Grade School cafeteria. The food had been unrecognizable and inedible. She'd begged her mother to allow her to bring lunch, but Nellie, ever the practical woman and only occasionally the empathetic mom, had been thrilled with the modern addition of a cafeteria where students could buy a hot lunch. Nellie would no longer have to slather peanut butter and jelly on Wonder bread and wrap up chips and fruit every night.

Realizing she could skim off one more chore from her already too filled night of housework after nine hours work at the EZ Way Inn, Nellie refused to listen to the complaints about slimy macaroni slathered in ketchup, unrecognizable chunks of meat in a gluey gravy over slippery instant mashed potatoes. Not wanting to waste time with the lengthy explanation of how tired she was at the end of a long day of cooking, serving, and tending bar, Nellie didn't bother to explain the reasoning behind her decision.

"Eat the hot lunch . . . it won't kill you," she'd said.

"My mom thinks it's more nutritious for me," Jane had said, stirring a mysterious mix of meat and rice, explaining to her friends who occasionally shared a cookie or orange segment with her from their own brown bags.

Jane, forgetting all about lunches, brown bag or otherwise, hummed as she walked carefully down to the basement, ducking her head and stowing her finds into a large plastic totebag that she carried with her to all sales. Thoughts of Nellie might have sneaked into the kitchen with her, but Jane refused to take her along as she continued through the house. Donna was still going through kitchen cupboards, and although Jane feared her rival would be the one to find the blue Pyrex mixing bowl that would complete the set that sat waiting in Jane's basement, she knew it was pointless to stand behind Donna and watch her. Better to strike off in a new direction. Better to sniff around in the basement.

She noted that her assessment of the owner, a nurse, had been correct. Objects did seem clean and well packed, neatly organized on crude, built-in shelves in all four of the spotless basement rooms. There was a little storage area off the laundry room that looked dusty and promising for boxes of unsorted odd dishes and holiday decorations, but Jane decided to scan the shelves left to right, top to bottom in each of the rooms first.

She moved off to her right and found herself in the middle of First Aid Central. Boxes and boxes of gauze bandages, sealed bottles of disinfectant and saline solutions, rolls of tape were stacked floor to ceiling. Two women, neighbors or friends from the sound of their conversation, were already in there, one of them cramming rolls of paper tape into a wicker shopping basket.

"Couldn't take it back legally, even if it was sealed. She said a lot of the patients and families just told her to get it out of their houses and donate it somewhere," said the one collecting the tape. "Mary said she was going to send it through the church to some places where they'd take anything, you know, any kind of medical supplies."

"Was the owner a visiting nurse?" asked Jane, breaking two of her rules—asking a question and getting distracted by the owner's history instead of the owner's stuff.

Both women looked at Jane, not surprised at all that someone might want to chat during the feeding frenzy of a house sale. Yes, they were Mary's friends and neighbors, amateurs, not dealers or professionals.

"No, not Mary. She was a nurse a long time ago, but it's her granddaughter who's a visiting nurse, gets these supplies. Mary just wanted them not to go to waste."

Jane nodded, enjoying the contact with Mary through these two old friends.

"Mary saved all of everybody's things. Her husband's stuff is in that other room, and he's been dead for nearly thirty years."

Jane tried to keep an appropriately sympathetic expression—after all, Mary's husband *had* been dead for thirty years—and not show the callous joy she felt when she pictured some of the vintage clothes and office supplies that might be in the adjoining room.

"Was Mary's husband a doctor?" asked Jane, spotting and seizing a buttery leather doctor's bag on the floor.

Both women laughed and the one who seemed to be in charge of talking for the pair said, "Oh no, dear. Bateman owned the Shangri-La."

When Jane shook her head and shrugged, the silent partner whispered, "It was a tavern. Bateman was a saloon keeper."

Jane hoped the women didn't think her rude, but she turned away almost immediately. She couldn't move quickly enough into the "Bateman" corner of the basement. A saloon keeper! Eureka! Pay dirt! Gold in them thar hills. If she had the flexibility of an animated cartoon character, she would have kicked up her heels and leapt into the next room. She sighed with pure rapture when she saw the similarly organized and shelved remnants of thirty years in the tavern business, all of it clean, boxed, folded, and tagged.

Jane wiped the corners of her mouth with her sleeve, just in case she had inadvertently drooled.

Don and Nellie, Jane's parents, had operated the EZ Way Inn in Kankakee for forty years. A ramshackle building across from the now-closed stove factory that had given the town so much employment, so much prosperity, the EZ Way Inn was as charming on the inside as it was tacky on the outside. Don had never been able to talk Gustavus Duncan, the owner, into selling the building.

For forty years, Don had paid rent on the flimsy shack, shoring up and improving the interior, praying that a heavy wind wouldn't blow it all into kindling overnight. Don always called himself a "saloon keeper," considering that to be the most honest description of what he did. He never gave up though. Each first of the month, along with his rent check, he extended the offer to buy. Four hundred and eighty offers finally worked their magic. Last month Gus Duncan had finally caved.

Don had called her, his deep voice trembling with excitement.

"I'm buying the place, honey," he said. "I guess now that the factory's been closed for twenty-five years, old Gus decided nobody's going to give a million to mow down the EZ Way and make it into a parking lot."

Jane hadn't asked if it was still a worthwhile investment since her father had lately talked about retiring at least once a week. She didn't want to do anything that would temper his excitement about this deal, this sale that would give him so much joy. She would leave that up to her mother, Nellie, who had been throwing cold water on Don's plans for thirty years.

"Now I'll be a tavern owner instead of a saloon keeper."

"Pay raise?" Jane asked.

"Pay cut, but I get a bigger office," Don said, describing the building improvements he was planning.

The improvements were scaled down considerably when Don realized that no credible carpenter would guarantee that the building wouldn't collapse if they tried to break out a wall or extend the roofline. Every contractor who had ever sipped a Miller sitting at the big oak bar inside the EZ Way told Don the same thing.

"Doctor up the bathroom plumbing and bring the electrical into the twentieth century, *mid*-twentieth century. Don't even consider the twenty-first. Any bigger improvements might prove disastrous."

"Hell, Don, I believe my electric drill could knock a wall down," said Eugene Smalley, a customer and cabinet maker. "Let's put in some bigger windows and add some lights so a guy can see if he has trump when he's playing euchre and leave it at that."

Nellie had told Jane last week that the carpentry was done and they were planning on having a grand opening next month.

"After forty years in this place, your dad's acting like a teenager with a new car," Nellie had said.

When Jane asked how it looked with bigger windows and improved lighting and bathrooms, her mother had snorted.

"All the better to see the dirt and dust with. We was better off when it was dark so you couldn't see where the walls don't quite meet or the cracks in the ceiling."

"Is Dad going to paint and redecorate?"

"Has to. Plaster cracked all over the place when they did the windows. I haven't been able to make a pot of soup in a month because of the dust."

By next week, the painting and plastering and pounding would be finished, and Don had promised Jane that she could come in and decorate. That is, she could decide where the beer distributor's big calendar and the bulletin boards where Don posted the golf league standings and the bowling league scores would hang.

"Same place, if you ask me," said Nellie during their "conference call," which meant Nellie was listening in on the bedroom extension while Don called Jane from the kitchen.

Jane had been planning some surprises though. She had found some great vintage signs, old beer advertising trays that could be hung, even an old high school trophy case that she figured could stand in the corner for a display of Kankakee photos and tavern memorabilia. She had collected Kankakee postcards for years, made inexpensive copies, and enlarged them to make a Kankakee River montage that she couldn't wait to show her dad.

And now she was smack dab in the middle of a tavern memorabilia collector's dream. It was only twenty minutes into the sale and a small-enough house that the first twenty or thirty shoppers were her only competition. Because the

19

other basement rooms seemed to be filled with vintage tools and a radio workshop—she spotted some great-looking Bakelite cases sitting on one of the shelves and another room had racks of spotless vintage dresses and hats—most of the dealers were keeping busy and out of Jane's way.

There were several neighbors, Jane now realized, milling around the basement, whispering about Mary and Bateman. Her two new friends from the medical supply storage corner had followed her, and one of them now pointed to a group photo, framed on the wall.

"That's Dorothy and me right there, the year our bowling team won the league." The more talkative of the pair took down the photo and held it close. In it, twenty women were grouped around a huge trophy. They wore silk bowling shirts, with individually sewn letters spelling SHANGRI-LA across the front. The black and white was so clear and well-preserved that Jane could read DOROTHY stitched over the pocket of the laughing woman with blonde curls and OLIVIA over the pocket of the much younger version of this now gray-haired fount of information.

"You're Olivia?"

She nodded. "Ollie, honey, just Ollie. There's Mary." She pointed to a voluptuous blonde in the front captured forever waving a cigarette and vamping for the photographer. Bateman, maybe?

"She looks like a movie star," Jane whispered, all notions of the plump, kindly nurse sending extra medical supplies to Third World countries disappearing and being replaced with a bad girl, B-movie starlet pouting in front of her martini at the Shangri-La.

"Mary was a beauty," said Dorothy. It was the first time Jane had heard her speak in a voice louder than a whisper. Ollie was clearly the talker.

"Still is. I bet she gets a husband by Christmas," Ollie said, and they both giggled.

Jane had found a kind of laundry cart or wooden dolly, a crate on wheels, and was loading it up while they talked. When she saw that they didn't want the bowling photograph—both said they had copies at home—she stuck it into the crate and kept filling. Boxes of old advertising shot glasses, Bakelite ashtrays, and a motherload of dice, decks of cards, and coasters.

"A husband?" Jane asked. "She isn't . . . she didn't . . ."

"Nursing home. Fell and broke her ankle and Susan, a visiting nurse and her own granddaughter, thinks she ought to live somewhere other than her own house," said Ollie.

"It's an assisted-living apartment, Ollie, and it's very nice," corrected Dorothy. "Susan can't care for her full-time, and she wanted her to be safe."

"Holy Toledo!" said Jane, using just the kind of archaic exclamation that her son, Nick, was trying to eliminate from her vocabulary, at least around his friends, and just the kind of expression that endeared her to Dorothy and Ollie.

"Punchboards," she told them. "There must be a dozen in this box. All sealed with their keys in the back."

The peaks and valleys of a childhood spent waiting in the tavern for your parents to end their day when the bartender arrived at six are few and far between. Waiting was mostly a plateau. A dry, arid, flat stretch of boredom and whining. Don would need a few more minutes to count out the register, leaving only a small bank for the night bartender. Nellie, roped into a euchre game as a fourth after all the soup bowls were washed and put away, all the ketchup and mustard bottles wiped clean, needed a few more minutes to win one with her partner. Jane wandered on the desert plain of waiting, reading, for the three hundredth time, the bowling scores posted on the bulletin board. It was a happy day when the jukebox man had been there in the morning, removing the nine-month-old hit songs and replacing them with three-month-old hit songs. Carp or Joe or Vince would flip her a quarter and tell her to pick out five, and she would take her time, drawing out the luxury of having new titles to read. Maybe if she took long enough, her parents would actually finish whatever they were doing and ask *her* when *she* was going to be ready. Maybe she would be able to shush them, hold up a finger, and mouth a patronizing "a few more minutes, that's all, just a few more minutes."

But the highest point, the peak that defined a mountaintop, was the day Don set out a new punchboard, a one-inch-thick piece of pressed particle board punctuated with a grid of foil-covered holes waiting for you to insert a key punch and push through a tightly rolled cylinder of paper. Was there ever a more satisfying activity? Pay your quarter, study the board for clues, cross your fingers, choose your spot, push the key hard through one of the holes, puncture the foil, force the paper out onto the bar, unroll, and read the numbers. Jane remembered that fives were usually lucky. A sequence with fives or multiples of fives was a winner. A box of chocolates, usually chocolate-covered cherries, was the prize, and there were few customers left at the EZ Way Inn by six o'clock who had anyone waiting at home who they wanted to surprise with a box of candy.

Bored stove factory workers, whiling away the time until the loneliest hours of their day were gone, would pay Don, Nellie, whoever was at the bar, a dollar and signal for the punch board to be brought over. Then they'd crook their fingers at Jane, calling her over for good luck, and ask her to punch out a winner. If she did, she got to keep the candy, a whole box for herself; and if she lost, she still got the glorious pleasure of punching out those tiny paper pills of hope. Don had once referred to a customer who played the board incessantly as having "gambling fever," and Jane hadn't known what he was talking about. Gambling was sweaty men in a backroom rolling dice, wasn't it? Or tuxedoed James Bond types at a Baccarat table, yes?

No, Don had told her. He described gambling fever, and she recognized her own symptoms—the tiny beads of perspiration that broke out on her upper lip, the intense need to swallow, and the fullness in her chest when Vince called her over and threw down a dollar. That moment of tension and release when he told her to punch out some winners, that satisfying fit of the key into the punchboard . . . *that* was gambling.

Jane held JACKPOT CHARLEY in her hands. Twenty-five cents could win you a dollar and a chance to punch out a jackpot winner, another five or even twenty-five dollars. ALL AWARDS PAID IN TRADE it read. Don had always had candy punchboards, but here in Bateman's corner of the basement, Jane ran her hands over money boards, radio and television prize boards, and a small, round MORE SMOKES board where you bought a punch for a nickel and a winning number got you five packages of cigarettes.

Jane snapped back to the present. She looked at Dorothy and Ollie, who had become energetic helpers, putting leather dice cups and Bakelite dice, boxes of glass jars, bar towels with SHANGRI-LA embroidered in rainbow colors into her makeshift shopping cart. Jane had been a picker only a few months. Timid and still distracted by the owner's history, she had often let the owners' property, what she was really at a sale for, slip away. She had to make a quick decision and the right offer. Prices were low in this room. Clearly the sales team expected to get their money from Mary's fabulous vintage clothes and the "smalls" upstairs.

Bateman's old inventory was nickel-and-dime compared to the stuff in the rest of the house. Because this was a separate room with a door, a sales representative stood with a clipboard and pencil, ready to add the cost of the odd shot glass to your ticket. Jane hoped this was an owner, someone in authority and not just a helpful friend of the sales team, wearing an apron for the day just for the opportunity for early bird shopping.

Jane went up to her and talked low and fast. "I'll give you three hundred dollars for the whole room." Jane hesitated only a second, then upped her ante, "Five hundred and we tape it off right now."

Jane had never made such a bold offer. She had seen rooms sold though. Once she had been at a sale during the last hour and tried to go into a bedroom, getting tangled in some string across the doorway where a Donna type had

24

barred entry with her body and waved her away. "I bought this room; it's all mine. See the string? I own the room."

This sale had only been going on twenty-five minutes at the most, and clearly this was a last-hour offer. Its appeal was the figure. Three hundred was a fair wholesale price for everything in this corner room, and five hundred was a fair retail price. Jane knew she would have to get the saleswoman's full attention. One of the other helpers was distracting her, telling her about some man who had tried to slip her a twenty to get to the front of the line. "Can you imagine?" she was saying. "Thought he could just buy me off? The people in line would kill me if I started taking tips like that."

"Look, Lois," Jane said, reading the name tag on her apron, "I'm a decorator and I'm doing a recreation room as a vintage bar. You're not going to get that much money for all this stuff even if you sell everything here individually for your asking price. And you know you're not going to get the tagged prices on all of it."

Five minutes later, Jane offered Dorothy and Ollie their choice of some of the Shangri-La souvenirs or cash if they'd help guard the door while she carried Mary's neatly taped boxes and bags out to the old van she and Charley still shared. They were terribly excited over meeting a real interior decorator and waved away any notion of payment.

"Mary'll be tickled pink when she finds out the Shangri-La is going to live on in some rich person's basement," said Ollie, and Dorothy nodded. In a moment of pure picker's rapture or the hallucination of gambling fever, Jane hugged them both, then proceeded to use Dorothy's roll of paper tape from the medical supply room to seal off the space. Crisscrossing the tape over the door frame, Jane sensed something familiar in the scene. What did this remind her of?

Shaking her head at someone trying to duck around her, she said, "No. Sorry, I just bought the room." When she turned and glanced over her shoulder, it only increased her giddy delight to see Donna slinking backward over to a sales employee and complaining about a whole room being sold so early. *Let her whine,* Jane thought, *it will only make the salespeople mad and less willing to bargain with her.*

She finished taping from the outside, sticking a sold tag on the center of the tape. She nodded at Dorothy and Ollie, who were both surprisingly strong, more than up to the task of pushing the boxes to the doorway for Jane to haul. Looking back at the older women framed by the strips of tape, she realized what it all reminded her of: a crime scene. She had just bought herself a crime scene.

2

"Chocolate chips or bananas?"

"Can we have both?"

"Dad, aren't you supposed to be watching your cholesterol or something?" asked Nick.

Charley looked up from the student paper he was reading and adjusted his glasses. Why in the world would his twelve-year-old son be concerned with his lipid profile?

Nick stood in the door, wrapped in a vintage blue gingham apron with a red duck embroidered on the pocket and gestured with a red Bakelite-handled spoon. "I just read an article in the *Science Times*," Nick said, popping a few chocolate chips into his mouth. "You're entering those *at risk* years, Dad."

Charley turned around in his chair to study his son, the chef and newly minted nutritional consultant. Earnest, handsome, average height, solid, compact frame, lightly freckled, and blessed (or cursed depending on just how honest you were being with him) with his mother's deep brown eyes that bored into your own, demanding hard truth and no compromise. When had he become such a worrier, a fusser?

"The potassium in the bananas is so good for me that

27

a few chocolate chips won't hurt," Charley said. "Besides, your mother says chocolate raises your good cholesterol."

"Right," Nick said, sighing, "haven't you noticed she makes stuff like that up depending on what we have in the house?" Nick headed back to the kitchen, calling over his shoulder, "Like when all we have is a box of Lucky Charms for dinner, she tells me they're made with whole grains and marshmallows are fat free."

Charley tried to go back to reading a freshman's description of igneous formations, the same paper he had read for fifteen years—not plagiarized, just the same old thing. Those igneous formations didn't change. He put the paper back on the stack.

He and Jane had to make some decisions. Their son was turning into their parent, and although Charley avoided reading books on child raising, he knew this had to be a bad sign. *How often,* he wondered, *are they having Lucky Charms for dinner?*

Even if he had read the books on child raising that Jane had suggested, he reasoned with himself, the authors probably wrote them assuming that parents were in a fairly stable state. He had glanced at the bookstore shelves that held those volumes, uniformly designed, *Your Child at Three, Your Child at Four,* etc. What about some truly valuable advice books, like, *Being a Parent in Your Forties If You Were a Child in the Fifties?* Chapters like "How Not to Look Bored at Little League," "Where to Look Up Basketball Terms If Your Son Likes Sports and You Don't," "How to Have Sex When Your Child Stays Up Later Than You Do," "How to Discourage Your Child from Early Experimentation with Sex When You're Preoccupied with Same," "How to Talk About Drug Use Before You've Had Your Required Twenty Cups of Coffee," and so forth, might have some real value.

Charley knew he and Jane had been pretty darn good parents when Nick was an infant and a toddler. They'd carried him everywhere, arguing over who got to cinch the Snugli pack around his or her waist. They rode bikes and picnicked and cooked healthy meals. Even when Jane put in long hours at the advertising agency or was out of town supervising a commercial shoot, they managed to work it around Charley's teaching schedule so that Nick's exposure to child care was minimal, just enough to teach him to socialize and just enough so that Charley and Jane could compare themselves to other parents and come out smugly on top.

Now he and Jane had entered some kind of bizarre second childhood. Only a year ago, they had watched some reality television show on MTV and been horrified at the twenty-somethings who whined and mugged for the camera.

"I hate these people," Jane had said, passing a bowl of popcorn to Charley. They had planned on watching a video but had caught this program flipping through the channels, and it had held them like a train wreck.

Blonds and red-haired beautiful people hugged each other and wept about their ungrateful boyfriends and Stair-Master addictions and their confused and empty lives. One olive-skinned beauty lamented the loss of her favorite moisturizer. "They took it off the market, do you believe it?" She was close to sobbing.

Charley and Jane had both looked at Nick, who was

glancing back and forth from the front window to *Sports Illustrated for Kids*. Was it their fault, their responsibility as a generation of parents who overindulged their children? His father's *Sports Illustrated* had been good enough for Charley. . . . Why did Nick and his friends have everything specially scaled to them? Why did they get their own magazine, their own demographic consideration, for god's sake? Had they fallen into the trap of grooming their children to be these people, these made-for-TV, solipsistic, body-conscious consumers who now shared their deepest, darkest feelings only with each other and the MTV audience?

"No!" Jane had cried out when the commercial came on. It was one of hers. The same tribe of beautiful people, drinking imported beer and discussing the market and playing darts, whom she had coaxed into intimacy on the set, now mimicked the very set of players on the show.

Nick jumped up at the honk of a horn and waved. "Love you guys: see you in the morning," and threw the magazine down on the couch.

Jane and Charley nodded at him and waved, but remained in a horrified trance, watching this community of youthful mannequins play themselves out around a kitchen table, pointing fingers at each other for being insensitive.

One year later, Charley thought, and twenty years older than those pretty boys and girls, and now he and Jane were sounding like those twits. *Jane's trying to figure out what will satisfy her and make her happy, and I'm trying to figure out why it wasn't or isn't me*, Charley thought, taking off his glasses to clean them.

* * *

"Breakfast is ready, Dad," Nick called.

"Why three settings?" Charley asked.

"Mom loves pancakes," Nick said, expertly flipping stacks of three onto the plates.

Was Nick so upset by their quasi-separation, their selfish searches for their real selves that he was fantasizing family meals? Charley knew he had to handle this delicately, so he gently picked up the third juice glass and turned to put it back on the counter.

"Thanks, Charley," said Jane, taking it from him and draining it in one gulp. "These pancakes look fabulous, Nick."

Jane had carried at least twelve boxes into the mud-room, but Charley had been lost enough in his work and his thoughts not to hear the truck, the door, the thuds of the cartons being stacked.

"Are there more?" Charley asked, pointing toward the garage.

Jane smiled and nodded. "Let's eat first. You're going to need all your strength."

Jane, flushed with both the thrill of the hunt and her room-buying victory, told them all about Dorothy and Ollie and Mary and Bateman. Charley interrupted only once, to ask where the Shangri-La had been.

"Howard Street, east of Western," Jane said, wiping her mouth after finishing every bite of Nick's pancakes. "Dot said the whole building's gone now, burnt to the ground years ago."

"Dot?" asked Charley.

"She insisted. We're buddies now. They want to take me to see Mary."

31

"Wouldn't that be weird? I mean you bought her old stuff and everything, and then you go to see her in a home?" asked Nick.

Jane nodded. It would be weird. Once she had left a house sale, carrying a great tan leather bag that had been stuffed into a basement closet. It was weathered and worn and stunning, and Jane couldn't believe anyone would have left it. The man running the sale had shrugged and asked for three dollars, which Jane handed over gladly. Walking to her car, Jane ran into a couple who stopped her, admiring the bag.

"That's the Crate & Barrel bag I could never find," the woman said, poking her husband in the arm.

"Isn't it great?" Jane said, gushing with house sale good humor, hauling it and another paper bag filled with dishes and weaving supplies to her car.

When she opened her trunk, she turned around and saw the couple arguing on the sidewalk, and it hit her. They weren't idle shoppers who remembered when the leather bag had been in the window, new stock, at Crate & Barrel. They were the owners of the house, the *former* owners who were moving and leaving all the old trappings behind. But they hadn't meant to leave that bag. Jane was relieved she hadn't bragged about the three-dollar price she had gotten, but that relief didn't make up for the guilt at carrying off something they hadn't intended to sell. She debated over offering it to them, but the man got into one car, the woman got into another, and they drove off in separate directions. Were they moving together or splitting up entirely, Jane wondered? Giving the bag back might have stirred up more trouble . . . one more object to divide fairly and squarely. *Maybe not*, Jane thought. Maybe they're just moving somewhere, leaving the old beloved house, and tensions are running high. Whatever the truth, both were gone, and Jane had an incredible piece of luggage for three dollars.

Would meeting Mary in the assisted-living facility leave her feeling guilty and more than a little dirty, coated with the scavenger dust that so many of her fellow pickers wore standing in line, sizing up houses, garages, Dumpsters parked in alleys?

By the time Jane, Nick, and Charley had unloaded the van, it was nearly noon. Usually, Jane wouldn't even be home yet from her Saturday round of sales, but she had blown more than her weekend budget on Bateman's storage room. Her plan, at least before she opened the boxes and fell in love with everything there, was that she would pack up most of it to send to Miriam in Ohio, but keep the really cool tavern paraphernalia to transform the EZ Way Inn. Tim, her best friend, was also a dealer and lived in Kankakee. He had a weakness for glassware. Tim would love to take this stuff off her hands . . . if she decided she could let him.

"I have to meet with a few graduate students this afternoon, Jane, so I . . . ," Charley said.

"Will you look at this adding machine?" Jane said, carefully lifting the heavy metal model from a box and setting it on the table. The black keys, rows of numbers were fat and solid and satisfying to press, the handle pulled down with an efficient ratcheting sound. The graphics on the machine were underlined with a deco style, and Jane traced the raised print with her long, slim fingers: VICTOR.

"Dad had one of these." Jane looked at Nick, who looked totally clueless. "It's an adding machine, Nick. He added up bills or checks that he cashed on this. Punched in amounts, then pulled down the handle, and it prints up here, see?" Jane asked.

"A precalculator," explained Charley.

"I'd hate to sell this. Someone would buy it and take it apart for the keys," Jane said, fingering them lovingly. "They're all solid Bakelite and would end up dangling as some cheap-ass ear wires in a craft show."

"Watch the language, Mom," said Nick, entering 999.99 and pulling down the handle.

Charley offered to empty one more box before leaving. He heaved a heavy carton onto the kitchen table and ran his fingers under the tape to loosen the flaps.

Jane reached in and wiped dust off a jar lid. She pulled out the wavy, pale blue glass, half-gallon jar and smiled. In raised capital letters, it read, THE QUEEN.

"That'll hold a lot of buttons, huh, Mom?" Nick asked, elbowing Charley to join him in poking fun at his mother's chief obsession. Both of them appreciated many of the things she brought home. Even if they didn't share her desire to own the objects, they understood and appreciated cool stuff when they saw it. Neither, however, could quite comprehend her lust for buttons. She couldn't explain it herself. Jane feared that her button and Bakelite lust was somehow linked to middle age and too close an identification with women in sensible shoes and fifties housedresses and didn't want to probe it too deeply.

She preferred to explain it away as a need to find and replace the buttons her grandmother had let her play with when she was young, her only toy at Grandma's apartment. The wooden sewing box, filled with the beautiful buttons, had disappeared after her grandmother died. When Jane had come home from college and asked about it, Nellie had shrugged and said Grandma hadn't sewn a button in years. Jane knew from experience that it was all the explanation she would ever get.

"Go ahead and laugh, boys," Jane said, "THE QUEEN is worth a pretty penny."

"Where do you get those expressions, Mom? 'A pretty penny'?" Nick said, again trying to get Charley to join in on the teasing.

"They're not all canning jars in here. Looks like some lab stuff, too." Charley pulled out a beaker and some glass measures. "Looks like Bateman might have brewed some of his own."

"This is promising," Jane said, pulling out two jars with black screw-on lids. "These lids are Bakelite, I'm pretty sure." She walked over to the sink and ran hot water, preparing to dip the lids in and give them the sniff test.

"What's in that jar?" Nick asked.

Jane looked at the one in her right hand. "Markers, maybe? Little disks with numbers. Maybe they played bingo or something." Jane shook the jar and held it up to the light. She dipped the other lid into the hot running water and held it up to her nose.

"Whew, that's Bakelite. Just like formaldehyde," she said, sniffing the air to get rid of the acrid smell.

"No, Mom, what's in *that* jar?" Nick asked, pointing to her left hand, his voice wavering.

"What's the matter, Nick?" She turned first to Nick, but both he and Charley were looking at the container. She held it up to the window above the sink, thumb on the bottom, middle finger on top, to see what was sloshing through the liquid in the glass.

"Move your hand, Jane, I—" Charley started, but cut himself off.

"Yuck," said Nick, clutching his stomach with both hands.

"Holy Toledo," said Jane, turning the glass in her hand, noting how much larger than her own was the finger floating in the jar.

3

Nick had turned pale as dough. He sat kneading his hands at the table, staring at his mother. He wanted to make a joke or laugh at someone else's attempt, but neither Jane nor Charley spoke.

Charley had taken the jar and turned it in the light of the window, studying the finger, which did its own slow float as Charley turned the glass. Jane shivered and recovered. This could not be a real finger. It was some kind of practical joke—a bit of a freak show in a bottle—that Bateman kept behind the bar as a sick little tease to play on a regular customer.

"It's not real, Nick, don't worry," Jane began, just as Charley nodded and said, "It's real, all right."

The finger, pasty white, almost blue in its whiteness, was perfectly preserved. Large, probably a man's second, third, or fourth finger—certainly not a thumb or pinkie—it took on a life of its own as Charley moved the jar: first beckoning, then turning away.

Jane did not want this to be the subject of Nick's nightmares or one more milestone in Nick's inevitable adult therapy sessions. She could hear some Freudian now. *Oh, yes,*

Mr. Wheel, was that before or after your mother brought home the finger in a jar? No, she had to nip this morbidity in the bud.

"Let's not get too excited about this, I'll just call . . . ," Jane said, then stopped. Who should she call?

Charley shrugged. "The police?" he offered.

"Yeah," Jane said, "they'll finally be able to solve that age-old criminal question, 'Where is Pointer?' "

Nick had his head down on the table and Jane saw his shoulders begin to shake. *Now I've done it,* she thought. *Turning the kitchen into a sideshow tent wasn't bad enough, I had to make the cheap joke.* Why did she always think turning things into laughs would work miracles.

When Nick looked up, however, she saw that this time, anyway, it had worked. Nick was laughing not crying, and shaking his head. "Shouldn't we finish unpacking before we call anybody? Maybe Ringman and Thumbkin are here, too."

"Where is Pointer? Where is Pointer?" Charley sang, slowly moving the jar from behind his back, bouncing and sloshing the finger until he held it in front of him.

"Here I am. Here I am," Jane and Nick joined in.

And for one golden moment, peering in on this cozy-late-Saturday-morning-early-afternoon-pancake-plates-still-on-the-table-Dad-and-son-still-in-flannels-and-socks tableau, anyone might have thought this was a Norman Rockwell painting of a perfect family scene.

Except of course, for the severed finger.

When the wholesome hilarity of the Wheel household had finally subsided, the coolest head among them prevailed.

"Call Detective Oh," said Nick, now able to actually

hold the jar and study the finger himself. "He'll know what to do." Nick had heard the story of the Balance murder case over and over when he and his father returned from the summer dig. His neighborhood friends told several versions, and he had listened carefully to them all. Detective Oh, stopping by to tie up a few loose ends, had impressed him mightily by treating him as an adult, telling the story simply, answering his questions honestly.

Jane agreed. Calling Oh was a good idea, but first she wanted to unpack the rest of the boxes. Charley and Nick both hesitated. Eight more cartons were stacked in the kitchen, each one of them large enough to hold an even more gruesome surprise.

"Come on, guys, I glanced through most of the stuff at the house. One of these has ashtrays and coasters. There's lots of glassware . . . shot glasses, old-fashioneds, stuff like that. I want to run them through the dishwasher here before I take them down to Kankakee.

"And punchboards. One of these boxes has unused punchboards," Jane said, her eyes glazing over.

Charley knew the look and knew that Jane would not be dissuaded.

"I have to meet a student in fifteen minutes, and I'm dropping Nick off at the Y to play basketball," said Charley. "I'll come right back here after the meeting and help you, I promise, but you promise me to wait. Forty-five minutes tops. I don't want you doing this alone."

Nick had already run up to change. Charley was standing in the doorway, buttoning a clean but wrinkled shirt he had pulled out of his duffle.

Jane agreed immediately.

"Okay," she said, washing her hands and placing a dish towel over the celebrated jar.

"Too easy," said Charley. "I mean it, Jane. There could be something dangerous in there."

"What? What's dangerous? Even if I found a whole pickled hand, what's dangerous about that?" Jane asked.

Charley winced. Jane was smiling, calm and collected, and already breaking the tape on another box. *Had playing detective this summer changed her that much? Had he just not been paying attention to who she had become in the last few years?* He watched her run the knife under the cardboard flap and before he could stop himself, he said, "You'll dull the knife."

She looked up at him. His beautiful, smart, stubborn, probably-soon-to-be-ex-wife just looked at him, and he knew without a doubt that the last thing she wanted to hear from Charley, from her once exciting and risk-taking husband, Charley, was the predictable and pedantic advice he had been dispensing over the last several years. When had he, like the knife he didn't even care about protecting, become so dull, and when exactly did Jane begin to notice?

"Ready, Dad?"

Charley nodded and didn't even try to stop himself from saying "Be careful," as he walked out the door because it was what he felt and who he was and what he had to say.

He even added, "Please."

Jane was careful. She only cut herself twice on cardboard as she opened the cartons that Mary Bateman had carefully packed away. The more glasses she unwrapped, the more towels she unfolded and refolded, the more old calendars and desk blotters she sorted through, the more she speculated about Mary herself. Dot and Ollie had told her that Mary had spent almost every evening at the Shangri-La, drinking a Tom Collins or an old-fashioned, and waiting for Bateman to close up.

"Not when Cindy was little, Ollie. She stayed home then," said Dot.

"That's true," Ollie agreed, then added loyally, "Mary was a good mother."

Jane asked the friends what happened to the daughter. The granddaughter, Susan, the nurse, was calling the shots on the house sale and Mary's move to an assisted-living facility, but Jane had heard nothing about the daughter's role in all of it.

Dot and Ollie both shook their heads.

"Gone," Dot whispered.

"Cindy and her husband got into a car accident when Susan was twelve," Ollie said.

"Thirteen," said Dot.

"Susan came and lived with Mary then, and they just took real good care of each other, I think," said Ollie. "Bateman had already passed, and I don't think Mary could have taken it, losing everybody like that, if Susan hadn't come to live here."

Jane wondered what it was like for Mary and Susan, living in that house, taking care of each other. Ollie had said Susan never went down to the basement, didn't want to see anything that reminded her of the Shangri-La.

"Wouldn't Susan have been too young to remember the place? I mean, too young for bad memories?" Jane had asked.

"Wasn't that," Ollie said. "Didn't and still doesn't approve of drinking. The car accident when her mom and dad were killed, it involved alcohol. Susan was old enough to remember and cling to it. Never forgave the drinking."

Jane carried the glasses she planned to ship to Miriam out to her shelves in the garage. She could repack them later. Jane heard a car turn into the driveway and opened the door to greet and draft Charley to help, but a strange car sat in the driveway, a big silver Oldsmobile or Buick or whatever make the current "Dad" or "Grandpa" drove—cars weren't one of her specialties. Two men were in the front seat, and the passenger leaned out with a newspaper in his hand.

"This 2303 Thayer?" he asked.

"No, you're four blocks south," she said.

"You having a sale, too?" the driver asked.

Jane shook her head and smiled. They saluted and backed out. Jane's racks of goods in the garage, her boxes and packing material, might lead anyone on this sunny autumn Saturday to assume she was in the garage-sale business. She smiled to herself. She felt so right with the world when like-minded souls crossed her path. Those guys, like her, were just out on the hunt. She immediately wished them good sale karma. May they find the perfect . . . what did they look like they wanted? One wore a baseball cap; one had a tiny stub of a ponytail. Driving a big-old-dad-car-four-door sedan complete with a college decal on the back window. Vintage record albums, she guessed, or maybe old radios?

She waved to them as they drove away down the alley. They were all members of the club. It was only when one of the neighbors watched her unload her trunk and asked in that bone-chillingly polite voice, "Been to another sale, Jane?" that she felt alone in the world, embarrassed by her passion.

She carried the cartons with punchboards and photographs and signs out to the van. She was going to Kankakee tomorrow, and she might as well bring everything she could carry. The EZ Way Inn was going to dazzle. It was going to be the quintessential neighborhood tavern, a tavern among taverns.

Charley and Nick were late. When Jane checked her watch, she saw she had been working for an hour and a half. Nick had probably roped his father into playing ball with them, and they'd stay until open gym time was over. They could be another hour or two.

Jane was going through the last of the boxes. Photographs, plaques, small bulletin boards with scores and newspaper clippings still pinned on were wrapped carefully in newspapers. Jane smoothed out a sports page from the *Chicago Sun-Times*, July 7, 1969. "Cubs Going All The Way?" asked one of the headlines. Had the Cubs actually been winners that summer? Maybe the newspaper itself was valuable.

What did Dot and Ollie say about this stuff? They said Bateman had been gone thirty years. Did Mary close up the place and pack it away, or did Bateman retire and pack up and drop dead? Who tucked all of this away so carefully?

Jane looked at the photograph she had just uncovered: a wedding picture. Standing in front of the Shangri-La, the neon sign just above their shoulders, were four adults. The bride and groom were smiling for the photographer, their arms around each other. Mary stood next to the bride, a younger version of herself, who had to be Cindy, her daughter. Jane assumed the balding man with the paunch and cigar clamped between his teeth was Bateman. He had one arm squeezed around the groom's neck in a mock headlock. Bateman's son-in-law, a long-haired, loose-limbed boy wearing, not a tux, but a shiny suit with wide lapels and no tie, looked a little scared. Cindy wasn't wearing a traditional wedding gown, more of a lace minidress, a tablecloth with a thin velvet belt around the waist, and carrying a bouquet of what looked to be roses and daisies. The groom's hand was clasped around the bride's, so it looked like they were both clinging to the flowers. Bateman was waving with his free hand and winking at the camera.

A happy, smiling family, celebrating a joyous occasion. Jane fought an urge to wave back to Bateman, to shake her finger at him, warning him about what was coming.

"Enjoy these years, Bateman," she'd say if he could hear. "Hug your daughter and say wonderful things to her. Be really kind to Mary. Make it last."

But Jane, looking harder at Bateman, thought maybe he didn't need warnings at all. He looked like a man who already knew what was coming.

"Don't worry about me, baby," he'd probably say right back. "I know what's what in the world." Then he'd wink and wave those three fingers at her, only three. Bateman wore a slightly stained bandage covering most of his hand, especially padded and bulky in the place where number four, his pointer, used to be.

Bruce Oh, until three weeks ago Police Det. Bruce Oh, had just come in from his morning constitutional. He'd gotten a late start and instead of seeing the sun rise, he contended with seeing every neighbor that he usually avoided by walking at 4:45 A.M. each day. He treasured his morning solitude and silence, what he called the rare and blessed anonymity of the hour before daylight.

This reverence for morning peace did not mean he was antisocial. At a party or picnic, he was proud of his camaraderie. That was the place for it, he thought, and he was a man who believed in a time and place for everything. He had a talent for remembering names and details; and at the Fourth of July block parties, he was a hit because he remembered the food likes and dislikes of almost everyone.

Efficiently handling the grilling tools, he'd smile at Mrs. Miller from down the block and say, "Not just well done . . . very well done, right?" and she would walk away with a charred square of meat formerly known as ground sirloin and wish that her late husband had been so thoughtful.

Oh also remembered what sports each child on the block participated in. Shin guards and baseball gloves usually provided clues, but nonetheless, parents seemed amazed that Detective Oh would ask if Little Jason had an RBI as Little Jason walked into the house, smiling and swinging his bat. If, on the other hand, Little Jason charged ahead, banging the front porch door, leaving his dad to carry the equipment, Oh would shake his head and shrug his shoulders, as if to commiserate with the family over the tough loss.

"People," Oh—now wearing the hat of a professor three days a week—would say to his class, "are never aware of what they reveal in their clothing, their walk, their choice of car. It is never a mistake to take note of the obvious. If we did not note what is in front of us, how would we notice when it is taken away? Hidden? Noticing the everyday becomes your baseline, your gauge for the extraordinary in human behavior."

Oh's students were never bored. His classes had waiting lists and had been written up as student favorites in campus publications. "It's like being in that show *Kung Fu*—he gives you this David Carradine nugget of wisdom and then just moves on. The only thing missing is him calling you grasshopper, which I really wish he would do just once," gushed a freshman girl who was quoted in one of the articles.

Because he loved to teach, he taught courses in criminal psychology and criminal detection at a few different Chicago-area universities. Oh didn't need the income. Because his investigative insights were much in demand by lawyers and insurance companies, he discovered that consulting fees easily paid the mortgage and monthly bills. His wife Claire's surprisingly successful antique business paid for any extras they might require, and the two of them required very little.

Oh much preferred the spare and lean style of living. That included minimal household decorating. Although he appreciated the many old, ornate pieces that his wife placed in front of him, he preferred to admire and learn from objects when they were safely ensconced in a glass case at a museum. Or when they were tagged and laid out on an examining room table in a murder investigation. When Claire complained that Oh only liked objects when they were clues, he smoothly pointed out to her that she only liked objects that were mysteries: old and abandoned.

Claire protested then that her art history background made her much more of a scholar in her pursuits and her M.B.A. made her a crack businesswoman, and he conceded both points. It was Mrs. Jane Wheel who adopted the orphaned objects, after all. His wife quite easily let go of her finds, her steady profit based on a constant buying and selling process. Jane Wheel, whom he had spent so much time studying when investigating her neighbor's murder, had told him that she was still learning how to let go. It was Mrs. Wheel who loved the forgotten and found meaning in the lost.

Mrs. Wheel also had something to do with his experimental retirement from the police force this fall, although he would find it hard to say exactly what that something was. He suspected it had to do with her constant searching. Her hunt was for objects that he didn't care about, yes, but perhaps she looked for more, found more than the physical stuff that filled her house. That was what her eyes seemed to say. Although he had never said it, even to himself, he knew it was what he had read in her eyes that had sent him off on his current search.

After the Balance case was ended, thanks in no small part to Mrs. Wheel herself, he had requested a leave of absence to devote himself to teaching. When his request was denied, he nodded, sat down at his desk for only five minutes, as long as it took him to type the letter, and tendered his resignation. He explained to Claire that he would be of more service in the classroom. She agreed, delighted that her husband would no longer be in the line of fire. He told her he also dreamed of writing a book about criminal detection.

"More pyschology than science," he had told her, explaining that the book would have a limited appeal to real police, who wanted hard facts and better techniques . . . what, when, where. Oh just wanted to know why.

"And occasionally how," he admitted, when she raised an eyebrow.

"Why," he asked aloud now as he searched the refrigerator, "can't Claire keep lemon yogurt in the house?"

Claire had left the house quietly at 4:00 A.M. for sales to replenish her antique stall, and he had uncharacteristically slept in. Taking his walk at ten-thirty had put him off balance, and now, trying to find his regular breakfast in the almost empty refrigerator set his teeth on edge. "She can find an eighteenth-century snuff bottle in someone's garage, but she can't locate the lemon yogurt at the Jewel," he muttered, knowing that he had no right to complain, now being on a flexible enough schedule himself to make the weekly trips to the grocery store. He straightened and took a deep meditative breath. Taking a small notebook out of the all-purpose kitchen drawer, he printed in precise letters, LEMON YOGURT.

I will make a list and go to the grocery store. This is what semiretired professor-type husbands do, he promised silently and brewed himself a cup of Irish Breakfast tea in a nineteenth-century, paper-thin, bone china cup, discovered by his wife, no doubt, holding greasy nuts and bolts in someone's garage.

Reading over papers in his study, Oh almost let the answering machine pick up when the phone rang. Claire had suggested it as a kind of discipline.

"You don't have to get the call. It's not a sergeant calling about a body, after all," she would say when he jumped to answer. "It's much more likely that it's someone who wants you to change your long-distance carrier."

Habits die hard, Oh admitted to himself, and this time it might even be Claire, needing his help at a sale. Besides, what was the harm in hearing about a different long-distance plan?

"Oh," he answered.

"Oh, hello," Jane said, and began laughing. "I mean, hello, Detective Oh. I didn't mean to be rude, I . . ."

"My wife says I am very foolish to answer the phone that way. Work habit, I'm afraid. How are you, Mrs. Wheel?" asked Oh.

"Caller ID?

"Pardon?"

"You knew it was me. Do you have caller ID, Detective?" Jane asked.

Was Mrs. Wheel working for the telephone company

now trying to sell Caller ID and get him to change his long-distance service?

"I knew you, Mrs. Wheel. No ID. You're well?"

"Yes. You?" Jane asked.

Both Jane and Oh felt the awkwardness of this call, but neither would be able to say why. There was nothing so tangible as a reason for it.

This past summer, Oh had found Jane Wheel engaging, intriguing. She was never a serious suspect in her neighbor's murder, but she absorbed a kind of community guilt, an overwhelming sadness over the crime that drew him. She became inextricably linked in his mind as one more victim of the whole mess. He had asked her many times about the collecting, the picking she did; and at the time of the questioning, he believed it had helped him better understand Claire and her world. In fact he hadn't even been interested in that world until Mrs. Wheel had given it her particular spin.

Jane had found the kind of listener in Detective Oh that she hadn't even known she craved. She had stopped chattering to Charley years ago, not because he had shown any kind of disinterest, but because she sensed that it wearied him. He had seen her enthusiasm, her spark, her youth, and now he was comfortable with tucking it away and filing it under memory. He didn't really want to hear about McCoy flowerpots anymore. He didn't believe there was that much more to say. Oh, on the other hand, wanted to know everything. Yes, he might have been hoping she'd incriminate herself as a murderer, but nonetheless, a good listener is a good listener.

They each tried to break through the stilted greetings and pleasantries.

"No more bodies, I hope," said Oh, trying to sound like he was joking, but realizing as he heard himself that he never sounded like he was joking.

"I'm not calling about a body," Jane said at the same time, then added, "just a body part."

Both waited for the other to speak. Neither wanted that embarrassing, out-of-synch double-talk again.

"How about coming over for a drink, and I'll show you?" asked Jane, unable to hold out as long as Oh. A good listener, all right, he could listen harder and longer than anyone she had ever met.

"Yes, that would be fine. And what is it you will show me again?"

"My body part," Jane said.

"Oh," he said.

"I know," Jane said. "I'll just see you at five."

Jane turned the cocktail shaker over and let it drip dry on a feed sack towel. She rinsed four glasses, dried them, and placed them on the matching tray. The glasses, shaker, and tray were part of a bar set that she had kept on her dining room sideboard for two years, admiring it every time she looked its way. Periodically she promised Miriam that she would pack it up and send it to her for a customer who would pay handsomely for this chrome-and-Bakelite martini set, the Chase manufacturing mark firmly engraved on the underside of the tray.

"Don't take forever," Miriam cautioned. "This Cosmopolitan craze will burn itself out when one of these newfangled hipsters gets cirrhosis and writes about it in a self-help magazine. Got to sell these puppies while they're hot."

Jane agreed that it was only a matter of time before the cranberry juice and designer vodka craze went down in flames. She had never been able to order a pink drink herself. If she even considered it, in her head she could see an entire row of EZ Way Inn customers shaking their heads and smirking. Still, she couldn't wrap up this bar set for Miriam. Not yet. Maybe she would never follow the Cosmo crowd, but she did love martinis. The shape of the glass, the whole "shaken not stirred" aura of them. Maybe the customers at the EZ Way Inn didn't drink them—the closest they got to a mixed drink was a shot and a beer—but when she went out to dinner with her parents after their long day of pulling draft beers and ladling soup, Don always ordered a martini, dry and straight up. Solemnly he handed Jane one of the olives, while Nellie shook her head and scowled over a cup of black coffee, her cocktail of choice. Don's martinis were made with Tanqueray gin and a whisper of vermouth. Jane made her own with vodka, Grey Goose or Ketel One, and merely nodded at the vermouth bottle she kept in a cupboard; but she, too, like Don, skewered olives onto a toothpick and smiled at the glass before her first sip.

"I don't even know if Detective Oh drinks," she said more to herself than to Nick, who was watching her try to stuff blue cheese into olives, the contemporary version of a task of Sisyphus.

"Where," asked Nick, "would someone get the idea to take awful-tasting things and stuff them with awful-smelling stuff? I mean it's crazy to think about eating them, but it's even crazier to think someone got the idea in the first place."

"Yeah, like artichokes," said Jane.

Nick stared at her. He was used to his mother's responses and their circuitous routes back to his own comments, but he didn't follow this one.

"I mean, whoever looked at an artichoke and thought it would be or could be edible? Who went to the bother of figuring out all the methodology?" said Jane, stabbing small skewers topped with Bakelite dice through the olives.

Detective Oh, as it turned out, did like an occasional martini and seemed pleased at the arrangement of vintage cocktail collectibles laid out on the table. He appreciated the clean design of the shaker and glasses, the whimsy of the olives, the tang of the cheese straws, and the irony of the centerpiece—a finger floating in its own little preservative of choice.

"It seems logical that the finger belonged to Mr. Bateman," said Oh, handing Jane back the photograph of the family.

Jane and Nick waited, but Detective Oh did not continue.

"That's all?" Jane asked.

Oh held up one of the delicate cheese straws, nodded, and took a tentative bite.

"Shouldn't we check it out? See how old it is or something? So we can tell if it was Bateman's?" asked Nick.

"I'm afraid that two months in formaldehyde would have the same effect as two years—or two dozen. There's no way to date it."

Oh noted Nick's disappointment and added, "Of

course, if there was any evidence of a crime or an old police report, maybe this finger could shed some . . ."

Rita, the German shepherd that had joined the household over the summer, perked up her ears just before Jane heard a knock at the door.

"Charley must have gotten out of his department dinner," Jane said, rising. She knew he had taken to knocking before entering so she wouldn't feel he was being too familiar, and she appreciated the respect. At the same time, though, it annoyed her that he couldn't just use his key and stop walking on eggshells. Then again, hadn't she laid the intricate eggshell parquetry herself?

Key or no key, it wasn't Charley. Even though he knew she adored forties tablecloths, complete with dancing fruit and jitterbugging knives and forks, Charley would not stand at the front door with a turquoise-and-red cowboy-print tablecloth over his head.

"I am the ghost of vintage hand-printed textiles. Treat me with vodka, or I will trick you with confusing machine reproductions."

"Timmy!" Jane hugged the wrapped figure. "What are you doing here?"

"Checking to see if you made your lucky five today," he said, shaking out and folding the tablecloth. "When you called me this morning, I was up in Kenosha at a monster sale, so I thought I'd pop in for sustenance on my way back to Kankakee. Who's here?"

Not waiting for an answer, Tim walked into the living room, saluted Nick, and raised an eyebrow at Detective Oh.

"Jane on another crime spree, Detective?" he asked, shaking Oh's hand.

"Hardly, Mr. Lowry. All quiet at your flower shop?"

"So quiet you'd hardly know I was in business. Kanka-kee is so provincial when it comes to shopping in places where bodies were found."

Tim took the drink Jane handed him and slumped into an overstuffed armchair.

"After the initial rush of customers who wanted to see how long a chalk outline really lasted—and they were all, of course, 'just looking'—my flower business has taken a turn for the worse." Tim sipped his drink. "However, in the perverse way of things, my antique sales and special orders have been through the roof."

"People might not want their wedding flowers tainted by murder, but an inlaid mahogany highboy chest that's tasted mystery only adds to the patina, yes?" asked Jane.

"Guess so. Got anything heartier than these cheese doodles? What's this?"

Nick, Jane, and Oh simultaneously shouted *no* as Tim reached for the jar.

Jane reached out protectively as Tim turned the jar in the lamplight. For her, the finger had ceased to be a freakish specimen and had taken on the personality of Bateman. He was, after all, a saloon keeper, and she knew something about them. She often bought photos and personal memorabilia around which she daydreamed and constructed whole lives from the spare parts she collected after the principals were gone. Should she feel less about an actual spare part?

"Tim, this is Bateman. Bateman, Tim," Jane said.

Tim struggled with what to say. He was neither appalled nor grossed out; he just knew he would never again have an opportunity like this. It was the perfect situation for the perfect smart-ass remark, and the pressure was overwhelming. He held up his free hand in mock protest.

"Jane, when I ask for *two* fingers of scotch, I mean *two*."

5

Jane didn't finish packing her car until after midnight. Tim and Nick had scrounged dinner, then disappeared upstairs to discuss Nick's summer with Charley digging for bones. Tim took his godfathering duties seriously. Even when Jane didn't need her best friend to help her solve mysteries or date an Eastlake chair or price a Monmouth stoneware elephant, he showed up with tickets to a concert or a ball game, charming Nick just the way he had charmed her when he sat down next to her in kindergarten.

"You look good in that color," he had said, seriously assessing her one-piece, romper-style playsuit, and a lifetime friendship had been born.

Jane packed the last box of Shangri-La napkins and coasters into the backseat, then thought better of it. She removed the box and took out just one coaster and a handful of napkins that had the name and address of the tavern and tucked them under her sun visor. She'd ask her dad if he'd ever heard of the place, if he'd ever met Bateman or Mary.

After Tim had arrived, Detective Oh had stayed for another half hour or so, explaining his private citizen status to Tim. When he got up to leave, he gestured to Bateman's finger, swimming in their midst.

"I will ask someone at the department to check if there was ever any open book on the Shangri-La, any assault charges filed by Bateman. The wedding photo is dated, so we have a time frame."

"But you said we can't date the finger," Nick said. Nick had engaged Oh in a discussion of dating dinosaur bones and was shocked that the finger couldn't be tagged and shelved with the same certainty.

"We can't exactly do a *when*, but we can probably do a *who* with that finger."

"How?" Nick and Jane had both asked.

"This finger still retains something very important," said Oh.

Jane paused to see if she would have to prompt him to tell them. He smiled ever so slightly. Jane realized he didn't explain further because he wanted to hear her speculate. Nick, too, looked at her for the answer. Jane looked at the finger, now the centerpiece of the cocktail tray. Tim looked up from his investigation of the cocktail picks. He had been rubbing and sniffing the plastic dice to make sure they were really Bakelite.

"Of course," she said. "The finger still has a fingerprint."

Oh had rewarded her detection by allowing his slightly upturned lips to relax into an almost smile.

Jane turned off the garage light, went into the kitchen, and noticed that the finger was still on the chrome tray. She wrapped the jar in one of her tea towels and went back to the garage. She carefully wedged it into her glove compartment, already brimming with area street maps and file cards and crossword puzzle books. The street maps got her to where the sales were, the file cards enabled her to make her many lists, and the crossword puzzles, the most challenging *New York Times* collection she could find, helped her pass the hours she waited in the car for a sale to open. Now the finger, Bateman himself, would give Jane some company.

Tim was checking out her new pottery and books in the living room when she came in.

"Nick asleep?"

"Pretty close."

Tim opened an Alice and Jerry reader, slightly dog-eared but in better condition than so many old textbooks. After all the years they'd stayed in a classroom and all the grubby, sticky fingers that had paged the texts, anxious to see what Mother would say when she found out that her favorite vase had been knocked off the mantle by Jerry, it was a wonder that any of them had survived. Tim banged the covers shut so the dust flew up between them.

"Get enough to eat?" Jane asked, flopping onto the couch.

"Never at your house. Do you only rummage? Don't you ever shop in a grocery store?" Tim flopped down next to her.

"Not if I can help it. There was stuff in there though. Charley gets food."

"No Charley tonight?"

"He had a department dinner or party or something; then he's packing up to come here for a week while I'm in Kankakee."

"When you get done decorating the EZ Way, you can help me with a project. I've talked the alumni association at Mac into a Show House fund-raiser."

Jane was astonished that anyone from their old high school would agree to such a plan. Casino nights, pot lucks, silent auctions, bingo, even a talent show, maybe, but a Decorator Show House? In Kankakee? Who would they get to decorate? Whose house? Would they get anyone to pay to walk through it?

"I bought the old Gerber place. Cheap. My old condo had too many memories. Time for a new start; new project. Gerber's was a mess, and I was going to do it over before I moved in, soooo . . . I offered it for the Show House."

"You bought Eddie Gerber's house? On Cobb? You're going to live on Cobb Boulevard?"

"Yeah. The fund-raising committee agreed pretty much because I offered the house and put a little spin on what the designers can do. No one can spend more than five hundred dollars per room—it's got to be all flea market and rummage. Only exceptions are some appliances and the new master bedroom bed, which I was buying anyway. And the designers are all amateurs, too. People were fighting to do rooms."

"I had my first kiss in Eddie Gerber's basement."

"What a coincidence! I'm decorating the basement."

"On that ratty tweed couch next to the Ping-Pong table."

"I'll put up a plaque."

Charley joined them for breakfast. He dumped his briefcase and boxes of papers into the study and poured himself an extra large mug of coffee.

"I might have to sit on a committee next weekend, fill in for Beegle. Any chance you'll be home?" Charley asked Jane.

"I'd like to be back on Thursday. That'll give me time

to do a lot at the EZ Way and do sales here on Friday morning. I have a bunch of packages to send out to Miriam, too."

Nick came in from the garage where he had been showing Tim his own collection of vintage bicycle parts.

"I'm almost ready to put it all together," said Nick, "just need another fender and maybe a better rear wheel. Tires shouldn't be any problem."

Tim nodded. "I bet I can find all that stuff in three sales. I've got the list," he said, patting his shirt pocket.

Jane gave Charley a kiss on the cheek and hugged Nick, reminding him of his weekly round of sports practices and guitar lessons. She reminded Charley that the calendar was on the inside cupboard door, and Charley nodded. He didn't remind her that he had filled out the calendar, and that he had always been better at keeping to the schedule than she had. Those reminders all seemed beside the point.

She was perky and happy and ready to hit the road. Charley kept asking himself what was so different about Jane now, but he couldn't put his finger on it. And he knew that until he could figure it out, he had no chance of putting their household back together.

"Don't forget to take care of Rita," Jane said, retying the bandana around the dog's neck.

"Like we could forget . . . ," Charley stopped himself. He loved this dog. Why did he find himself speaking lines out of a script that cast him as the grumpy old husband? Especially now that Jane seemed, more and more, to be playing the ingenue?

More hugs, reminders, kisses, smiles, and Jane was ready to take off. Tim had already left, racing off with a quick promise to call her at her parents' house later.

Jane, on the road, was daydreaming of Don and Nellie's tavern, trimmed out as a post-WWII hangout, swing music blaring from the jukebox. She saw the café curtains unfurling at the windows, a breeze wafting through the barroom. Napkins, anchored by sweating beer mugs, fluttered, then fell. The soft buzz and flutter of cards being shuffled and dealt, and a baseball game turned down to a low murmur provided the soundtrack. It was when she pictured Dot and Ollie, sitting at the bar in their bowling shirts, that she realized she was picturing the Shangri-La instead of the EZ Way Inn. That couple, twirling around behind the bar, enchanted with each other and making merry with the customers, wasn't Don and Nellie, it was Mary and Bateman. That damn Bateman, winking at her and waving his jaunty three-fingered salute. What was he trying to tell her?

6

"That son-of-bitch. I don't give a damn what anybody says, that guy's a son-of-a-bitch. He'd swindle his own mother, then sue her for fraud. I hate that son-of-a-bitch."

Jane came in through the kitchen door of the EZ Way Inn on the last son-of-a-bitch, but had heard her father's tirade in its entirety as she came in from her car. His voice had carried outside through the screen door and set her teeth on edge.

Don was a gentle man as well as a gentleman. He had always cautioned her never to use the word "hate." Kill 'em with kindness had been his motto, and he had tried to instill it in both Jane and her brother, Michael. She had only heard him use the word hate about one individual and that was his landlord, Gustavus Duncan.

Gus Duncan had been the thorn in her father's side for as long as Jane could remember. He owned several buildings in the Kankakee area, nothing fancy, but spots of property here and there. He collected rents from saloon keepers and restaurant owners and, Jane assumed, shopkeepers, barbers, any type of business tenant who wanted a small, unkempt storefront, badly managed by an absentee landlord. Gus would collect the rent on the first of the month, then disappear through one of the cracks in the plaster sure to appear in any of his properties every time a truck rumbled by or a clap of thunder shook the foundation. Gus did not employ a handyman, a plumber, a painter, or a carpenter. He rented out the shell of a building and promised nothing. Unless you considered his growled, "See you next month," a promise rather than a threat.

Don had treated the EZ Way like some kind of semi-precious gemstone. A stone, that although rough and ordinary on the outside, could be polished into luminescence on the inside. *An agate,* Jane thought, *or maybe more of a geode, bumpy and dirty on the outside, cracked open to reveal a sparkling world of wonder.*

Some might not see it. The massive oak bar, cleaned and polished daily to a warm glow. Nellie's café curtains in a cheery print adorning the spotless windows. The top of the line paneling on the walls of the small excuse for a dining room connected to the bar area. But Jane never failed to see the shimmer and shine of her parents' loving care of this ramshackle old building. Her brother, Michael, had once remarked that their parents took better care of the EZ Way than they did of them, but Jane had shushed him.

"It's their work," she told him. "It's what they have to be proud of." Michael, only twelve at the time, looked up at his adored older sister, clearly puzzled. "Shouldn't they be proud of us?"

Don was still muttering under his breath when Jane came in and faced him. "Daddy, aren't we supposed to avoid the H-word? I wasn't allowed to hate anyone," Jane said, setting down two bags that she had carried in and putting her arm on her father's shoulder.

"It's okay to hate one person. Just pick out one guy and concentrate on hating him so purely that you don't have any left to spill over on the rest of your life," Don said. "In fact, it's okay for everyone to hate Gus Duncan. He can be the one person in the world that everyone hates."

Don moved around behind the bar to get a glass of water. Jane looked at Nellie.

"Mom? A clue?"

"Gus called a meeting and didn't show up. Who cares? Papers are signed. Nobody can get out of it," Nellie said, shrugging. "I don't know what he's so mad about."

"The guy has jerked everyone around for fifty years, and he's still doing it."

Through a combination of her father's rants and raves and her mother's shrugs and grunts, Jane figured out that Gus Duncan had scheduled a meeting with all of the former tenants turned owners, ostensibly to give out any extra keys or paperwork he had in his files. He had, apparently, offered to buy everyone breakfast at Pinks Café, the kind of uncharacteristically generous gesture that Nellie hadn't trusted in the first place.

"Don't know what he's all excited about," she said, pointing her elbow at her husband. "Gus hasn't picked up a check for fifty years; he ain't going to start now."

"Gus still live in the shanty?" Jane asked.

Gus lived in a four-room house, made of the same tar-paper-and-trash construction that the EZ Way Inn boasted, about three blocks away. He owned three identical houses—called the shanties by everyone in town—on the same block; and even though his rental properties must have made him a wealthy man, he had never moved away or traded up. He bought bars and shops, one by one, on the west side of town, usually from desperate sellers, and added to his seedy little empire, never changing his own address, his surly manners, or his dirty clothes.

Jane and her dad drove slowly over to shanty number one and parked in front. Duncan's fifteen-year-old truck sat outside. Jane shook her head and thought about a house sale at this place. She had always shunned the precautions that she noticed that some pickers took, but even she might don a mask and gloves to enter this one.

"I bet that son-of-a-bitch has mattresses stuffed with money in that rathole."

"Have you ever been inside?" Jane asked.

Her father stared at the house. Jane, too, looked at the broken outer door, the grime-streaked windows and torn screens. Everything about this eyesore screamed, "*Get a tetanus shot!*"

"Never."

Jane, made bold only by wanting to appear that way in front of her father, knocked loudly on the door. "Mr. Duncan? Gus?"

Don banged his fist on the door. "Duncan? Open the door."

Jane turned the latch on the screen, and the door fell aside. The house unlocked and all the windows open—was he inside, ignoring them?

"Could be in there drunk, I guess," said Don, quieter now.

"We'd better check," Jane said.

The living room, or main room or family room or whatever you'd call the space that the front door opened onto, was furnished with two filthy couches, their stuffing spilling onto the floor, and three broken chairs. A large television sat in one corner. It was on, tuned to a cable sports channel, the sound muted. The floor was littered with pizza delivery boxes, sandwich wrappers, and greasy brown paper bags. Slimy green-and-brown vegetation was piled on the floor by the couch. Aquarium plants? Jane cautiously approached and bent over to examine it.

"Guess Gus doesn't like lettuce and tomato on his sandwiches."

The smell inside the house was as horrible as it was indefinable. Spoiled food, yes, and unwashed clothes, naturally, but what gave the air its peculiar pungency, its nauseating weight?

Jane and her dad cautiously weaved through the room, picking up and replacing their feet carefully to avoid the debris on the floor.

Cats? Was it the smell of kitty litter? A dead or dying dog?

"Did Gus have any pets?"

"I don't think he was high enough on the food chain to actually care for another . . ." Following Jane through the kitchen door, Don let his voice drift off.

This was a stage set. Sam Shepard or David Mamet? Jane tried to remember what play she had seen in Chicago with John Malkovich throwing dishes and hurling plates and silverware. Any number of them, she guessed. This was the set for something that would involve half-wit brothers fighting over worthless property. Here was a prop master's dream of pots and pans and cans and boxes, stacked and balanced. A torn linoleum counter was covered with months, years of grease. Dirty cups, empty fifths of Jack Daniels, and prescription medicine bottles were shoved out of the way into wads of dirty paper towels to make a small work space by the sink.

Mismatched dishes, crusted with food and cigarette butts, covered nearly every surface and every inch of floor space. Jane pushed away old soup bowls with the toe of her canvas shoe, so glad she hadn't worn sandals or slides on this warm September day.

Who saw Gus first? Impossible to tell since Jane and her dad both inhaled sharply at the same time. A crumpled heap of dirty laundry in front of the sink? That's what Jane hoped for, but she knew better. Too solid and bulky a pile for just clothes. Although the light was dim, Jane saw that the shaggy, dark shape farthest from her feet was a head. Gus was curled on his side, and his head was tucked, chin to chest. She followed his profile, her eyes moving down his body and focusing on his hands. Palms were up, his hands cupped toward his face. A supplicating pose? Had his hands fallen open in prayer? A pitted, crusty, serrated knife lay next to him, as if he had dropped it there when he fell.

When she heard her dad heading out of the room, muttering something about calling the police, Jane took out her cell phone from her back pocket to call 911.

"Don't touch anything, Dad. I'll call on my phone." She heard her father come back and felt him touch her shoulder.

"Don't look at this anymore, honey. Come on," Don said.

"But . . ." Jane squatted down next to Duncan, holding her breath as tightly as she could. Removing a tiny credit card-shaped flashlight from her vest pocket, she shined it on Duncan's hands. They were slightly open, stiff, as if displaying some object, illustrating some point of conversation. The right hand, half-curled in death, seemed no longer human. Now it looked as if it were carved out of marble. The left hand, less sculpture, more flesh and blood, was not marble, merely carved. The left middle finger was pointing toward the thumb, not simply curved or angled toward it, actually turned on its side, lying flat against the palm, the dirty fingernail touching the pad of the thumb. A digital contortion that would have been impossible, as Jane kept proving by trying to get her own middle finger into the same pose, had Gus Duncan's left middle finger not been almost severed from the hand itself.

7

"Duncan was a lowlife. A slob. He was overweight, ate junk by the crate. You can tell by the bags and wrappers all over the house. Everybody who rented from him hated him, but lots of people hate their landlords. They don't kill them," Tim said, picking up another sandwich from the tray Nellie had set on the table.

Jane heard her father agreeing with Tim, but she could tell, even from her parents' bedroom where she was using the telephone, that Nellie's grunts and groans and mono-syllabic responses meant that she heartily disagreed.

When Detective Oh picked up the phone and answered with his last name, Jane was prepared, greeted him with her own, and quickly got to the point.

"The thing about this body, this Gus, is that his finger was almost cut off," Jane said. "As convinced and convincing as they're trying to be, I just can't agree with the police here that he had a heart attack, then continued slicing a tomato or something and nearly cut off his own finger."

Jane had been so absorbed in the dangling finger that she forgot to be uncomfortable or embarrassed or whatever one should appropriately *be* when meeting a policeman over a dead body for the second time in a matter of months.

Detective Munson, if surprised to see her again hovering over a corpse in Kankakee, did not show it. He didn't really show any emotion, observing Duncan's body from as much of a distance as he could professionally manage. Jane, although somewhat surprised at his apparent squeamishness—after all, he had chosen to be a police officer—could, in this particular case, understand it.

Gus Duncan was a hideous corpse.

No corpse could be beautiful. Living hard and dying young wouldn't guarantee it. Nor would a virtuous passing in one's sleep. No matter how peaceful the death, how pure the soul, spirit, or whatever your belief demanded to be pure, no death could come without extracting some type of toll.

Jane had been to enough wakes where she had heard friends and relatives murmur how beautiful in death someone looked, how natural. She had listened hard, with a great measure of hope, to nuns tell her that in death people met God and were at peace. And if it were all true—Jane's private jury remained locked on the subject—these ghostly souls might be as beautiful as anything Sister Kelly or Sister Galvin could imagine, but the shells they'd left behind, those empty bodies, were never pleasing to look at. It was only when animated with life, with breath and flowing blood, that a body made sense. Once that life stopped, the body was a bulky, badly designed container. Even the perfect features of an individual celebrated for his or her beauty—luscious lips, a perfectly straight and pert nose— looked silly and incongruous—faintly ridiculous add-ons to an oddly shaped package.

And Gus Duncan was never a beauty. Even Jane Wheel, celebrated among her own friends and colleagues for her blindness when it came to physical imperfections, had a difficult time looking objectively at Gus Duncan, alive or dead. Jane, self-educated and well-read even in youth, had her models of beauty formed by the masters. Not Titian or Rembrandt, but the cover girls of *Seventeen* and *Mademoiselle*. As shallow as any teenager, she curled or straightened, wore short or midi, went matte or shiny as the fashionistas dictated.

At college, though, her world changed. The people she found the most interesting, the most attractive, were those who shunned mirrors and makeup. She fell in love with the artsy crowd, the sensible shoes and flannel shirts who were committed to inner beauty and intellectual honesty. She fell into the arms of men who were among the uncombed and unwashed, who were far too busy talking and thinking, changing the world, to worry about holes in their sweaters or socks that matched. She shunned the pretty boys with wrinkle-free shirts and seamless faces and searched for character and bad boy scars. She swooned for brains.

She totally understood how Julia Roberts could marry Lyle Lovett.

As a producer of commercials, which she had been in her last career, she was famous for casting actors with unusual, out of the mainstream faces, ones who were remembered and believed because intelligence shone from their eyes. But even Jane, the nonjudgmental, had trouble looking at old Gus Duncan.

In life he had had the face of a fighter, a losing one: cauliflower ears, pouches, and scars on his cheeks and jowls. Pummeled and shapeless, his bulky form was usually poured into dirty nylon running pants and topped with a polyester print shirt stretched tight across his fat middle, the buttons straining. His eyes were small and piggy, his lips thin over stained and broken teeth. Jane, who could find character in the least likely places, turned her head when Duncan, who refused to accept checks in the mail or direct bank transfer—deposits, came into the EZ Way Inn on the first of every month to collect the rent.

Bruce Oh tried to grasp all the information Jane was giving him. An ugly and nasty man was dead. The police seemed to believe that he had had a heart attack, the profile was right for that, but Mrs. Wheel felt that it was certainly a murder. Why? Because of another finger. This one, not in a jar, but almost detached. Even though Gus Duncan and Mr. Bateman had no other links that she knew of, Mrs. Wheel wanted to investigate.

What would Oh tell a student who came to him with this passion for discovery? He would say, as he did now, with a small sigh, follow your instincts. If the police won't listen, find out what you can on your own. Then he added what he had never and would never add to an answer for a student, "I'll see if I can help you."

Jane returned to the living room, picked up a sandwich, tore off a corner, then replaced the rest of it on the tray. Tim knew she had gone off to call Oh and looked at her, waiting to hear Oh's take on the Duncan death.

Jane nodded. "He's on the case." She chewed the corner of sandwich that she planned to call dinner. "With me. He's on the case with me."

"There's no case, honey," Don said. "Duncan dropped dead. Probably had a feeling about it, and that's why he was going to give all of us the records and keys and stuff."

Nellie picked up the mangled sandwich Jane had torn apart, put it on a paper plate, and set it in front of Jane.

"Finish what you started; you're looking anemic," she said, then turned to Don and Tim. "She's right and you're both wrong."

"Look, I have another friend who just bought her place from Gus Duncan, and she hated him, too. She said when he came for rent, he had a hacking cough and told her he had congestive heart failure," Tim said.

"Yeah, he claimed to have lung cancer, too, last time he came in the EZ Way," said Don.

"Did he ever go to a doctor? Did he ever say a doctor told him that or was it just self-diagnosis? Besides, I'm not saying he couldn't have died of natural causes; he was a mess. I'm saying he didn't saw off his own finger." Jane looked at Nellie. "Is that what you think, too, Mom?"

It was so rare that Nellie ever agreed with or supported anything that Jane said, she actually felt a rush of warmth as her mother poked at the sandwich and gestured again for Jane to chew more and talk less.

"Nah, I just think people get what they deserve. That's God's way, ain't it? It's simple. Gus Duncan deserved to die a horrible death, begging and pleading for his life. That's what happened," Nellie said, brushing crumbs into her apron and walking them over to the garbage can. "He didn't deserve a fast and final heart attack." Nellie measured coffee into the pot for tomorrow morning. "And he didn't get one."

"Exactly who does your mother pray to?" Tim whispered.

"Some Catholics remain devout in spite of history—you know papal corruption and scandal—stuff like that.

Mom's Catholic because of her admiration for the Spanish Inquisition," Jane whispered back.

"Nellie, that's just plain stupid," Don said. "Want me to show you in the paper all the horrible stuff that happens to people who don't deserve it? By your logic, every earthquake or flood that happens anywhere is to punish sinners."

Nellie raised an eyebrow. "Yeah?"

"Dad, Mom *does* think natural disasters come along to punish sinners," said Jane.

Jane was unpacking one of the Bateman/Shangri-La boxes she had brought in from her trunk. Her father said he vaguely remembered a tavern called the Shangri-La in Chicago. "I might have met him at one of the liquor dealer association meetings," Don had answered when Jane questioned him about Bateman. "Drunken brawls more than meetings if you ask me," Nellie had chimed in.

Jane took out one of her many prizes from the Bateman sale.

"Look, Dad," Jane said, holding up an unused punchboard, "it's Jackpot Charley."

Twenty-five cents a punch—170 winners—proclaimed the red-and-yellow board. Tim reached his hands out.

"Don't touch the key; it's still sealed onto the back."

"Where the hell did you . . . ?" Don started to ask.

Nellie shook her head and put her hands up as if warding off a hex, ignoring Jackpot Charley altogether. "I'll give you another reason that Gus died a terrible death," she said.

"I want this talk stopped. Finished." Don stood up quickly, bumping the sandwich tray. "Gus was a terrible man. He did terrible things. That doesn't mean he was killed," he said. "He died, that's all." Looking at Nellie, he added, "He might have deserved to die, but that's not how the world works and you know it. This isn't a cowboy movie where somebody needs killing and—" Don stopped, distracted by the punchboard that Tim was running his hand over.

"Dad," Jane said, softly, "what is it?"

"I don't want that thing in the house. Punchboards are illegal," Don said and left the room.

Nellie hurried over to the coffee table and picked up the spilled sandwiches, wiping up crumbs with an unused napkin. Tim raised an eyebrow, but kept quiet. Jane looked around the living room. It was meticulously neat. Early American furniture, all reproductions Jane was sad to note, traditionally placed. The few knickknacks that Nellie allowed, the ceramic Lord's Prayer planter and three vases that had come from Don's mother, were spotless, never having held a bouquet of flowers or a sprig of ivy. Nellie didn't like cut flowers. "They just die and make a mess": Her all-purpose gripe against most living things.

In the small unspectacular house that Nellie kept dust-free, airtight, and dimly lit with forty-watt bulbs, Jane suddenly could not catch her breath. She felt as if she had inhaled talcum, powdered sugar, ragweed. Something in this house had just given off microscopic particles that whirled through her system and made her cough and choke. She stood up and stepped out onto the front porch.

September was still summer in Illinois, but the nights were cool and clear. Stars shone, and Jane looked up, trying to count them so she would not think about the look she'd seen on her father's face. The anger and impatience she had seen before—the hatred for Gus Duncan had burned in his eyes many times—but the look he gave before he left the room was a new expression. She couldn't define it precisely; it was a mixture, an emotional cocktail made up of many parts: guilt, memory, pain. They were all there. What else? What was the base of this complex formula?

"Why is your dad so scared?" Tim asked, suddenly standing beside her.

Fear? Was that it?

The next morning, unloading boxes at the EZ Way Inn, Jane tried to bring up Gus Duncan. Don changed the subject. When he saw Jane pushing her finger unnaturally toward her thumb and showing her mother while Nellie was slicing onions and tomatoes in the kitchen, Don said quietly but firmly that he wanted to erase the image of Duncan from his mind.

"I hated the sight of that man alive, and I thought nothing was uglier than his mug when he showed up the first of every month; but now I've got to live with something even uglier," Don said, shaking his head. "Leave it, Janie."

Whatever Jane had seen in her dad's eyes the night before had passed into something else. Acceptance? Relief?

Don and Nellie allowed Jane to unpack most of the boxes from the Shangri-La. They stored funny cocktail napkins and coasters with outrageous cartoons, hung old calendars with vintage beer and whiskey ads, usually involving a woman in a bathing suit, and Don ran his hands over the old ledgers with "Shangri-La" printed neatly at the top. Those Jane knew they wouldn't keep forever, but wanted to hear her dad exclaim over the wholesale prices of thirty years ago.

Nellie vetoed the shot glasses with the black horse head profiles, protesting that they didn't match the plain ones they already used.

"Besides, the more glasses you have, the more you end up having to wash," Nellie said. "Sell those to Tim. He pays a lot of money for junk, too."

Don made it clear that he wanted no gambling paraphernalia. When Jane tried to point out that the punchboards and horse racing bar games were examples of fabulous vintage graphics, just for display, her dad had remained unmoved.

"Pack them up, honey, and take them home," Don said. "No gambling here."

"I don't see why he's so against this stuff. We had it around all the time when I was a kid," Jane said to Tim as they walked around the basement of the Gerber house, Tim's new project and site of the Bishop McNamara High School fund-raiser. He handed Jane a round metal compact and sent her to the other end of the room.

"Measure those windows, honey, while you're talking," Tim said, sketching out the room in his graph notebook.

Jane looked down at the object he had put in her hand. In the center of the green disk was a gray leverlike piece. She pulled up on it and realized it was a crank. "Oh," she said, realizing this wasn't a compact, but an old tape measure with a silky worn tape that pulled out from a substantial metal loop. When you finished measuring, you wound that center lever/crank, reeling in the tape. Ah, the satisfaction of it all. The weight and heft of the piece. The sheer impracticality of a heavy metal measuring tape over three inches in diameter. She wanted it badly.

"Can I have this?" she asked.

"If I say no, are you going to Malcolm it?"

Jane wished she had never told Tim about Malcolm Morgan, the sweet blond boy who had lived down the block when she was four. His parents were wealthy and indulgent and had furnished him with a playroom separate from his bedroom filled with every imaginable toy. Once, when Jane was playing there, she had found an old purple velvet ring box with a white pearlized button, which popped open the lid with a satisfying snap. Jane had never seen anything so marvelous. She could not stop rubbing the velvet, snapping the lid.

"Can I have it, Malcolm?" she'd asked.

Malcolm offered Jane toys daily—anything she enjoyed he told her she could have, but she had always said no. Nellie had told her to accept nothing.

"Mark my words, later they'll say you stole it," Nellie said, waving a paranoid finger.

But surely this old ring case was something she could accept. It wasn't even a toy. It was just an old thing that someone had accidentally tossed into the well-stocked toy chest.

Malcolm had looked at the ring box, then at Jane's desperate eyes.

"No-o-o, I don't think so," Malcolm said, shaking his head.

Jane's mouth had dropped open. He had blocks and animals and art supplies and every jack-in-the-box, building set, and game manufactured in the past ten years. He was a generous and kind boy. But Malcolm, even at five years old, understood desire and value.

Jane's deep brown eyes, filled with need, had raised the value of this throwaway to priceless.

"My mom gave it to me, and she might want it back. I better keep it."

At four o'clock when Jane left for home, she and Malcolm stopped making the clay animals for the zoo they were building and walked down the winding staircase of his enormous house. Jane said good-bye and thank you to both Malcolm and his housekeeper and quickly walked the two houses back to her own.

The purple velvet ring box pulsed in her pocket.

That night, sleepless, tossing and turning, she called out to Nellie, who came and stood stonily at her bedside.

"If you had a friend who took something from her friend because she really wanted it but knew she had to give it back because she felt sick, what would you tell her to do?"

Nellie stared at Jane for what seemed like hours. Under the blankets, Jane snapped the ring case open, then coughed to cover the soft popping sound.

"I would say that when I was playing with it, I put it in my pocket and forgot about it, and then I would hand it over," Nellie said, uncharacteristically smoothing back Jane's hair over her worried forehead.

"And I would do it tomorrow," Nellie added.

Jane repeated the well-rehearsed lines to Malcolm the next morning. He barely looked up from the clay zebra he was finishing.

"Oh, well, you can just have it, I guess I don't really want it anyway."

Tim loved that story. The fear and desperation of Jane, the theft, the unknowing callousness of Malcolm, the uncharacteristic gentle wisdom of Nellie. It had everything. He brought it up to Jane every chance he could. His only regret was that Malcolm had moved to Indiana before they would have all met in first grade. Tim had a feeling that Malcolm would have been his second-best friend.

"If you help me measure the whole basement, I just might give you the tape measure," Tim said.

"I've outgrown Malcolming, you know," Jane said, looking down at the carved Bakelite ring on her finger. She *had* taken it from Richard Rose's store when there was no clerk on duty, but she had sent full payment in the mail the next day. No, her grown-up conscience was far too scrupulous to allow Malcolming.

She jotted down the uneven window measurements. "I think I kissed Eddie right over there. That was where the couch was."

There was no furniture left in the Gerber basement. It had been stripped of everything, including the old linoleum, and Tim was now throwing down flooring samples and sighing. "If the old stuff hadn't been damaged, I would have kept it. It had the look I wanted, that's for sure."

"You can find vintage flooring, Timmy, I . . ."

Jane and Tim both looked up at the sound of a door closing and footsteps above them.

"Tim, is that you down there?"

"Be right up, Lilly," Tim said.

Tim had told Jane that Lilly Duff was coming over. She had been three years behind them in high school and was now serving on the fund-raising committee with Tim.

She had even agreed to decorate a bathroom in the McNamara Flea Market Show House, now being referred to around town as "the McFlea." Jane remembered her not as a classmate, but as a fellow traveler. Her father had owned a bar just down the street from the EZ Way Inn. Like Jane, she had grown up waiting for her parents in backrooms, hoping the bartender wouldn't be too late. Unlike Jane, however, she hadn't broken the pattern. Duff's Bar was now Lilly's Place, and Jane was most curious about why she had decided to take on the family business.

As soon as Jane saw Lilly, sitting at the built-in breakfast bar, circa 1959, in the Gerber kitchen, she realized that now might not be the right time to ask her about her chosen profession. Lilly's hair was uncombed, her eyes circled with dark, puffy clouds.

"I have seasonal allergies," she said, sniffing softly and extending her hand to Jane. "I know you. We were in Sodality together at Mac."

Tim passed her a box of powdered sugar doughnuts and poured a cup of coffee. The coffeemaker, Tim's spare from the flower shop, was the only thing in the kitchen made after 1962. The Gerber house was frozen in time, just the way Jane wanted it to be. Now all she had to do was convince Tim that things should not be changed or redone, just enhanced.

"I can't do any redecorating, Tim," Lilly said. "I'm going to be really busy at the bar. I've got to let a lot of help go and do some longer hours for a while."

Lilly explained that buying the building from Gus Duncan had pushed her to her financial limits and that now there would be even more expenses, bringing the building up to code, taxes, and so forth. As plausible as it all was, Jane sensed that some part of her excuse for backing out of the fund-raiser had more to do with her puffy, sleep-deprived eyes than having to work longer hours at the bar.

"Sally Turney really wanted the first-floor bathroom anyway, so you should give it to her," Lilly said.

"Who'll take the kitchen then? It took me all night and a bottle and a half of decent Merlot to get her to agree to that," Tim said.

Jane had taken a rag from the box of cleaning supplies Tim had brought and was polishing one of the knobs on the old Chambers's stove. She turned it slightly and laughed out loud when the hissing of gas proved the stove still worked.

"This is priceless, Tim. I can't believe they left it in the house for you. They could have sold these appliances to a dealer for a small fortune."

"I do know how to write up an offer, honey. I bought the place as is."

"More like 'as was,'" said Lilly, rubbing her eyes as she sipped her coffee.

"Claritin?" Jane asked, turning back to Tim and Lilly, both seated at the wooden breakfast bar. She walked over to her backpack where she always carried a stash of what-ever Nick was taking or needing for his allergies.

Lilly stared blankly.

"For your hay fever," Jane said.

"Oh no, thanks," Lilly said. "I'm allergic to penicillin."

"It's not . . . ," Jane started to say, but realized Lilly was not listening to her. She had turned to Tim and whispered, purposely loud enough for Jane to hear. "I think I know someone who could take the kitchen so Sally could have the bathroom."

"Absolutely," said Tim, grinning at Jane.

"Full plate, baby," Jane said, shaking her head.

Tim laughed. "I don't want to be unkind, Janie, but may I remind you that you no longer have that advertising job that made you so nasty and busy all the time. You're carefree, with an independent son and a flexible husband."

"There's the EZ Way Inn to finish. Fall is major rummage and sale season, and I *do* work as a picker for Miriam. Nick still needs me around whether you think so or not . . . even if it's just to drive him to his soccer games. And since Charley and I are separated, he's not as flexible as you might think."

"Separated?" Tim snorted. "He still sleeps at your house."

"Of course he does; his stuff is there. We are *psychologically* separated, which is much more important than our physical arrangements," Jane said, starting to wonder if Lilly really needed to know about what she was beginning to think of as her living *derangements*.

"Besides, I'm going to be busy until Gus Duncan's murder is cleared up."

Lilly dropped her coffee cup. Jane and Tim both turned to her, Tim jumping up for a rag to sop up the liquid. No one said anything; then everyone said something.

"I'm sorry, I . . ."

"Let's get that before it . . ."

"You didn't know . . ."

They stopped, Tim holding up his hand. "Three-way stop. I yield to my right," he said, pointing to Jane with his coffee-soaked rag.

"Gus Duncan was murdered sometime yesterday. Maybe the day before . . . I don't know for sure yet. My dad and I found him at his house."

"I heard that he'd died, but . . ." Lilly stopped and wiped furiously at her eyes. "He wasn't murdered. He had a heart attack or something. He had high blood pressure. He was always complaining . . . he was sick."

"There are a few things that need to be explained before that's . . ."

"No, my brother knows somebody on the police force, and he told Bobby that it was a heart attack," Lilly said, standing up.

"Oh, Jane's got a theory about the whole finger thing, that Gus couldn't have almost cut his own finger off the way . . ."

"I might have Allegra in my backpack, do you want Allegra?" Jane asked.

"*What* are you talking about?" Lilly asked, her voice pitched high. "You think you can come back into town and just take over things like the know-it-all you were in high school? The police know what they're doing here. They don't need you to complicate matters."

Jane and Tim both looked at Lilly, who seemed now to want to take back her outburst but was uncertain how to begin.

"I didn't mean that," she said finally.

"It's okay," Jane said.

"You were just really smart and you seemed to have a lot going for you, even though you and I both—oh, I don't know—both came from the same place."

"The tavern?" Jane asked.

"Yeah. I knew who you were, a tavern kid just like me, but you were such a goody-goody and smart, too. President of all the clubs and stuff."

"Lilly, you were very popular in high school," Jane said, thinking that this was sounding more like an intervention than a show house fund-raiser meeting.

"Yeah, with the boys. I got them beer out of my dad's outside cooler."

Tim put his arm around Lilly. "Baby, you had tons more fun as a bad girl than Jane ever had as a good girl. Trust me on this. I had to take her to the prom for god's sake. The guys figured she'd never . . ." Tim stopped when he felt Jane staring a hole through the center of his forehead.

"This bad-good stuff makes no difference now, Lilly. We're all grown-up."

Lilly nodded and stood. "I'm still sorry I acted like a jerk. I've got to go back to work."

She let the screen bang shut on her way out of the kitchen.

"Hay fever, my eye," Jane said. "She no more has seasonal allergies than that"—Jane looked around for a definitive nonallergic object—"than that ironing board closet? Oh, Tim, you have a drop-down ironing board. That is so adorable."

"Yeah, yeah, you can feature it in your design. Now, what's the big deal playing pharmaceutical detective with that girl? Could you use a . . . Claritin, little girl?" Tim twirled an imaginary moustache and whirled around. "Or maybe an . . . Allegra would be more to your taste?"

Tim flopped down into a kitchen chair. "What the hell was going on, Nancy Goody Two-shoes Drew?"

"She didn't even know what a Claritin was, okay, so I figured she had been crying or was upset about something. Then I thought maybe Claritin wasn't the prescribed cure of choice around here, so I took a chance on Allegra; so it was clear . . ."

"It was clear that she had been crying and didn't want to give us an explanation. I'm an acquaintance not a friend, and you're barely that. You're a face in the yearbook, that's all, and, I might add, one with a lot of little clubs and award thingies under your name, which she obviously resents. Why would she want to tell you that her fourteen-year-old daughter stayed out all night with her boyfriend or her husband whacked her last night when he came home drunk?"

"I didn't know her daughter . . ."

"She doesn't have kids, but something's possible, isn't it? People have messy lives that screw them up, so they make excuses."

Jane started to nod but stopped. People did cover up hard lives, but Lilly Duff had actually driven over there and come to talk to them in person. Covering up involved phone messages left when you knew no one was around. Lilly could have called Tim's flower shop and left the message that she had to drop out of the project. She didn't have to show up where Tim had told her that he and Jane would be working. Jane had heard Tim tell her on the phone last night. Lilly had walked into the house hoping to find out something about Gus Duncan or make sure that Jane and Tim knew that the police were satisfied with natural causes.

"If Lilly has problems that make her cry and lose sleep, then she's used to making excuses. She might pick allergies, but it would be because she read an ad for Claritin or Allegra in *Family Circle* or *Women's Day* that described watery, itchy eyes and so forth. This was a last-minute, spur-of-the-moment excuse that someone uses because she's really desperate or determined or scared . . ."

"Okay, Nancy, what's she scared of? That we'll find out she murdered Gus Duncan, who after all those years of holding out finally agreed to sell all his property. People have wanted to kill that guy for at least thirty years. Why now *after* he's signed all the papers?"

She shrugged and went over to the refrigerator, opened it, and inhaled sharply when she saw small, square, GE glass refrigerator dishes neatly stacked inside.

"I'll do the kitchen," Jane said.

"Knew you would."

9

Jane measured the kitchen of the Gerber house with loving care. Using Tim's big green tape, she smoothed her hands over the window frames with worn, wide sills, just big enough for a few McCoy flowerpots with blooming African violets or trailing English ivy. She measured the depth of the pantry shelves, thinking about the vintage tins she might be able to find to fill them. She decided on the perfect spot for the beaded board spice rack she had at home waiting to be hung.

Tim knew her paperwork was in order, but nonetheless he'd asked her about the prices of all the pieces she already owned. A five-hundred-dollar limit he had said at least three times. To Jane, who had nickel-and-dimed her way through a hundred or more rummage sales, it was a lottery jackpot. She wouldn't even have to worry about walls since the painting was all to be donated by a Bishop Mac alum.

"You have a limited color palette," Tim told her, "but if you can choose today, the whole place will be done in a few days. Bill promised me a double crew doing a double shift. The second floor is already finished."

"Floors?" Jane asked.

91

"Not free, but a deep discount, babe. That's one of my donations to the project. Refinishing all the hardwood on the first and second floors. Everybody's got to live with the wood floors. The vintage baby black-and-white tile in the bathrooms—can't do better than the original—so we're keeping that. Just cleaning it up."

Jane nodded her approval. The bathrooms were gigantic, with room for a comfy chair and lamp; or, she supposed, for the more practically inclined, a treadmill and an exercise bike. Although why anyone would want to rack up no-distance miles when you could, instead, inhale the perfume of your child's bubble bath, curl up in a garage sale stuffed chair, and read aloud a chapter of *Charlie and the Chocolate Factory*, was beyond Jane's imagining.

Tim offered her black-and-white vinyl tile for the kitchen floor—he could get that from one of his magical discounters—but she shook her head. "I'll stick with the wood," she said, "if you'll let me paint the pantry floor."

"Deal."

She chose her wall color in three minutes. A rich off-white. Heavy cream that would allow the color in the room to come from all the kitchen linens and culinary objets d'art that she had by the boatload in her own kitchen and in storage. It was the exact color of the old stool that sat in a corner of her garage, milky paint peeling, waiting patiently for the *right* corner, which was right under the window she had just measured. Tim sighed when she tossed the paint card down on the table.

"Ah, *Buttermilk*. Thank you so much for not going jade-ite green, dear." Tim taped the color card into his notebook and put the rest of the samples back into the file.

"That jadeite stuff is pretty played, don't you think?" Jane asked. "Or maybe I'm just sick of it from the tavern."

Long before Martha Stewart popularized the pale green Fire-King kitchenware, Nellie had chosen the heavier restaurant version for the EZ Way Inn. Jane had sipped enough coffee and spooned enough chili out of green jadeite bowls to last her a lifetime.

"It's funny," Jane said, helping Tim pack up his supplies and check all the window locks on the first floor, "so much of the stuff I lust for is from my childhood, and yet that green stuff Nellie has at the tavern doesn't do a thing for me."

"Doesn't take a genius, dearie, to figure that one out. The jadeite is always greener on the other side. I mean Nellie's *got* all that stuff, so you don't need to replace it, do you?"

"Maybe," Jane said, pocketing the tape measure that Tim had agreed she could now "Malcolm."

"Maybe, nothing. You wander through all those sales of yours glassy-eyed, reliving every Saturday cleaning rampage Nellie ever went on, getting rid of your beloved stuff."

Jane shrugged but didn't argue. She knew Tim was half right. She did try to replace objects she remembered, objects she had loved. But what about the high school yearbooks and autograph books and photo albums that belonged to complete strangers? Why did she have box after box of those packed and labeled on shelves in her garage and in her attic? And the glass flower frogs? Nellie had never arranged a flower in her life.

The mania for sewing stuff and buttons, that probably came from Grandma; but all the rest, the skeleton keys and old locks, the Bakelite jewelry, the fishing lures, the turned wooden boxes, the folk art carvings, the sweet little beehive string holders . . . ? And on and on?

Poor Nick. He would have a hard time doing any family research when he went through her stuff. Who were all these people whose memories his mother had so lovingly cleaned and kept? She made a mental note to change the labeling on the boxes of photos from her wry EXTENDED FAMILY to the more explicit, NOT RELATED TO YOU, NICK. It was the least she could do.

When she returned to the EZ Way Inn, Jane witnessed the rare sighting of a sitting Nellie. Her mother was famous for perpetual motion. While Don might relax at the small desk behind the bar, going over the books or whiskey orders, Nellie manufactured some physical labor to keep herself moving. Wiping down the bar, cleaning the windows or glass on the jukebox, dusting the lamps that hung over the tables where the boys gathered after work for a quick euchre game or two before heading home . . . those were Nellie's reflex movements. Standing in front of the stainless-steel bar sink, as natural as breathing, she soaped, she rinsed, she wrung. She emptied ashtrays twice as fast as cigarettes burned.

But this afternoon, Nellie sat at the bar, sipping coffee from one of those thick jadeite cups, running her hand over something Jane couldn't quite make out as she slipped in the back door of the kitchen.

"Coffee break, Ma?" Jane asked, risking tirade number seven, "Who has time for a coffee break?"

But Nellie looked up slowly and shook her head.

Jane came over and saw that her mother was studying the punchboard, Jackpot Charley, that Jane had dropped back into a crate after her father had refused to display it.

"I haven't seen one of these things in a million years," Nellie said. "Where'd you say you got it again?"

"House sale, a tavern owner and his wife. He's dead and she's gone to assisted living, and they had all this stuff from the Shangri-La in their basement."

Jane poured herself a cup of the coffee, even though she knew she wouldn't be able to get past one swallow of the tarry paste her mother's coffee became after sitting on the warmer for six hours.

"Why is Dad so touchy about this stuff?"

"How am I supposed to know what he's thinking?" Nellie said.

"You know everything, that's why."

"Gambling hurt a lot of people. Lot of old friends."

"How'd it hurt Dad?" asked Jane.

Nellie looked at the board for at least thirty seconds before looking up.

"Who said it hurt *him*?"

Nellie hopped down from the bar stool with the agility of someone half her age. Jane knew that this signaled the end of the rare conversation with her mother. Rare since it didn't involve a dust rag; a conversation since Jane was allowed a sentence or two.

Hell, thought Jane, *she moves with the agility of someone half my age.*

Jane knew she shouldn't feel insulted by Munson's refusal to discuss Gus Duncan's death with her. She hung up the phone but continued to stare at it. He was right—she was not the police. Nor was she a member of the coroner's staff.

She was not even a reporter for the *Kankakee Daily Journal*. She was not a relative of Duncan's. She was not a PI. She blushed slightly, remembering just how high-handed Munson had sounded when she had interrupted his litany of what she was not, to ask what a PI was.

"That would stand for 'private investigator,' Mrs. Wheel, and you are clearly not that either."

Why am I not that? At least why am I *clearly* not that? Jane packed up all the tavern stuff rejected by Don and Nellie. She planned to drop it off for Tim, who might want some of it. She would then inventory the boxes, photograph some of the more interesting finds, and send the listing off to Miriam in Ohio, who would tell her what to pack up and send to her. Jane was Miriam's prime picker, and Miriam was Jane's professor in the study of buy and sell. Antiques, collectibles, vintage memorabilia, junk. Killer stuff. Miriam taught her what she needed to know and provided her with the trickle-down paychecks of other people's manias.

Jane bought it for a dollar. Miriam gave her two. Mr. Collector gave Miriam five. As long as someone wanted a handmade primitive shoeshine box with an art nouveau brass last fastened on the top, and as long as Jane could spot it and grab it at the Saint Nick's rummage sale for a dollar, Jane would have a job. Sort of. A picker. It wasn't exactly a job, she knew—more of a calling. She was good at it, though, and getting better. She hadn't quite made enough to prove to herself—or Charley or Nick for that matter—that she could actually pay the mortgage, but she was getting better.

She did come pretty close last month when she turned over some room-size hand-braided rugs that she had bought at an estate auction for just a few dollars. Most of the big dealers had gone to a more desirable sounding sale in Wisconsin, and Jane had stayed to the bitter end of this little under-advertised gem, picking up a lot of American primitive and country stuff, all hot now, and all at bargain prices. It had gotten her close to being able to actually pay some bills. She had also picked up a trunkful of old photographs, calendars, seed catalogues, and Elmira Selfridge's elementary schoolwork. *The family had been pretty proud of Elmira,* Jane thought, *since it appeared that every spelling test, every composition, and every arithmetic assignment had been carefully saved in a University of Illinois Agricultural Extension binder.* Naturally, Charley and Nick had asked more questions about the why of the trunk rather than the how of the truly profitable work of acquiring the rugs. Jane couldn't blame them. She couldn't explain to herself why she had to keep Elmira's colored maps and state capitals quiz. She couldn't explain her passion for purchasing the nonsensical things she often came home with that Miriam would not ever want to buy.

The best she could come up with was *If I don't conserve Elmira's work, who will?*

And that, she knew, was a tough sell.

Now, driving back to Evanston a few days ahead of schedule, she sifted through the events of the weekend. The thrill of finding Bateman's Shangri-La packed into boxes and hers for the picking seemed like centuries ago. Discovering Bateman's pickled finger also seemed like ancient history. Something about finding a dead body, or even, for that matter, a dead finger, threw off the mundane time schedule, the 24/7 of daily life. Everything slowed down because it was so important to sift through every minute, every second in order to piece together the why and how of the body, the death, the discovery. Or, if her hunch was right, the victim, the murder, the crime scene.

Jane called Oh on her cell phone and smiled when she heard his careful message. "This is Bruce Oh. Your call is important to me, so please say and spell your name, and repeat your phone number twice, slowly and carefully, and tell me, please, the best time to call you back."

"I'm on my way back to Evanston, so I'm on my cell; but I should be at home in, wait, did I say this is Jane, Jane Wheel, and my home phone, if you get this after an hour or so is, but wait, you have that, I'll give you the cell number first. It's new, I switched carriers, but I can't retrieve the voice mail on it yet, so . . ."

Oh's machine clicked off.

Jane had never gotten the hang of the succinct message. No matter. He would figure it out and call her back within five minutes of her arrival at home. Dropping her worn leather duffel on the floor by the back door when the phone rang, she hurried in and answered, "What took you so long, Detective Oh?"

"I am so sorry, I must've misdialed. Please forgive me," said a woman whose voice sounded familiar. "I hope there's no trouble?"

Jane recognized it on the second worried but curious remark.

"Is that you, Ollie? This is Jane Wheel speaking."

"Thank goodness. I thought I'd lost even more marbles and that I had copied down your numbers wrong. It was so teeny tiny on your card, I made a new listing for it in my big book. Now I've got this number and your portable one big enough so I can *see* them," Ollie said, clearly another one who hadn't gotten down the succinct, get-to-the-point telephone manner. "What? Oh, Dot says I'm rambling, and I shouldn't be bothering you."

Jane could picture Dot talking so quietly, her lips barely moving. She remembered giving them one of her old business cards and crossing out the firm's number, printing her home and cell phone number carefully under her name. Miriam was right. She did need to get some new cards, some cards that said Jane Wheel, *picker* or *dealer* or *vintage items bought and sold* or something that reflected her new status in the world.

"Are you busy with a client right now?" Ollie asked.

Jane remembered her little lie to the house sale worker about being an interior designer.

"No, no, I'm not busy at all," Jane said, not sure why she was so thrilled to be hearing from the Shangri-La ladies. She got out a handfull of Cheerios and began feeding them to Rita, her adopted German shepherd, who had been sitting obediently waiting for some attention. Rita munched while putting one giant paw on Jane's lap, keeping her close. Out of habit, Jane, like any good commercial producer, picked up a pencil and began doodling, ready to take down numbers, notes, complaints, whatever seemed necessary.

"We were just over at Mary's new place, that is, me and Dot, and we told her all about the sale and meeting you and how you bought up all Bateman's Shangri-La stuff, and she was saying how she'd love to meet you . . . what, Dot? Oh yes, Mary's a little bored in the assisted-living apartment. It's a slower crowd than she's used to, you know? Anyway, we told her we had your number, and we'd try to get you to come over and see her, maybe tell her about the place you're designing that's going to have a little Shangri-La in it?"

Even though it was against all Jane's rules to meet an owner or seller, she agreed to meet Dot and Ollie in the lobby of the Grand Heritage at three so they could introduce her to Mary. She avoided sellers, but not for the reason that a dealer had given her while making small talk one Saturday morning standing in line at a huge estate sale.

"Relatives always want to charge you more. They think their parents' junk is worth a million, you know. They watch those bozos on the *Roadshow* and suddenly think that their daddy's old pencil sharpener—the one that sharpened the pencil of the nephew of the guy who ran against so and so for state comptroller—is worth a mint. So I want it 'cause it's got a Bakelite base and I can sell it for five or ten bucks, and they got a twenty-five-dollar price tag on it, you know?"

Jane knew. It was the same twenty-five-dollar price tag he'd put on it himself when he got it to his booth at the antique mall. Maybe he'd even charge thirty or thirty-five.

Jane didn't mind the relatives because of overpricing. She found that just as often, they were sad-faced and apologetic, asking a dollar or two for plates or vases that were clearly worth more to anyone who turned them over and read the markings for California Pottery. Jane had found two Griswold cast-iron baking pans in the basement at an estate sale. They were so heavy and bulky that the family member who checked Jane out wanted to just give her the "filthy old things." Jane had pressed a five-dollar bill into her hand and sped to her car like a thief. Miriam would price the pans at eighty-five dollars and probably accept seventy-five. That meant she'd give Jane thirty or maybe forty dollars each. She was generous to Jane, her protégée, and Jane was grateful. If she could only get over the guilt that the families didn't know what they were selling. The guilt was why she avoided the relatives.

"Look," Tim had lectured her, "you gave them five dollars more than they would have gotten if they had put them in the alley or, for that matter, if they had given them to anyone else. Another picker might have faked it a little, like, 'Oh, maybe I could use 'em for screws or something in the garage or give 'em to my grandkids for the sandbox' then strolled off to his truck cackling over his *find*. *Finds*, my dear Jane, depend on a good eye, which you have, patience to sift through rubbish and get dirty, which you also have, and luck."

"Which I have, too, don't I?" Jane asked, while Tim took a breath.

"Luck is a two-part invention. The first part is being at the right place at the right time. Figuring out the best sale to start with, being the early bird, and so forth. You've got that part down pretty well."

"And part two?"

"Acceptance," Tim said. "Picking up the butterscotch Bakelite cowboy-hat pin with the dangling boots, which, I might add, are dangling from their original strings, out of a child's junk jewelry box and handing over the requested dime, putting it in your pocket, and continuing to poke around instead of blushing beet red and looking like you're going to be arrested at any minute."

"I don't . . ."

"I've watched you, babe. In this situation, your eyes would roll back in your pretty head and you'd be thinking about the girl's grandma giving her this pin that she picked up in a dime store for some spare change when she was a little girl and then when her little granddaughter said she liked horses, Grandma gave it to her and Little Sally wore it every day; but now she's a big girl and wants to buy flared jeans, and she's selling out Grandma and her whole history by letting you buy this pin for a dime. She'll regret it, oh yeah, and spend her adulthood going to rummage sales and auctions trying to find a pin just like the one Grandma gave her."

Jane wanted to tell Tim to shut up, but she was afraid her voice might crack.

"Luck is acceptance, Jane."

Jane had been poking around in Tim's flower shop while he was giving her his "picker's tutorial," and she picked up a small, Redware pitcher, noting a tiny chip on the spout. Just a fleabite, but it explained why Tim had it among these lesser vases for his loose and blowsy arrangements.

"Okay," Jane said.

"Okay what?"

"I'll accept luck when it comes along."

"Too easy."

"I'll accept luck," Jane said, finally smiling, "because when Little Sally grows up and finds that she needs

Grandma's cowboy-hat pin more than anything in the world, more than new clothes, more than eating in restaurants, more than advancements in her career, she'll start going to rummage sales and thrift stores and flea markets and she'll find stuff that she likes and admires and has to buy; but it won't be quite the thing, you know, so she'll keep going and one day, she'll be at a house sale and it'll be there, in a jewelry box, and it won't cost a dime anymore, but she won't mind because she'll know that the money was spent in paying someone to be the caretaker all these years."

"Gag me, please," said Tim, "and are you hovering over the house as an angel, watching your estate go to all those deserving little boys and girls now grown up?"

"Don't be ghoulish. You and I are financing our apartments in a very fancy senior complex, where we will live happily ever after."

It wasn't the usual guilt clouding this meeting with Mary Bateman. Jane knew that she had paid more than the going price for much of the Shangri-La merchandise that was now being hung or displayed or washed and dried and racked up at the EZ Way Inn. Jane's guilt was too strange to discuss even with Tim. As she sat in the parking lot of the Grand Heritage, ten minutes early for her meeting, she was in serious debate with herself over the finger still in her glove compartment. On the one hand, why would you bring up something so disturbing to an elderly widow in a nursing home?

"Oh, by the by, Mary, I've come across a finger you might like to have . . ."

There's a conversation starter.

On the other hand, this finger was surely Bateman's, and even if Mary didn't want to keep Bateman's finger, she might not want someone else to have it.

"And I don't want to give it up," Jane admitted out loud, looking at the glove compartment.

Why she didn't want to part with it, she couldn't say. It was a curious attachment, and even Jane, who was a master of the creative, long-winded explanation for the whys and wherefores of keeping the stuff she did, could not put her finger on the reason she could not let Bateman's finger go. Not yet.

Dot and Ollie parked and got out of a small, silver Saturn on the other side of the parking lot. Ollie was talking a mile a minute, and Dot was staring straight ahead, nodding occasionally. The sight of the two women, both wearing the senior uniform of pastel jogging suits and running shoes, made Jane smile. Just as she began opening her car door, her cell phone rang. "La Cucaracha." Nick had been at the "menu options" again.

10

"I have found two pieces of information for you, Mrs. Wheel. I'm not sure that either one will shed enough light to be valuable, but perhaps, together, they will lead your way."

Jane slid down in the driver's seat, not wanting Dot or Ollie to spot her and come over until she'd heard what Detective Oh had to tell her.

"There were no police reports filed regarding an attack on Mr. Bateman, no descriptions of an incident over an injured or severed finger."

"Not much light there," said Jane, printing "no police report" in her small notebook.

"There was information about Mr. Bateman in the files though. He served a short time in prison on a gambling offense," said Oh. "Six months only. He was released, apparently, because of some missing paperwork on his case."

"Is that common? Losing paperwork gets you out of jail?"

Detective Oh hesitated. "Not common, exactly, but possible. There may have been some kind of deal struck after the fact. Or perhaps, something was not on the up and up from the beginning. These gaming charges were confusing. Seems the state laws and federal laws were in conflict, and many tavern owners, holders of Illinois liquor licenses, were implicated in these so-called gambling raids. The paperwork is incomplete and sloppy in Mr. Bateman's case."

"Is there some way to find out more details?" Jane asked.

"It has been my experience that when paperwork goes missing, it stays missing," said Oh. "Most of the principals in this particular case are long gone . . . the judge, the lawyers. Perhaps if you had a way of talking to Mrs. Bateman? If you could somehow be put in touch with her, in some non-threatening role? A friendly conversation can reveal the most astonishing facts."

Jane sat up straighter. Dot and Ollie were standing by the large, double-doored entrance to the Grand Heritage scanning the parking lot. Jane opened her car door, stood up, and waved at them.

"I'll see what I can do," Jane promised.

Mary Bateman was like no one else. She was the paradox you encountered at a party, exotic yet familiar. Someone who enchanted you with her unique personality, her unconventional look, but someone with whom you felt totally at home. When she took Jane's hands in hers, she radiated warmth, but the handshake itself was firm and cool. If Jane had to explain it to Nicky, she might try out the term "soul mate," which would no doubt cause him to roll his eyes all the way up into his head, shudder and whis-per, "Not the sixties, Mom, please, don't flashback to the sixties, Mom."

"Leonard, say hello to Dot and Ollie and Jane," Mary said, introducing her visitors to her euchre partner. "Len and I just whipped the Bagwell twins, didn't we, hon?" Mary asked, pointing to two women—dressed in identical red warm-up suits—walking arm in arm toward the large coffee urn set up on the other side of the parlor.

Leonard was an elegantly dressed octogenarian. Tan slacks, a navy blue silk shirt, and a red-and-navy striped tie, perfectly knotted at his collar. His hands were folded over his cards, a soft crepe tent, and he slowly lifted one of them and bent his already curled fingers into a wave. His movements, the wave, a slight turn of the head, all came with some effort; but his eyes were quick, darting from woman to woman to woman, resting finally on Mary. His whole body sighed as if he'd like to keep those eyes resting on Mary for a good long time.

"Leonard doesn't speak," Mary said. "Stroke. But he still knows his left bower from his right, don't you, dear?" she asked, gesturing to the jack of clubs played in the last trick. "See you later, baby."

Jane thought she might have seen tears gather in Leonard's eyes, but a younger man quickly came and wheeled him away from the card table as soon as Mary turned toward the hall.

"They're on the ball here," said Dot. "They've got an attendant making sure you're not stuck alone for a second."

"That's Leonard's private nurse, dear," said Mary. "Around here, it's the only way to fly."

"He was somebody, I bet," said Ollie. "Does he dress like that every day?"

"Don't be a sucker, Ollie. Any moron can tie a tie. Or pay someone to tie it for you, as the case may be."

Mary exuded lithe energy, despite the clumsiness of the walker she had begun to use for exercise. She led them down the hall to her neat one-bedroom apartment. Her silvery hair was long and wavy, and during Jane's visit, Mary put it up in jeweled hair sticks, took it down and rewound it into a french twist, shook it out yet again, and nimbly braided it into a single tail that hung down her back. The mere fact that she could use her fingers so ably and hold her arms up to do the braiding showed an admirable dexterity and a near miraculous lack of arthritis.

Jane ran her own hands through her thick, short hair. She understood Dot and Ollie's dismay at Mary being assigned to assisted living. Mary seemed capable, not only of taking care of herself, but assisting several others at the same time. When Ollie began describing one New Year's bowling tournament where they had all gotten snowed in, Mary raised both her hands in protest.

"Hush, Ollie, you're boring our guest to death with tales of the old Shangri-La," drawled Mary. "That place's dead and buried, child, dead and buried. Tell me about the rebirth, Ms. Wheel."

Mary had blue eyes. Normally, Jane trusted brown eyes. She felt they somehow demanded truth, both from the speaker and listener. Humble, yet rich. Deep, yet vibrant. Yes, brown eyes were the reliable feature of the true soul mate. Mary's eyes, though, threw everything Jane had believed out the window.

It was now that sparkling blue that commanded attention. Jane was mesmerized, riveted by Mary's stunning eyes.

The old black-and-white photos had captured her movie-star allure, but that was nothing compared to the spell she cast in full living color.

"It's going to be a humble rebirth, I'm afraid," Jane said, "but a loving one."

"Do tell," said Mary, folding her manicured hands and sitting up straighter to listen.

Jane explained that she was a picker, not a designer, but that lately the picking was leading her into some designing projects. She told her about the McFlea House fund-raiser and Tim, and found herself talking about Charley and Nick and her confused marital status and con-fused professional status, and after running on for longer than Ollie ever had, she realized she was near tears.

Mary had not stirred. Dot had gotten up and poured Jane a glass of water, and Ollie had nodded and clucked through the entire story. As Jane drank the water, she real-ized that she had explained how Tim had convinced her to decorate the kitchen of the McFlea, and that Tim would use Shangri-La collectibles in the basement party room. She had talked for several minutes and explained much in great detail, but she hadn't yet mentioned her own tavern connection. She hadn't told Mary she was a saloon keeper's daughter.

"I don't know why I've rambled on so," Jane said. "Sorry."

"Did you find the punchboards?" Mary asked. "Do you know what they are?"

"Yes, yes, I found them," Jane said. *Here it comes. I babble on to sympathetic ears, and now I hear her story of how she wants everything back.*

"If you don't use them in your show house, dear, you can sell them on Ebay for good money. My granddaughter says there are idiots out there who will buy anything."

Jane nodded. She was too familiar with those idiotic Jane Wheel types.

Jane tried to direct the conversation to Bateman himself and the golden days of the Shangri-La.

"Golden days?" Mary said. "Some people think whatever anybody else does must be fun or glamorous or romantic or some such stuff. I'll tell you what running a tavern was like, honey. It was plain hard work, serving drunks and layabouts who couldn't hoist their lazy butts off a bar stool to get home to their wives and kids."

"Mary."

Dot spoke so rarely that when she said her friend's name, it had the effect of a major chord being struck in an auditorium. Everyone turned expectantly, waiting for her to begin the concert.

"The Shangri-La was a nice, clean place, and there were plenty of wonderful people who came there just to be a part of something, especially when times were tough. Bateman always welcomed everyone, and we all felt like it was our place, you know. Not fancy, but . . ." Dot seemed to lose her place for a moment, "fun and friendly."

"'Where everybody knows your name,'" Jane said, quoting the *Cheers* theme song.

Three pairs of eyes, a combined total of more than two hundred years of vision, stared a hole through Jane.

"It's from a television program," Jane said. Why did she feel like she should apologize?

"Of course it is," Mary said.

"I did know everybody's name," said Ollie, "and if I didn't know somebody, I went over and asked what the hell he was doing in our bar."

Dot nodded. Apparently her defense of the old days of the Shangri-La was enough talking for one day.

Jane envied these three old friends, their brains uncluttered with the debris of television theme songs and advertising jingles. Their memories of who came up with the design for the bowling shirts or who decided what to serve for snacks on euchre night were perhaps just as trivial as some of Jane's, such as the name of the actor who played Diane's professor on *Cheers*. These women's memories seemed, at least to Jane, more important, more real. Maybe it was because those stories that they told and retold truly belonged to them. How many conversations did Jane have with people her age that began with, "Remember on *Seinfeld* when George . . ." The memories she shared with her peers she also shared with millions of others whom she had never met, would never meet. *Television*, she thought, *where nobody knows our name*. Even conversations with Tim, with whom she had shared her childhood, her real life, were often peppered with television and movie and song references. *It keeps us at a distance from each other*, Jane thought; *we wear it like armor*.

"I do feel a little guilty about that, I guess, but that's the only thing," Mary was saying to Ollie. "I was on painkillers, and I guess, truth be told, I was a little mad at Susie for arranging everything so fast."

"The pictures," Mary said, turning to Jane. "I told those house sale people it was okay to get rid of everything I'd left in the basement, but I didn't think about the pictures."

"I'll bring them back to you," Jane said.

"You bought them, too?" Mary asked. "Why on earth?"

"They were there," Jane said.

Blank stares again.

"You know, when someone asks why someone climbed a mountain and he answers, 'Because it was there'?"

Nothing.

"I buy stuff. Collect stuff. I'm not always sure why I buy what I buy. Sometimes it's because of my childhood memories, something I remember from our kitchen or something of mine that my mom got rid of.

"But sometimes, it's somebody else's memory, a dream of what somebody's life is like. I hold an old cake breaker with a red Bakelite handle and I like it because it's Bakelite, but I also like it because in someone's life, somewhere, a mother or an aunt baked an angelfood cake and used this little outdated tool to divide it up and put it on little Lu-Ray pastel dessert plates, sharon pink, I like to picture, and spooned fresh-sliced strawberries over it and sang "Happy Birthday" to someone they all cared about, then . . ."

Uh-oh, thought Jane, *they're thinking about how to get me to the locked ward.*

"I'm just a little nuts about this stuff," Jane said, apologizing. "Sorry."

"No, dear, you shouldn't apologize," Mary said. "It's beautiful what you said. It's nice to know somebody cares about preserving the past, telling the stories."

"Even if you make them up yourself," agreed Ollie.

Dot nodded and patted Jane's hands, which were clasped tightly together in her lap, just like a good schoolgirl waiting for Sister Rose to dismiss her for lunch.

Jane did a quick mental inventory and realized that in less than an hour, she had told the three women about her marriage, her current career status, and revealed herself as a raving lunatic, but had not found out one thing about Bateman and the bloody bandage in the wedding photo.

"I had a feeling someone might care about those photographs," Jane said, smiling at Mary.

"Not me, honey. All my photos are right here." She pointed to her head; "and when they're not here or they get fuzzy, I don't want the evidence that I'm losing my marbles right in front of me."

"Pictures would help your memory, wouldn't they?" asked Ollie.

"I'm not going to be the old broad, jabbing at a wrinkled picture saying that was your Aunt Minnie, or was it her sister-in-law, and, wait a minute, was that in forty-three or forty-four? Nope, when I forget it, I'll make me some new memories, girls," Mary said. "Jane here is a born caretaker; she's like one of those people who make up the displays in the museums and use them to teach history or something. Not me."

Mary opened a beaded black bag on the table next to her and took a lipstick from its ornate gold container. She outlined her mouth, using the tiny, narrow mirror hinged to the case, then continued.

"Nope. The photographs are for Susie. She's the one who needs to make sense of her past. It was thoughtless of me to let all the pictures of her mom go. I should have given her a chance at them before I waved good-bye."

"I'll pack them up for her," Jane said. "There are wedding pictures in there that I'm sure she'd like."

"Maybe so," Mary said, closing her makeup bag. She drilled her blue eyes into Jane's. "Not me, though. I couldn't care less about the whole mess."

As Jane drove home, she tried to organize her thoughts about Mary Bateman. Mary had gone on to tell Jane that if she ever got sprung from assisted living, she wanted a loft. "Just a big open space with some simple, straight-back chairs and a new record player, CD player, whatever they've got that's the best. Music and a phone to order takeout Chinese. And a good bed, simple, new, and clean. I don't want to be one of them old-timers who can't throw out the garbage," Mary said, wrinkling her nose.

Dot and Ollie both giggled when Mary mentioned the good bed. Raised eyebrows and winks passed among them.

Jane wasn't sure whether or not Mary was entirely forthcoming. She might have talked the clean and uncluttered talk, but a few things in her room belied her walking the walk. Jane had noticed the book by her bed, a romance novel that lay open. Mary's bookmark was a photo strip, the old-fashioned, black-and-white kind where people posed in a dime store booth. The four photos on Mary's bookmark were pictures of her with Bateman, their heads touching, smiling first at the camera, next at each other, and in the last two kissing. Mary's head was tilted back, and she kept one hand on the top of her small feathered hat to prevent it from falling off. The photo was wrapped in clear plastic and taped on its sides. Home-made lamination. It was done with the kind of care that someone uses to protect something precious; yet the fact that it was clumsy and makeshift told Jane it was done by someone who covered up all sentiment, someone who professed to the world that the past was past, someone who didn't want to ask her granddaughter where you got something laminated, someone private, so protective of her memories that she could not frame the photo and display it for the world.

Jane also noted that Dot and Ollie referred to Bateman by name in all their talk about the Shangri-La. And although Mary might say a few words about the bowling league or the Christmas decorations they put up every year, she never spoke Bateman's name. It was a deafening omission.

And then, of course, there was the lipstick, a nearly new tube of Clinique Earth Red Jane had noted before Mary had put it back into her bag. But the gold case she'd slipped it into! Vintage Cartier. Thirties? Mary might have a little curator in her after all.

11

Jane threw together some dinner from what she could find in the cabinet. Pasta with a sauce made up of artichokes, black olives, roasted red peppers, and a jar of pesto. She hadn't wanted to cook at all, just make the announcement, "Animals in the Jungle," which meant that it was every Wheel for him or herself—you find it, you kill it, you eat it.

Nick had been pleased to see her home a few days earlier than expected. Happy to sit at the kitchen table and talk about his day, his homework, the teacher who hated him, the teacher he hated. Jane knew if she didn't cook, didn't busy herself around the kitchen counter, she'd lose him to television. As long as she could pour things into pans and stir, she seemed to be able to hold him there. She rummaged for cookie ingredients.

"I'll break the eggs," Nick offered.

He was almost as tall as she was, but he still liked to do those "first" chores, those little jobs that every child started on, standing on a stool, wrapped in an apron at the kitchen counter. His voice had deepened, and he spent a long time combing his hair every morning, sure signs that he was growing up and away; but still, Jane thought, he still likes being here with me.

"Dad's coming home for dinner, right?" Nick asked.

Us, Jane corrected herself, *he likes being here with us.*

"I suppose," Jane said. "I didn't tell him I was coming back, so he'll be coming home to you."

"And we'll surprise him with this great dinner," Nick said.

"Whatever you say, Nick."

Jane felt hope rise off Nick's body like steam.

"Dad and I are always going to be together for you, Nick, even if we're not always together for us. Know what I mean?"

"Sure, whatever," Nick said, shrugging and not looking at her while breaking up the egg yolks with a fork. "Can I do the mixer?"

Later, after dinner, Jane went over a schedule with Charley while she inventoried their kitchen. She knew that much of what she would use for the McFlea House could come from her own store of supplies. Tim wanted assurances from everyone that they hadn't gone over their spending limit, but he wasn't too worried with Jane.

"I know you're a nickel-dimer, dearie," Tim said. "When you start hauling in the rummage, folks will be throwing money at you to go out and buy something new and real, for god's sake."

Still, Jane knew that stuff added up. It used to be that those sweet little crocheted pot holders cost a nickel or dime. That's how she'd got hooked on them. She remembered her grandmother sitting in front of television, small needle clicking away. No one ever used these handmade treasures. They sat in a drawer, hung on a wall. Now she picked them up out of other people's drawers and cast-off boxes, thinking of herself as the conservator of crochet. All that work and no granddaughters or grandsons wanted to at least make room in their own drawers in order to let the color brighten their day. Sure, they were too small to be useful and too delicate to handle one of those heavy enameled cast-iron pans that the foodies nowadays hefted onto the stove for their bouillabaisse, but couldn't these yups just tuck them into a drawer?

"Great-grandma made those," they could say to their own kids, when they asked to crack the eggs or do the mixer.

Charley rinsed the dishes as he always did when she cooked. A pale blue scalloped-edge platter of still warm cookies sat on the counter. The scene was domestic bliss and Jane, sorting through boxes of stored kitchen collectibles at the table, realized she could have sold any number of household products had this been a commercial she had produced.

"Nick's in a tournament in Wisconsin this weekend, and the Conners offered, so I was thinking of just letting him go and stay at the motel with them," Charley said. "Okay with you?"

"I guess, but . . ."

Jane stopped counting out place settings of red and green and butterscotch Bakelite flatware and looked at Charley. "Don't you like going to those? I thought you . . ."

"Of course. Love it. But this weekend there's a little get-together with all the people who were on the dig this summer, and I wanted to . . . you know . . . go," Charley said.

Was he blushing?

"Sure, of course," Jane said. "I'll call Jill and ask her the details and help Nick pack a bag and all that," Jane said.

"I talked to her already, and we're all set. They have a half day of school on Friday, so they're leaving then. If you want to go to Kankakee for the whole weekend, you're free."

Jane nodded.

"Free as a bird," Charley added, cursing himself for sounding so stupid. Perhaps he should have made a neon sign that flashed, "I'm going to go to a party and flirt with graduate students."

Jane smiled and turned back to the flatware.

"Okeydokey, then," Charley said, wondering where that expression had come from, wanting to slap himself in the forehead. "P.S.," the neon would say, "it's just so I can remember who I was."

When Jane was about to call Detective Oh to tell him that she had learned nothing and something from Mary Bateman, the phone rang.

"Jane, my little sleuth, you're going to love my news," Tim said, singsonging the last part.

"You've decided to give me that Roseville vase that you never liked anyway?"

"Better."

"Lily called and admitted that she had never had an allergy in her life and that she killed Duncan?"

"Better."

"Give."

119

"Duncan had a nephew; he's the only living relative. And Duncan had already put two of the shanties in the nephew's name. The only thing Duncan owned when he kicked was the shack he lived in."

"How is this so good?" Jane asked.

"The nephew, Bill Crandell, stopped in at the shop and asked T & T Sales to empty out the shanties. He took one peek and said he wanted to torch them, but thought better of it and hired Tiny Tim."

Tim was crowing, and Jane was confused. She knew that there were three shanties in the block south of the EZ Way Inn. Duncan lived in one, and, she assumed, he rented the others.

"Nah, Duncan lived in one until it was filled up with crap, then moved to the next one. He lived in the first one about ten years, the second one six, and he had lived in the one where you and your dad found him about three."

"What kind of crap? He died in the middle of garbage. Was that what he left behind in the other houses?" Jane asked. Despite her negative words to Tim, she noticed she was feeling a small tingle of excitement at the back of her neck.

"Lots of garbage, but according to Crandall, there're boxes of papers, dishes, letters, books, you name it. When he bought buildings . . . you know, taverns and restaurants and whatever, previous owners left lots of stuff. Crandall says Gus never threw anything away, just boxed it all up and brought it home," Tim said. "So I thought you and me, baby, might . . ."

"We can't do a house sale at a crime scene," Jane said.

"My poor, sweet deluded Jane," Tim began, "no one, not

one police person, civilian, enemy, or friend of Duncan has suggested foul play."

"He had no friends."

"Doesn't mean he was murdered, oh daughter of Nellie," said Tim. "You're sounding more like your mother every day."

"He did not slice his own finger to the bone while . . ."

Jane stopped. What had the police, her father, Lilly, Tim all said? They'd all insisted that he was making a sandwich and accidentally cut his finger while slicing a something, probably a tomato, had a heart attack, and collapsed. Or had a heart attack and, as a kind of bizarre reflex, kept slicing away. Okay, maybe it was possible. *It wasn't*, she thought, *but if it was* . . .

"Tim, I'm not guessing; I know I'm right about this."

"I'm listening."

"No tomato."

"No tomato?" asked Bruce Oh. He was admiring the three-compartment dish Jane had set out with blue cheese-stuffed olives, pickled onions, and lemon slices. Oh knew nothing about barware or kitchenware per se. Claire tried to educate him on what was collectible and what was junk. Jane Wheel, on the other hand, preached that nothing was junk; all was collectible. He liked this snack dish, with its shiny chrome and modern shape. The handles, solid bars on each side, were rich red, line carved. He tapped one with his index finger.

"Bakelite?"

"Chase," Jane said, nodding.

Why did he often feel that a conversation with Mrs. Wheel might not always take place in English?

"Not Bakelite?"

"Sorry, yes, the handles are Bakelite. It's a Chase chrome tray," Jane said, picking it up and holding it high enough for Oh to see the Chase symbol, the archer, half-man, half-horse, etched into the bottom. She picked up two olives that had spilled out and popped them into her mouth.

"I probably wouldn't bother with martinis if they didn't come with so many accessories," Jane said.

Charley was going to say that what Jane drank—Grey Goose vodka on the rocks with a toothpick full of olives soaking in it—was hardly a martini since it contained no vermouth, but thought better of it. It had been such a pleasant evening, coming home to find Jane and Nick making dinner, the smell of home-baked cookies in the air. And even if they were doing this upside down, having martinis after dinner, it was a comforting ritual, wasn't it? Jane would say it was more fun to do it this way, upside down, and Charley knew that it was what he had found so charming in the first years of their marriage. Jane liked conventions; she just didn't like to perform them conventionally. Why now, after years of adoring her quirky charm, did he hear his own voice, impatient and weary, correcting, scolding, lecturing?

"What is this missing tomato?" asked Oh again. He had hurried over when Mrs. Wheel called. A drink would be nice. Claire was working at her stall at the antique mall, unearthing all her Halloween and Thanksgiving collectibles and rearranging displays.

"Munson or one of the detectives dismissed Duncan's cut finger, saying he was cutting a tomato or something when he had a heart attack. He was on the floor in front of the sink, holding the knife, and his finger was nearly cut off. But there was no tomato out on the counter. No food. The sink was piled with crusty dishes, looked like a lot of unrinsed cereal bowls or something, some moldy. Lots of glasses. This place was a shrine to filth, so a tomato, a fresh red tomato, would stand out."

"I know you have the eye for observing details, Mrs. Wheel, but it didn't really have to be a tomato. The policeman there might have just meant, because it was a serrated knife and he was found where he was found, that he was preparing to slice something, to fix some kind of food," said Oh.

"Tomato as metaphor?" offered Charley. He had been gathering papers to take back to the apartment for the night but found himself drawn to the discussion.

Oh nodded.

"Metaphor for what? Lettuce? That's the first thing I saw when I went into the dump. There were fast-food sandwich wrappings all over the place, on the floor, covering the coffee table and chair arms. The 'works'—you know, lettuce, tomato, pickle—all that stuff had been peeled off the sandwiches and lay rotting in the wrappers," Jane said.

She took a long, thoughtful sip of her drink and set it down.

Jane turned to Charley and Oh. "Look at this bar," she said.

"Charming," said Oh. In spite of his protests to his wife

that he abhorred objects, too many things cluttering up their house, he had to admit that the tableaus set up by Mrs. Wheel were quite seductive. On this wooden table, with the black cast-iron base, she had set out three brass and Bakelite trays. Chase, she called them. A round ice bucket with penguins circling its middle sat between the trays. Cocktail forks with tiny Bakelite dice attached to the handles poked out of a red-and-butterscotch Bakelite deck of cards base. The olives and onions and lemon peel all seemed more delectable in their surroundings. A drawer in the bar was open, overflowing with an appealing stack of mismatched, embroidered cocktail napkins. Detective Oh noticed with a start that the bar was really an old sewing machine table. Mrs. Wheel had removed the sewing machine that would have unfolded from the top and saved the life of this outmoded piece of equipment.

"If all the olives were left in the dish, and if you saw my glass with my fingerprints on it over there on the table with the drink gone, but the olives on a toothpick thrown out next to it, you'd probably figure I didn't eat olives, right?" Jane didn't wait for an answer. "So if you found me dead with my hand stuck in an olive jar, trying to get the last one out, wouldn't you find that strange?"

Neither Charley nor Oh said anything. Nick had come in to say good night around the time of *the tomato as metaphor* and had been puzzled enough to stay quietly in the corner and listen. Now he forgot that he was being silent so no one would notice him and send him to bed. "No, Dad likes olives," Nick said.

The three adults turned to look at him.

"We'd just figure you were getting the last olive for

Dad. Or Detective Oh," Nick said. He came over and leaned in toward his mother, brushing her slightly. It was this year's version of a hug. "Night."

"Do you suppose the police checked to see if there was any food in the refrigerator? Anything he might be preparing to cut or fix?" Charley asked.

"Munson mentioned that the refrigerator was filled with packages of leftover take-out food, all old and spoiled. You had to see this place," Jane said, shuddering a little. "He hadn't throw away newspapers or junk mail. He hadn't taken out the garbage in weeks."

"Langley Collyer syndrome," said Oh. When Jane and Charley shook their heads, he continued. "Two brothers in New York, Homer and Langley Collyer were found dead in their apartment surrounded by their accumulated possessions, newspapers, garbage. Langley took care of Homer, who was blind, but he got tripped up by one of his own booby traps and they both starved to death. Took days to haul out enough stuff to get to the bodies."

Charley looked around their living room. Forties flowerpots, planters, and vases; stacks of vintage luggage; small, wooden children's chairs piled high with elementary school readers from the '40s and '50s, old calendars, boxes of punchbowl sets, and trays full of pressed-glass tumblers; hobnail glass bottles; wooden sewing boxes; tins of Bakelite buttons tucked into the niches in the bookcases, waiting to be sorted. And more, always more coming in every Friday when the weekend sales began, Thursday if there was an early start rummage sale.

"Uh-oh," he said.

"I still take the garbage out," Jane said.

Charley picked up a crudely carved beakless duck with a hole in its head. Perched on its base, it was surrounded by pickets, but no fence.

"Some would beg to differ," he said.

"That's not garbage," Jane said, snatching it from him. She picked up a pair of scissors from the coffee table where Nick had been cutting out a science article from the newspaper for homework and placed the scissors through the hole in the duck's head. The blades formed the beak. Charley realized then that the tiny dowels sticking up on the base were meant to hold spools of thread. It was actually a charming, cleverly carved sewing caddy. Folk art, a collector might say.

Detective Oh softly cleared his throat. "About your hand in the olive jar?"

Jane smiled. She, too, was thinking about how brilliant her son was.

"Yes," she said, "I would be getting an olive for someone else."

If Gus Duncan was really going to *slice* something other than his own finger, which Jane still doubted, he would most certainly be doing it for someone else. Someone else had walked through that landmine of foul trash, sat in his kitchen making small talk, and waited for him to die. Made him die. Why? Was it just because they wanted another finger?

12

The Kankakee police were unconvinced. At the urging, gentle and completely unofficial, of Bruce Oh, they agreed to go over the Duncan kitchen one more time for evidence of visitors, but both Jane and Oh knew it would be cursory and without much investigative curiosity.

"So all police detectives aren't curious? I would think that would be part of the job description," said Jane.

"You would think," said Oh. He spoke with care, choosing his words so carefully Jane thought they might have been rehearsed. "Some police are too knowing. Periods at the ends of all their sentences instead of question marks. It gives people confidence; makes them feel that the matter is under control. So perhaps they don't try to help as much, don't make themselves remember," said Oh. "Someone who is trying to solve a crime must begin by knowing nothing, asking everything. Only then will others try to find the answers that only they can provide."

"That sounds wise," said Jane, adjusting the phone under her chin as she merged onto the expressway. She might have to break down and get one of those headsets that she and Tim made fun of if she was going to have these conversations on the road. Then again, she could just stop having these conversations on the road. She didn't even believe that cell phones saved time or made things easier and safer, just contributed to the national high-anxiety level, like E-mail and faxes. Yet here she was, on her way to Kankakee, having a heart-to-heart with Detective Oh.

"Wise might be excessive, Mrs. Wheel. My wife says that when I make pronouncements like that I sound like a fortune cookie. She doesn't like me to fall into any language that sounds stereotypical. Even though I keep assuring her that no one would stereotype a man with one *Japanese* parent by accusing him of sounding like a *Chinese* fortune cookie."

"She's protective," Jane said, thinking of how she tried to help Charley break habits like leaving his glasses on top of his head, then searching for them. She didn't want his students to write him off as the absentminded professor.

"But isn't she the one who maintains the stereotype in the first place? If she is the one who hears the cookie talk, as she calls it?" asked Oh.

"Oh," said Jane, now wondering if she cared about Charley's image or was just impatient with the habits of her husband. Was *she* the one who was writing Charley off?

Jane dropped off several boxes at the Gerber house, where Tim was supervising painters. He helped her unload her carefully taped cartons labeled KITCHEN in red marker and tried to coax their contents out of her.

"This smells like copper," Tim said, sniffing the air. "Very seventies. You're putting up a rack and hanging scads of copper pans, all perfectly patinated. You think it'll go with the thirties and forties theme you've tricked me into believing in. You'll sneak the little sauciers and sauté pans in so the hordes of people walking through will be seduced and suddenly become copper zombies. They will storm kitchenware departments, their arms outstretched, their hands clutching Visa cards, chanting, 'must have copper, must have copper.'"

"Why, Tim, why would I create this run on copper?" Jane asked, laughing as she piled the boxes neatly into a corner, covering them with an old piece of oilcloth.

"Easy. You and the mysterious Miriam, who I'm not even sure I believe exists, bought a boatload of copper from some old hippie-turned-capitalist estate and now you've got to create a market for it."

"Pretty clever of me to have befriended you in kindergarten, knowing that someday you'd be in charge of this ridiculous fund-raiser, and I could worm my way into decorating the kitchen to create a copper market," Jane said. "I *am* an evil genius."

"Okay, so maybe it's Fiestaware. No, you wouldn't let that stuff out of your sight if you could find any for the chump change you're willing to pay," Tim said, tapping his finger against his lips. "Let's see, you were willing to go with the creamy walls and leave wood floors, so . . . I know . . . Lu-Ray! Ever since you ended up with all those boxes from that Wisconsin rummage sale, you've been trying to convince me to embrace it."

"This little guessing game is tons of fun, but might we get back to Gus Duncan's murder?"

"When were we discussing that? Murder? Are we back to 'The Secret in the Old Shanty,' Nancy Drew?"

"Munson's going over the kitchen, and I'm talking to him this afternoon. Bruce Oh convinced him to meet with me. I'm not sure what he said, but whatever it was, it worked."

Tim started to complain about Jane's obsession, but she picked up the phone and dialed, shushing him. "I'll be over there late this afternoon, Mom. I've got some great advertising signs to hang on the south wall."

"We got enough stuff on the wall now," Nellie said, loud enough for Tim to hear across the room. "Another coat of paint would collapse it."

"Just to look over, Mom. I won't be hurt if you don't like them."

"What? Yeah, yeah. Your dad says don't bring any more of them punchboards."

Tim had a fresh pot of coffee brewing in the kitchen. The painters had finished the downstairs, and Jane admired their work, agreeing with Tim that they had done a spectacular job in record time. Tim wanted the place ready for the preview on Sunday, and it looked like they really might make it.

"My dad still doesn't want the punchboards," Jane said, accepting a cup.

"I'll take them," Tim said.

"Really?" asked Jane. "You of the sneering-countenance-over-anything-I-find-first."

"You wound me. I only make fun of the junk. Punchboards are cool. The graphics are neat, the whole idea of them, you know, luck, hidden prizes, all that. I thought they might be cool hung in the basement here. I'm doing the rec room with a bar down there, and they'd be neat hanging under the old beer signs and stuff."

"Have you spent a lot already? On those signs and that neon waterfall thingie?"

"Let's just say I'm getting close to my limit."

"How can you afford my punchboards then?" Jane asked.

"Come on, you didn't pay anything for those," Tim said.

"Who says? You have no idea what I paid. Besides, they're cool. You know, neat graphics, hidden treasure, all that." Jane sipped her coffee.

Tim narrowed his eyes. She was learning. He had showed his hand too early. He had let her know that he wanted them. He had actually mentioned the place they would hang, which meant he already, in his mind, owned them. If he didn't get them now, he'd see enormous gaps in the wall, the blank spaces where they should be.

"What I have helped to create, I can destroy," Tim said, in his best Dr. Frankenstein voice.

"Relax, buddy, I'll deal," Jane said, grinning.

"Not the Chase tea set," Tim said firmly.

Jane *did* want the Chase tea set. He always knew what she wanted with her transparent longings and deep sighs, but she didn't want it right now. That's not what she had in mind. She shook her head.

"Not the autograph coverlet," Tim said.

Jane wanted that, too. One of the names stitched into the wool was "Nellie," and Jane thought she ought to have it to pretend that Nellie had contributed to this cozy blanket. She thought it would fit very nicely into the puzzle of her missing childhood, even if it was invented memory. "Creative nostalgia," Jane liked to call it. Jane consoled herself that a reconstructed history was better than none.

"Nope."

"Okay, let's flip over all the cards. What is it? My baby grand piano?"

"Don't be silly," Jane said. "How hard is it to find a piano? No. What I want is your willing suspension of disbelief. You have to just trust me and help me get to the bottom of this. Gus Duncan was murdered. If you come along with me to meet Munson, I'll get more information."

"Munson hates me."

"I know. It'll distract him, and he'll give more away."

"How many punchboards?"

"Two. I want to keep Jackpot Charley for Charley's office."

"Okay, it's a deal," Tim said quickly.

"One more thing . . ."

"I knew it."

"If you're convinced by the end of the day that Duncan was murdered, I get to pick something from your house . . ."

"No. Absolutely not."

"That has a book value of under twenty-five dollars," Jane finished.

Tim thought for a moment, doing as rapid a mental inventory as possible, and decided Jane's taste for the sentimental and peculiar would not rob him of any irreplaceable treasure.

"Deal."

Munson said she could have ten minutes if she agreed to meet him at Duncan's place. She knew it was because he didn't want her at the police station, did not want to give this meeting any kind of official stamp, but she was delighted with the opportunity to get inside Duncan's house again.

Tim walked around to the back door and called Jane up the wooden steps to the porch.

"You can see right in. Not much of a window-treatment guy, was he? Where did you find him?" Tim asked.

"Crumpled in front of the sink. Clutching the knife in his right hand. And the finger on his left hand was kind of like . . ."

"I know, I know. You've told me a hundred times. Are you sure he was right-handed?" asked Tim.

"Positive. He signed his name hundreds of times in front of my dad. Ashtrays and side tables by the chairs in the living room were all on the right side. Had a watch on his left hand," Jane said. Still peering into the kitchen, forcing herself to see the whole picture again.

"What kind of watch?" asked Tim, not expecting an answer.

"An old Bulova. Clunky, but kind of cool. I'll bet it was fifty years old."

Tim had to admit that Jane did have an eye for detail. Having a dead body to concentrate on put her off her game in terms of kitchen merchandise though.

"Janie, you didn't tell me about the table," said Tim.

Jane hadn't seen the table before. It had been covered with junk mail and newspapers and smeared glasses and plates. It still was for the most part, but both she and Tim saw now that it was a gorgeous red formica table flecked with gold. It looked like it was in fine shape, perhaps protected by its layer of grime and debris. It would clean up beautifully. And there were four matching chairs, the seat cushions that were visible, plump and unripped. They were still oohing and aahing about the fifties kitchen set when they heard a gravelly voice behind them.

"This is all about a dead guy's stuff, isn't it?"

"Detective Munson, what a pleasure!" Tim held out his hand, and when Munson reluctantly put his out, Tim grasped it with both of his. For a minute, Jane was afraid he was going to go too far and kiss it, he made such a scene.

"I've been trying to tell Janie that she's crazy with her worries that there's a murderer loose in Kankakee. And even if there was, we wouldn't have to worry with you on the case."

Was Jane crazy or did Tim bat his eyelashes at the dumbfounded detective? She knew Tim hated homophobes and tried to bait them whenever he could, but this was the most outrageous performance she had ever seen him give.

"Yeah, that's . . ." Munson took his hand back, looking like he wanted to wash it immediately, but settled for a not so subtle swipe on his pants leg. "Let's go in the house."

Jane wanted to jump with joy. He was bringing them in. Then she realized what that meant. It was not a crime scene. They had found nothing.

The house smelled foul, almost as bad as it had when

Duncan's body was still there. Munson opened the window over the sink and shook his head, looking at the dishes on the table. "We found nothing to convince us that Duncan died of anything other than natural causes, Mrs. Wheel." Munson added an insincere, "Sorry."

"No evidence of visitors? Nobody else was here in the kitchen?" Jane asked.

Tim was not being a help or a distraction, Jane noticed. He had taken out a tape measure and was eyeing the kitchen table.

"Oh no, there were visitors. There were lots of finger-prints on the dishes, the glasses. He hadn't washed any-thing or cleaned anything in months. Anyone who ever stepped into this house left something behind. Meter read-ers, delivery people. I talked to the Chinese take-out place, and they said Gus always left his doors open and when they delivered to him, they were supposed to deliver *to him*, right to his chair. Sometimes he'd ask them to bring him a beer from the refrigerator or a soft drink. Some of the high school kids who delivered wouldn't come here. Said he creeped them out. They didn't care how much he tipped."

"So you've run prints of . . . ?"

"I talked to Lou Wong. He had personally delivered food the night before Duncan died. I brought him into the kitchen this morning, and it was just as he remembered it. He described it to a tee in the car on the way over here, and nothing was different from the way he said it was."

"But what about the knife? If he had Chinese takeout the night before, what was he slicing at the sink?" Jane knew questions were futile. Munson was done with this.

"Egg rolls. There were two old cartons of them in the refrigerator cut up in little pieces. There was a carton on the kitchen counter. Uncut," Munson said. "Lou Wong said he always cut food up real tiny. Had trouble swallowing. Duncan told Lou that he thought he had cancer, but he wasn't going to let the doctors make a penny off him."

"Did he?" asked Tim. He had come up behind Munson and stood so close behind him that Munson jumped forward into the kitchen counter.

"Did he what?" Munson shouted.

"Have cancer," Tim said.

"No. Blood pressure probably through the roof though. Enlarged heart. Thickened walls. Nephew says he was taking pills a year and a half ago when he saw him last. Made a big deal about taking Lasix; said he peed like a racehorse. We found his meds, and the coroner said he had taken them. His potassium level was up, so he had even taken the supplement, like you're supposed to with a diuretic."

"He smoked, too. Look at those ashtrays," Tim said.

Jane knew Tim wanted her to notice that he had dozens of Bakelite ashtrays, advertising businesses that hadn't operated in Kankakee for sixty years. She noticed.

She also noticed that there were a variety of cigarette brands that had been stubbed out in the various ashtrays. For a guy who was loyal enough to get takeout food from the same place every night, he was certainly fickle with cigarettes.

"So it's natural causes, Mrs. Wheel, plain and simple."

Jane could almost hear Detective Oh whisper in her ear. "It's never plain, and it's never simple."

She thanked Munson as he was getting into his car. Tim waggled his fingers and smiled a big goofy smile. She was going to have to talk with him about being a distraction. He was supposed to put Munson off balance, not lead her offtrack. She was pushing him toward the car when Munson rolled down his window and called out to her.

"When you see your dad, be sure to tell him it was natural causes. Nothing to worry about."

13

Jane entered through the EZ Way's kitchen door, but instead of walking straight through and stepping up into the bar, she took an immediate right into the backroom. It had been called the backroom forever, and it served as storage area, alternative office space, cooling-off room when someone started a friendly bar argument that threatened to escalate. The room contained a small desk and a twin bed wedged into the back corner, the head of it wedged under an alcove, dangerous to any regular customer whom Nellie had pushed in there to sleep one off who happened to be a fast and vertical riser. Don had put an old La-Z-Boy recliner into the other corner for his own catnaps, and Jane could draw from memory a map of the cigarette burns on its worn arms.

Jane didn't pay any attention to the room's furnishings now. She went directly to the metal cabinet on the west wall. Stacked neatly on the shelf were packages of lightbulbs. Forty watts, forty watts, forty watts, and finally, hidden behind the front two rows, a package of one-hundred-watt bulbs. Jane went over to the single light in the room, a hanging sconce over the desk, turned off the switch, and with a clean, dry bar towel protecting her hand, unscrewed the bulb and replaced the hot forty with a cool new hundred. When she switched the lamp back on, the room glowed. It still wasn't enough light for the size of the room, but after making do with so little, it was dazzling.

The backroom of the EZ Way Inn could be a dangerous place for Jane. She had spent hundreds of hours there as a child. After school, Don picked her up and brought her directly to the tavern, where he and Nellie were in the midst of the afternoon rush hour. Roper Stove had blown its afternoon whistle and assembly line workers—wasted after eight hours of screwing on doors, wiring ovens, welding on racks—crowded the bar, downing bottles of beers and glasses of draft as fast as they could. Jane, too, needed a little something after her long day at the desk pushing the pencil, coloring in the workbook, memorizing the capitals; and Nellie, tapping her foot and wiping her hands on her apron, would appear at the door of the backroom where Jane was sitting at the old wooden desk.

"Coconut cream," she'd say, wasting no time with small talk about life in the second grade, setting down a wedge of pie next to Jane's book bag. "Sold all the chocolate cream at lunch. Milk?"

Jane hesitated. She hated milk, but consented to drink it with desserts. Sometimes, though, if her mother was distracted enough, Jane could ask for Pepsi with her pie and get it.

"Come on, come on, I'm busy out there," Nellie said, looking toward the bar.

"Pepsi?" Jane asked.

Her mother often shrugged and dashed back to the bar, where she and Don opened, poured, served, wiped, collected, and made change as fast and as gracefully as any piece of choreography adult Jane had ever bought a ticket to see. If Nellie got too busy to bring the soda back to her right away, Jane would give up, go into the kitchen, and open one of the huge double doors of the institutionally sized refrigerator and pour herself a glass of milk. Then she would eat her pie, drink her milk, and settle in at the desk. If she had a library book with her, she squinted in the dim light and read happily for the two hours before her parents would be ready to leave. If she had forgotten a book, or if she only had a chapter or two left, she was forced to while away the afterschool hours creating some kind of backroom game.

She sometimes lay on the daybed and just dreamed, imagining herself as a nightclub singer, a movie star, a homesteader in the Old West, all of which she wanted to be when she grew up. Other times she kicked back in Don's La-Z-Boy and sketched the EZ Way Inn customers on one of the dozen scratch pads Don kept in the old desk drawers. Her father was sure she'd grow up to be an artist.

"Looks just like Chuck," he'd say to Nellie, showing her one of Jane's portraits. "Look how she puts in every hair in his crewcut."

The backroom was dangerous to the adult Jane because she crossed the threshold and became the second grader again, lonely and hungry. Jane the pessimist, a shy sad-sack, the fatalistic Eeyore. Or, as Tim was fond of pointing out, she was in equal danger of becoming the giddy, deliriously happy Jane—the lucky girl whose mother handed her pie and Pepsi and gave her time and space to let her imagination guide her through the barely navigable waters of elementary school.

140

Independence and neglect were doled out to Jane in equal measure, she supposed, and it was up to her what she chose to look back on as her childhood. Wasn't it? Right now, Jane was not thinking about pie or fantasizing on the daybed or coloring in a map of the United States. Jane was concentrating on getting enough light over the desk so she could see into her father's eyes when she asked him the question.

The question? Who was she kidding? She had a battery of them. But the one she would start with would be this. "Why, if you were so sure that Gus Duncan died of a heart attack, did you call Munson this morning to confirm that the investigation had turned up nothing suspicious?"

Once she got him to leave the whiskey orders on the bar and come into the backroom, Jane found the question wasn't so easy to put to him.

"Hey, what'd you do back here, honey? I can see, for god's sake," Don said, looking around in a kind of wonder. "There's that case of matches. I told Barney they hadn't come with the rest of the order."

Don began looking through the other boxes stacked next to his chair and muttering about Nellie and her goddamn low-wattage lightbulb fetish. "She had a twenty-five watt in here until a month ago. I finally told her they didn't make them anymore. She'd have to go forty. This one'll probably blind her."

"She keeps one package of a hundreds back here, Daddy," Jane said. "I made her start when I was in the eighth grade so I could see to do my homework."

Jane showed him the package in the back of the cabinet.

"I'll be damned," he said, stroking his chin. He grinned,

his whole face lighting up. "Think she's got any other secrets?"

Jane paused and swallowed hard. "I think you do."

Don sat down in his recliner and held his hands out, palms up. "A few. But I don't think they're very important anymore."

Jane wanted to say, "Because Gus Duncan is dead?" But the words stuck in her throat. This wasn't some bit player in a film noir. She wasn't living out her movie-star fantasy as a Humphrey Bogart Sam Spade. This wasn't Sydney Greenstreet, for god's sake. This was her dad, easygoing, honest, all-around-nice-guy Don, the man who wouldn't let her use the word "hate" as in "I hate my teacher." He said it was just as bad as any swear word, and he never wanted to hear her say it. "Kill 'em with kindness," he always told her when she'd complain about cliquey girls and nasty boys. And now Jane, with some girl detective fantasy playing in her head, was going to grill her own father under a hundred-watt lightbulb in the backroom of the EZ Way Inn to get him to confess to the murder of Gus Duncan, the only man he'd ever said it was okay to hate?

"Daddy, the night Gus Duncan died, did you . . . ?" Jane began.

"For Christ's sake, Jane, get that look off your face. You look like you seen a goddamn ghost. Your father didn't kill Gus Duncan," Nellie said from the doorway. "He just wanted to."

Jane hadn't heard her mother at the door, but that wasn't surprising. Her brother, Michael, her father, and she had always maintained that Nellie wore silencers on her shoes. She was always appearing behind them or at their

bedroom doors, catching them doing something embarrassing and silly.

"Mom, I never said Dad . . . ," Jane started at the same
time Don began. "Nellie, this is between . . ."

Nellie stopped them both. "I killed Gus Duncan."

Jane wanted very badly to faint, swoon, actually. She felt
this was the proper moment for it if there ever was one. She
at least must have looked like she was going to fall because
her dad jumped up and guided her into the La-Z-Boy.

"Nellie, what the hell's the matter with you?" asked
Don.

Nellie gave a tight, satisfied smile.

Don went into the bar and got Jane a glass of ice water
and double-checked the front door to make sure it was
locked. The grand reopening wasn't for a few days, but that
didn't mean that the regulars failed to show up. In fact, Don
and Nellie had welcomed customers in every day, serving
them a bottle or glass while carpenters hammered or while
Nellie hung curtains. Nellie hadn't seen any reason to close
in the first place.

"Nobody's going to notice anything anyway," she had
said, when Don had hung the CLOSED FOR TWO WEEKS OR
SO sign on the front door.

"For Christ's sake, Nellie, look how you upset Janie."
Don took his daughter's hand and wrapped it around the
water glass.

Nellie had stayed in the doorway. She generally wore
pants now with elastic waists and comfortable pastel sweatshirts; but as Jane watched her there, she pictured her in

143

one of her fifties shirtwaist print dresses, a belt around her tiny waist, and an apron to wipe her hands on. Jane half expected her to offer her a piece of cream pie. After she had swallowed some water and handed the glass back to her father, she found her voice.

"You did not," she said.

Okay, so it wasn't a rebuttal worthy of the shocker that had prompted it, but it was the best she could muster.

"You and your dad don't think I can do anything. Just because I didn't have an education and don't read books doesn't mean I'm helpless, for Christ's sake."

Jane looked at her father. He could sometimes help with translation; but he, too, was at a loss to see where exactly someone could jump into this conversation.

"I went over there right after you did, Don. I saw you come out and I went in. Gus was in the kitchen laughing his ugly head off. Didn't even look surprised to see me. Just kept laughing. Then he waved that knife at me and said he'd tell me the same thing he'd told you—that he was selling us the building 'cause he could still own us, us and all the others. So I went right up to that ugly face of his and told him I'd cut his . . ." Nellie hesitated for the first time, looking at Jane, seeming to decide whether or not Jane was old enough to hear what she had said to Gus Duncan.

"I said I'd hurt him really badly if he tried any more bullshit. We'd had enough. It was over and done. His face turned bright red, and the veins on his neck looked like they were going to explode. I walked out, but I knew I'd taken care of him. Next thing you know, you two are telling me he's dead. And now I'm telling you," she said proudly, "that I killed him."

Nellie blinked and looked around the room. "Why the hell's it so bright in here?"

Jane smiled and shrugged.

Nellie grunted and picked up the towel on the desk to protect her hand. She unscrewed the lightbulb and picked up the forty watt that Jane had left there. In the moment in which the backroom went dark, they heard a thud, breaking of glass, and another thud in the front of the EZ Way. Nellie, then Jane, then Don ran into the barroom and saw the front window broken, jagged glass now framing the neon DON AND NELLIE'S that hung independently in the window. A brick lay on the floor, and Jane picked it up, untaping the paper wrapped around it.

```
I KNOW WHAT YOU DID. I KNOW WHERE THE
     BODIES ARE BURIED. SAME MONEY.
        SAME TIME. SAME PLACE.
```

"Call Jimmy," Nellie said, getting a broom.

Don nodded, sighing and shaking his head.

Jane's heart was racing. "Mom, why don't you ask him to send Munson over, too? This probably has to do with the Duncan case, right?"

Both Don and Nellie stared at her.

"Jimmy sells glass. He'll get someone over to fix the window," Don said. "He'll get someone over here right away."

"Mom, you have to call the police. Somebody's trying to blackmail you, and you didn't do anything," said Jane. "Just because you tried to put a voodoo scare into Duncan doesn't mean you killed him."

"Oh, yeah?" Nellie said. "I killed him all right. I scared the daylights out of him."

"Okay, Mom, okay. If it means something to you to be a murderer, by all means, you can take the credit for it. But no one can blackmail you for it," said Jane, holding the dustpan for her mother.

"Yeah, I know. Move the pan, hold it flat," said Nellie.

"So call the police, Dad."

"No, honey, not just yet," Don said.

What was going on here? Jane had gone through a lot of ups and downs with Don and Nellie over the years, but this might be the strangest stretch of roller-coaster track yet. First she'd worried that Don had killed Duncan. He had certainly worried enough about the police investigation of Duncan's death to ask Munson about it behind Jane's back. Then Nellie confessed, bragged about scaring him to death, which under some circumstances Jane might believe was possible. Her mother was a force of nature, after all. But now they were both totally unfazed by an unknown blackmailer who had flung a brick through their newly installed front window. And what was the brick thrower planning to blackmail them over since as far as Jane could tell, no one present had killed anyone?

"Relax, Janie," Don said, after he had arranged for the window repair. "I was worried that it might get complicated if the police knew I had gone to see Duncan. I just asked Munson to let me know what they found out, if it was natural and all," Don said, "which I was sure it was. I didn't even know about your mother going over there. Which was really stupid, Nellie," he added.

"So why would anyone want to blackmail you?"

"Same old, same old, don't you think?" Nellie asked Don.

"I suppose," he said, with a long sigh.

"Will you please explain this to me," Jane shouted, "before I go nuts!"

"It's nothing. Gus had been blackmailing your dad and me for years. Not much money. We just made it part of expenses. Like a mortgage. It was no big deal," Nellie said. "Sounds like somebody just took over the business, that's all."

"At least the money's the same," Don said. "Thank god for small favors."

Jane felt dizzy. She knew she'd get it out of them eventually, if she could just keep at it, but her endurance was wearing thin. They had said they were discussing blackmail, but it would sound to any outsider like they were discussing car insurance rates or the price of barrels of draft beer. And Jane was rapidly feeling like the most outside of the outsiders.

"One more thing, Mom?" Jane asked.

Nellie stopped sweeping and looked at Jane.

"What did you tell Duncan you were going to cut off?"

"What do you think, for Christ's sake? His . . ." Nellie, who had never hidden from Jane the most grisly details of any news story, whose description of the facts of life could make your hair stand on end, hesitated, then said, "His manhood, of course."

Jane smiled with overwhelming relief. She, in fact, laughed, only half listening, as her mother went on to describe exactly what she'd said she'd do with said "manhood," her plan involving a sack and the Doberman next door. It was almost a pleasure to hear her mother wax poetic about her violent intentions as long as the "cutting off" she mentioned didn't have anything to do with Gus Duncan's finger.

14

Bruce Oh agreed with Jane Wheel that there was now a motive for someone to kill Gus Duncan. He was a blackmailer. Oh also felt it was only right to point out to Jane that it was her parents, Don and Nellie, who had the motive. Jane had thought of that but seemed untroubled.

"Duncan owned at least five buildings, probably more. Maybe there were other tenants he was blackmailing. Maybe one of them—or maybe more than one—decided that they weren't going to pay rent *or* the little extra he had been charging every month," Jane had said when she phoned.

Oh agreed with Jane Wheel about that as well. When he spoke with her, he found himself swept along in her investigative fervor, although now, as he made tea and prepared to read a student's paper on DNA evidence—*why were all of them obsessed with the same topic?*—he realized it might be more helpful for Jane if he had disagreed with her.

There was, after all, no real investigation. Munson had done everything he was supposed to do and had found no reason to call Gus Duncan's death anything other than heart failure. He might be interested in the blackmail, but so far, Jane couldn't get her parents to agree to report it.

"Why would we report blackmail? So everyone would know what we paid Gus not to tell?" Nellie had said, shaking her head, muttering about money wasted on fancy college educations for children who didn't seem to have the sense they were born with.

"We have things under control, honey. You forget about it. Some of us did something stupid years ago, and we deserve to pay something for it," Don had said, somewhat kinder, but just as firm.

"Your father's exact words, Mrs. Wheel?" Oh asked.

"I think so. Under control, that's what he said. But he didn't mean anything ominous by that. My father couldn't . . ."

"I was thinking about the 'some of us' part," said Oh. "Who are 'some'? What group would he put himself in?"

"My dad's a joiner. He's an Elk and a Kiwani, I think." Jane realized she didn't even know what those groups meant or signified. "He has a golf league that operates out of the EZ Way Inn. And he sponsors bowling teams," Jane said. "Is that what you mean?"

"Anything else? Did he have friends with whom he invested money? Did he own property with a group? Did your parents travel?" Oh asked.

"Why? I mean they didn't, but why would that matter?" Jane asked.

"Perhaps they were in a group and witnessed a crime; perhaps one person in the group made a mistake, and all agreed to keep the secret?" Oh said. "I'm just throwing these out and seeing if anything sticks, as my colleagues used to say."

Jane had hesitated then. Oh had heard her breathe in

sharply, but knew the breath was not coming out as quickly. She had remembered something. She had an idea.

"Yes, Mrs. Wheel?"

Then Oh had heard a sound that was one of the several banes of this modern existence. A click had sounded, meaning Mrs. Wheel had another call. She had asked him to hold, had come back on the line and begged him to forgive her, but she had to take it. Now he had to wait until she called back. He had to think about her little breathing noise and sit here and drink his tea, and most disturbing of all, he had to read his student's paper.

Jane hadn't wanted to cut off Detective Oh, especially since she had just remembered the conversation with her mother at the EZ Way as they looked at the Shangri-La stuff together. Nellie, who never reflected, never waxed nostalgic, never romanticized had been lost in the past as they sat at the bar together. A lot of people had been hurt, she had said. Some of their friends. What did she say had hurt them? But she felt she had to take this call.

"Mary, how are you?"

"I've been better, doll," Mary said. "The girls gave me your number. Hope you don't mind me calling you during work."

Jane smiled. A business card with your cell phone number on it did wonders for your career. People assumed you had an office, an income, a professional life.

Jane assured her that she wasn't interrupting a thing. Mary told her that she had talked to her granddaughter, and Susie would be interested in the photographs if Jane wouldn't mind. They'd be happy to reimburse her, give her whatever she had paid the house sale team.

"I couldn't begin to tell you what they cost. They were just part of the room, so don't worry about money," Jane said. "I'm delighted to know that they'll be where they belong."

"Part of the room?"

"I bought everything in the room where the Shangri-La stuff was boxed up. All the barware and ashtrays and cards and euchre boards and cribbage boards and . . ."

"The whole room?" Mary asked, interrupting Jane's inventory.

"Yes."

There was silence on Mary's end, and Jane debated with herself. Now was the time to bring up Bateman's finger. Mary was thinking hard. The silence was what thinking sounded like. Was she remembering that Bateman had left his finger in a jar, and Mary had packed it away in a box with the Shangri-La glassware?

"How about the other rooms? Did you buy them, too?" Mary asked, sounding more amused than concerned.

"No, I picked up a few things here and there, but when I saw the tavern stuff, I forgot about the rest of the house."

"Why?"

Jane had been waiting for that question. If Mary asked her directly, she knew she could tell her about the EZ Way Inn. As long as it wasn't Jane who brought it up—that she was the daughter of tavern owners—she could talk about it. She had been afraid, she realized, because Mary had lost her own daughter; and Jane would be a glaring reminder that while someone you loved died, someone else lived. She wanted to be friends with Mary, she wanted Mary to like her, not think of her as just another one of the scavengers who descended on a dead guy's stuff like flies on a dead guy. Jane wasn't sure why it made her more of a vulture to be a tavern owner's daughter, but somehow it did.

"My parents own a place called the EZ Way Inn . . ." Jane began, then heard a click. She had another call, and she had always promised Nick that she'd pick up. No matter what. No matter if she was in the middle of a tug of war over a box of vintage linens, hand embroidered, signed and dated, even if she'd lose a box of canning jars that had one rare amber-tinted quarter pint under a sea of the ordinary green full pints. No matter what, she had promised her son, she would always answer the call-waiting. "Can you hang on a minute, Mary? I'll be right back."

"Jane, it's an emergency, can you meet me at the shanties? We've got a doozy on our hands," Tim said, sounding high as a kite. Gus must have a boatload of good stuff under the garbage.

"Hang on, I'll be right back," Jane said, clicking back to Mary, but she heard only silence. She had either disconnected her, or Mary had hung up.

"Tim, I have to make a few calls before I . . ." Jane said. She could hear Tim singing when she came back on the line. She had to remind him not to make fun of her giddiness over a good sale. He was obviously over the moon.

"What is it, Tim?" Jane asked.

"Honey, I'm not sure I should care, but we have the whole history of Kankakee here. Newspapers and junk, but mostly photographs. You wouldn't believe. Group photos in big old wood frames, you know the kind you love. I'm guessing Gus bought a building that had a photographer's studio in it or something. And we got your Bakelite, baby. Boxes of unopened button cards, jewelry, drawer pulls, the works. Looks like the inventory from a dime store, circa 1932. Right up your alley. This is the most unbelievable stash. I feel like Ali fucking Baba and I just open-sesameed the cave."

Jane felt her heart race, her pulse pound, her hackles raise, her flesh creep, and all the other cliched but true visceral reactions to Tim's news. He—and she—because he was letting her in—had struck gold. They would be the first ones to see it all, to catalogue it, to price it, to sell it. Or to buy it? Could she do that? Or did the T & T Sales policy prevent her from buying the objects she was supposed to sell?

"Do I get first dibs, Timmy?"

"We'll cross that ethic when we come to it. Listen to this. I opened this wooden crate that was nailed shut and . . ."

The phone clicked. Yes, she had said to Nick, even if I am reaching for a red, carved Bakelite bracelet, two inches wide, and if answering the phone means one of the damned book guys gets it instead, she had promised Nick, even then, I will answer my call-waiting.

"Hang on, Tim," said Jane. "Hello?"

"Yeah?"

"You called *me*, Mom. You're supposed to say hello," said Jane.

"Yeah, hello. Are you driving? Because I don't want you in a car and on the phone," said Nellie.

"No, I'm not driving but I'm on the other line," said Jane. "Hang on."

"Pull over," said Nellie.

"I'm not driving. Hang on a minute," said Jane. "Tim, it's my mother. I'll be there as soon as I can."

"Where are you?" asked Tim.

"Parking lot of the Jewel. I stopped for some orange juice and decided to call Oh from here."

"From the Jewel parking lot?" asked Tim, confused.

"Instead of from my parents' house," said Jane.

"Oh, yeah, I get it," said Tim. "Detective talk. Private."

Jane clicked back to her mother who was talking to someone else, yelling at someone.

"Mom, I'm back. Quit yelling at Dad," said Jane.

"Dad's not here. Get off the lawn, you kids. There's a park down the block. Play ball there."

"Mom, Halloween's coming up. You're going to get your windows soaped," Jane warned.

"Yeah, let 'em try something like that. They got no business being in other people's . . ."

"What did you call about, Mom?"

"Your brother called," said Nellie.

"Okay," said Jane.

"From California."

"Mom, speak up, there are cars next to me and I can't hear," said Jane.

"Stop driving. I'm hanging up," said Nellie.

"I'm parked in a parking lot!" Jane screamed. "There are cars around me. Moving cars. What did Michael say?"

"He's coming home for Thanksgiving."

"Okay," said Jane. "That's good."

"So I didn't want you making any other plans."

"Mom, I'm five minutes away at the Jewel," said Jane. "And it's September. Who would I make Thanksgiving plans with? The produce man?"

"I told Michael I'd make sure . . . What's that noise?"

"I've got another call," Jane said, grateful for the first time that call-waiting had been invented.

"Janie, I've been thinking about this whole blackmail thing," Don said.

"Hang on, Dad, let me get off my other call," Jane said. "Mom, I'll call you back."

". . . because I can't lift the damn pan," her mother was saying, and Jane realized her mother had been talking the whole time she had been answering the other call.

"I'll call you back," Jane yelled into the phone.

". . . don't know who I'm paying, and I didn't like that brick business," her father was saying. Don hadn't stopped talking either while she was finishing up with Nellie.

"Dad, wait. I didn't hear the first part. Will you tell . . . goddamn it," she screamed as she heard another click. "Daddy, I have another call and I have to get it because Nick made me promise . . ."

"Jane?" It was Ollie. "I'm so sorry to bother you during work."

"No problem at all, Ollie," Jane said, pleased that Ollie imagined her sitting behind a big desk instead of hunched over the steering wheel, trying to open a carton of orange juice.

"Mary called me and asked if I'd drive her to your office

to pick up the photographs, and I realized your card didn't have an address on it," Ollie said.

"This is my cell phone. I work out of my car a lot," Jane said.

"Out of your car?" Ollie asked.

"On the road, you know, visiting clients and all. I'm in Kankakee right now, working on that Flea Market Show House I told you about," Jane said.

"That's in Kankakee?"

"Yes, where I'm from. Where I grew up," Jane said. "Didn't I tell you about doing the house?"

"I don't believe you mentioned Kankakee."

"Do you know it?"

"Oh, yes. We've bowled there and visited and all. Used to play ball there. Sure, Mary's got . . ."

Call-waiting clicked, and Jane banged her head on the steering wheel.

"Please hang on, Ollie, I'll be right back on the line," said Jane, nearly weeping.

"Hello, Jane, Tim gave me your number. This is Lilly."

Jane asked Lilly to hang on but felt certain that Ollie wouldn't be there when she went back to her. She wasn't.

"Yes, Lilly?" Jane said.

"My brother, Bobby, said maybe we should talk to you. He heard from his friend at the police department that you went back to Duncan's and met with Munson," Lilly said, "that Munson was going back over the place."

"Yes?" Jane was going to tell her that Munson still didn't think anyone murdered Gus, but she stopped herself. She had learned from Oh that if you don't say anything, someone will try to fill in the silence. She was trying hard not to be the someone.

"I can explain why I was there," Lilly said. "And I didn't . . ."

Jane heard a different kind of clicking than her own call-waiting.

"Lilly? Is that your call-waiting? I'll hold," Jane said. The dead silence told her, however, that Lilly had not put her on hold. The screen on her cell phone confirmed it.

"Call disconnected."

15

The three houses that Gus Duncan owned, the ones that locals called the shanties, were lined up, one, two, three on the 800 block of Linnet Street. All three of the houses were the same, small frame cottages with postage stamp–sized front porches. The pointy roof and symmetrical front windows made them look like the models for children's drawings. A pencil scribbling of smoke emerging from a chimney was all that was missing.

Linnet Street was only four blocks long, a zigzag that broke up the monotony of the grid of streets just south of the EZ Way Inn. Jane had driven by the shanties almost every day of her Kankakee life: eyesores, piles of rubble, dumps. That's how most townspeople described them. Gus was clever though. He let the front lawns with their tangled vines and grasses get just so high, just weed clogged enough, littered with just enough car parts rusting in front to annoy, frighten, and horrify the other residents of Linnet Street. When the properties were just a rat hair away from the city being able to start condemnation procedures, Gus would call in a ragtag crew in a pickup truck and have them haul away just enough debris, have them mow the weeds just barely under what was acceptable, and then he'd park his enormous self on a folding chair on one of the front porches and dare anyone to show him written complaints from the neighbors.

At the Jewel that morning, Jane had overheard a checker and her customer talking about how soon the shanties would be torn down. The implication was that a bulldozer had been parked down the block, gunning its motor for years, and now it could do its work.

Jane parked in front of 801 Linnet Street, right behind Tim's Mustang. This was the farthest away from where Duncan had been living at 805. She stood outside her car, leaning back with arms folded, and looked at the three houses. She appreciated the way the town saw them. Rotted-out buildings, barely habitable, and then only by someone like Gus himself. A big storm would knock them to bits. Maybe even a gust of wind. Oh hell, you could huff and puff and blow them down.

But still . . . Jane pictured them painted, with picket fences and rosebushes that would climb up the wrought-iron porch supports. A fiber mat in front of the door with a hand-hammered metal knocker, the lawn green and mowed, the sidewalk swept, a fruit tree in the front yard. Green shutters lidding the windows. She clapped her hands against her shoulders to wake herself up. She was one step away from scribbling in the wisp of smoke from the chimney.

"I know, I know. You were thinking why couldn't you buy these up and fix them, and I could live in one and you could live in one, and . . ." Tim stopped. "Who would live in number three?" He stood inside the first house, behind the shredded screen in the front door.

"Tim, where do you get these romantic notions?" Jane asked, all wide eyes and fluttering lashes.

"Yeah, right. I saw you out there, redesigning and landscaping in your head. Your lips were moving, babe. It's your tell," Tim said.

"What?" Jane asked. "I have a tell?"

"When you want something, honey, your lips start moving, like you're reading a prayer book or saying a rosary. At an auction people probably think you're about to have a seizure when a box lot of McCoy flowerpots comes up."

Jane had wondered if anything gave her away. She had noticed all the dealers, the other pickers give in to shakes and shudders and rapid blinking when they saw their oh-so-necessary object come into view. When Charley was looking at rocks and fossils and he started to click his tongue, she knew to start oohing and aahing. When Tim saw his heart's desire, he patted his wallet pocket.

"What took you so long?" Tim asked, pulling her inside the house.

It would have been darker and smellier and scarier, but Tim had already performed the big three. He'd opened all the windows. He'd sprayed industrial disinfectant into every sink and drain. And most importantly he'd set up four of the dozen metal work lamps he'd bought at Home Depot and trained more wattage into the house than it had ever seen. Yes, it illuminated the filth, but somehow the dirt was less intimidating when you could see it—and what did or did not live in it. He handed her thin plastic gloves and a paper mask.

"It's really not so bad. The basement is actually fairly

organized. A million boxes, but stacked and marked and fairly dry. That's the amazing thing. Looks like the Kankakee River barely made it into these basements, which is almost impossible to believe. Are you listening to me, dearie?"

Jane took out her cell phone and found a place to plug it in. Her battery had taken a beating in the last hour, and although she had tried to call back all the people whose calls she'd lost or cut short, no one was now available. She needed to talk to Oh, she needed to get back to Mary and Ollie, and she was most anxious about Lilly. She had tried to call her at home and at her tavern, but gotten no answers.

"Is there a working phone here?"

Tim shook his head and handed her his cell. He also checked his ever-present day planner and gave her a third number for Lilly.

"Her boyfriend's? Her brother's? I don't know," said Tim. He had gotten lost counting out place settings of silver.

Jane leaned over his shoulder, breathing heavily. "It's not . . . ?"

Tim shook his head.

They both sighed. Tim and Jane loved hotel silver and serving dishes. Both were mad to get silver from the Hotel Kankakee, long gone from downtown. Jane had managed to find six silver dessert bowls and one larger bowl, a salad, she and Tim had decided. Tim had hit the mother lode at one of his house sales. A former employee of the hotel, Mrs. Slagmore, had been offered much of the merchandise before it was auctioned, and she'd left it boxed and unmarked in her basement. Tim had trays, condiment servers, some silver utensils, and a tea service that Jane would dearly love to claim as soon as Tim acknowledged Duncan's murder. Its book value, however, was a good deal over twenty-five dollars.

"It's hotel, though. Where did Gus . . . ? The monogram is an L," Tim said.

"L?" Jane asked, then smiled. "Pay dirt."

"Yes, yes, yes. It's from the Lafayette Hotel, and there's tons of it." Tim performed a kind of jig around the box. Jane would have described it as an end-zone dance. He had the glee and the stomping feet of a player who had just scored a touchdown, but Tim was no running back. He was just a tall, handsome man with a taste for quality vintage tableware and whose last name began with L. It was a touchdown *and* the extra point.

Jane walked into the kitchen of Duncan's shanty number one and wasn't surprised to find it as dirty and garbage strewn as the one he had been living in. The quality of chaos was slightly different. Not as much abandoned as ransacked. In fact, as Jane scanned the room, left to right, top to bottom, just as she would at a house sale, she noticed the drawers had been pulled out and barely closed, with some linens still spilling out. Upper cupboards had been opened and the doors left hanging. The pattern of dust was disturbed, too. Fingers had trailed through the grime recently.

"Have you been going through the kitchen?" Jane asked.

"You get first crack at that. You need stuff for my place, right? I mean the McFlea," Tim said.

"How were the doors secured? Regular deadbolt or were they padlocked?"

"The back door, believe it or not, was open. I'm guessing Bill Crandall just left it for me. He didn't have real high hopes for the stuff."

"Who?"

"Duncan's nephew. He owns the places, but Duncan didn't want him messing around here while he still lived at 805. Told me that Uncle Gus was always eccentric and said he had to do some filing and packing, then Bill could do whatever he wanted. Burn the joints down, Bill said. That's what Gus always said. Just burn 'em."

Maybe Gus had started to do some filing and packing in this kitchen.

Jane forgot that she had come in to call Lilly, to try her at this other number, and instead, began going through boxes that had been stacked to the left of the back door. Maybe Gus had emptied some of those cupboards recently and boxed things to move. He had sold all his properties and given the shanties to his nephew. Maybe he was leaving town or at least leaving Linnet Street.

"Tim!"

Tim came in with a large white linen napkin, a large maroon L tastefully embroidered on its corner, tucked under his chin.

Jane was crouched over a wooden crate, squatting in the picker's pose. Tim would have to tell her that pretty soon her knees were going to go. She was going to have to lift those boxes up to table height. After all, she wasn't a catcher who could go nine innings; she was a forty-something whose arthritis was hovering around the corner.

Jane was holding a MORE SMOKES punchboard. Red, white, and blue graphics laid out the rules. Red tickets with numbers that ended in five won five packs of cigarettes. White tickets that ended in zero won five packs of cigarettes. Jane held it up to the dim light of the kitchen. Tim hadn't put any stands of lights here yet, but some sun came through the grimy streaks of the small window over the sink. When Jane held it up, Tim saw that this board had lost value. It had punches pushed out. Jane was twisting it and turning it in the light, looking at the pattern of holes.

"What a pack rat! He saved *old* punchboards, I mean ones that were punched," Jane said, shaking her head.

"Yeah, what a nut!" Tim said, laughing. "I'll just toss it."

Tim tried to take it from Jane, but she gripped it firmly.

"I'll put them in your car, pack rat," Tim said.

"Ms. Pack Rat to you." Suddenly remembering Lilly's call, Jane dialed the number Tim had given her. An answering machine, male voice. Jane hung up.

Tim loaded up the punchboards and several other boxes of kitchenware that Jane wanted to go through at Don and Nellie's. It would be impossible to wash things clean enough in this filthy kitchen to see what they were, to judge their condition. Jane had found some iced tea spoons with Bakelite handles that were charming and pristine, never removed from their box; but for the most part, Gus Duncan's stuff had sat under cobwebs and greasy dust for decades. Jane knew her mother would holler when she saw the dirty boxes hauled in, but Jane also knew the deep satisfaction it would give Nellie to help her daughter clean the stuff. Nellie might not want to accumulate, but she dearly loved to sanitize. Tim was still trying to decide whether they should try to clean one of the shanties well enough to have the sale inside.

The McFlea preview was this weekend; then he turned it over to the ticket takers and tour guides. He could be ready for the shanty sale in two weeks if Jane would help, or so he said. He was toying with setting up a tent in the yard. Both he and Jane were willing to plow through old musty basements and attics, pick their way through rusted hardware and moldy Tupperware, but Tim wasn't sure he could convince Kankakeeans—and the Chicago dealers he might be able to draw if he found anything interesting—into Duncan's caves.

Bill Crandall poked his head in briefly. He shook Jane's plastic-gloved hand, and Jane offered him a pair for his own use. He declined, saying he didn't plan on going through any of his uncle's trash. He just wanted top dollar for it.

"Gus didn't strike me as a man who knew the value of anything he had. He just didn't want to get rid of stuff," Crandall said. He was a big man, too, although much fitter and trimmer than his uncle. There was some facial similarity, but where Duncan was dark-skinned and dark-haired, his nephew was fair and sandy-haired.

"Gus Duncan Lite," Tim said, describing him as they watched him leave in his Jaguar.

"Showy car," Jane said. "What's he do?"

"Told me he was an entrepreneur like his uncle. Owns some properties downstate. Lives in Chicago, some south suburb. Doesn't look like he works with his hands," Tim said. "Did you notice his diamond pinky ring?"

Jane nodded. She had also noticed that his fingernails, neatly and professionally manicured, she was sure, were in need of a touch-up. His white linen shirt was going to need some special attention, too. He might not want to borrow a pair of gloves to do it, but he had certainly been going through his uncle's trash.

Jane made sure that Tim catalogued everything she packed into her car. She knew it all had to be accounted for before the sale. In addition to the kitchen kitsch she wanted to clean and examine, she took the old punchboards. There were at least thirty of them. And a file box full of random papers, old clippings of places for sale, foreclosures. Jane also took a bagful of yellowed sheets, old handwritten papers marked by Tim for trash. She could use the old papers for her McFlea project. Poking around in the bag she saw paper squiggles. Gus must have eaten the cookies that came with his takeout but hung on to the fortunes. Jane smiled—she could use those, too, in the pantry.

Jane wanted to look over some of Gus's scratchings. Were those his rental agreements? On the backs of napkins and matchbooks? Maybe she could afford to keep a place here in Kankakee, store and sell her overflow, stay there when she was visiting her parents and Tim. She'd still live in Evanston with Nick and maybe Charley, if that worked out, if they got through this malaise or cold war or whatever it was they were suffering from. But she'd have this place, too. Maybe that was the key to a good marriage, a healthy family: separate houses. Some happily married couples had separate bedrooms. Some of her own friends and neighbors did, she knew. The bedroom, though, she liked sharing with Charley. That's the room that seemed too lonely as a permanent single. But the kitchen, the study, the living room? Those she might like to rule: alone.

Jane and Tim had made a schedule. They would work at the McFlea after a dinner break; then if they weren't too tired, they'd come back and continue going through the shanties. Tim brought lights over to 803, but didn't set them up. They'd be lucky to finish 801 by tomorrow. These cottages were small, but densely packed. Tim thought this one, 801, had the most paper ephemera. Old calendars, maps, Jane's kind of stuff. No. 803 had more restaurant wares, cases of cards and dice, cartons of 78-rpm records, all the basement leavings of a saloon that might have gone bust in the forties or fifties. Jane and Tim were both high and giddy on old-stuff fumes, the dust and must of their addiction.

"What about 805? Gus's place?" Jane asked. "Have you been through there?"

"Bill doesn't own that one," Tim said, "yet. He's the only relative though. He will."

"Yeah, but have you been through it?"

"I checked to see if the keys fit. I had a feeling since 801 and 803 were the same lock, he'd just keep it easy on himself," Tim said.

"And?"

"The keys fit," said Tim, "and yeah, I skimmed it."

"And?"

"Nothing, really. It was all his living stuff, you know? Big, ugly clothes. A pretty raunchy video collection. Stuff like that. Seems like everything we'd be interested in is in these two."

"Except that kitchen set?" asked Jane.

"Right. There is some furniture and the television. That kind of everyday junk."

Jane and Tim worked together for another hour,

methodically writing down what they found, sorting stuff in piles. Jane was humming loudly, lips occasionally moving trying to find words to a song. Tim patted his wallet pocket rhythmically.

Jane offered to tackle one of the two small bedrooms, while Tim started on the basement. He gave himself a spritz of his inhaler—his "career-related" asthma flared most frequently in basements, but he was unable to resist them. Jane put on the paper mask, since the closets promised clouds of dust every time she pushed a hanger farther along the bending wooden pole.

There were a few items of clothing that Jane knew would interest Tim. Two gorgeous wool coats with enormous Bakelite buttons. The wool was miraculously moth hole free. Jane wasn't sure what had spared these garments. She opened men's hatboxes marked DOBBS and found three felt fedoras. She placed a gray one on her head and bent the brim down in what she hoped was provocative Raymond Chandler style.

"Jane! Jane!" Tim called.

Tim had set up an additional bank of lights in the basement. It made it look much more like a stage set than an actual living space. An old farm table with a white porcelain top and a sweet little narrow drawer held three boxes that Tim asked her to dip into first.

"This is a sample of the kind of stuff Gus was sitting on."

Jane lifted out photograph albums, autograph books, and high school yearbooks. These could have belonged to the original owner of this little house or to any number of people whose property Gus had descended upon. Turn-of-the-century photos of families, their gatherings and special events, and Kankakee buildings were in excellent condition. An autograph book held good luck messages and poems, all addressed to Darling Minna. Jane began reading, but Tim told her to keep going. His goofy smile told her that he had left something in the bottom he wanted her to find.

It was a photograph. Inside the oak frame, the black-and-white print measured ten by twenty-four. It was a large group of people posing outdoors. Were they in a parking lot? Some scrubby trees in the background were leafless, but there was no snow on the ground. The coats and hats looked more late fall than early spring. November? The photo might have been taken from the top of a ladder since it seemed to look down on those standing in front of a ramshackle building almost hidden by the group. A car was parked to the right of the group. It looked like a Cadillac, 1944, '45?

Tim bounced up and down on his toes. He waited for Jane to recognize the photograph or someone in it. She was enjoying his excitement as much as she was the photograph. It had all of her requirements: crisp black-and-white quality; a large group of individuals; clear shots of faces, even if they were too far away for great detail, a few goofy mugs; a man trying to kiss a woman who seemed to be squirming away. A lot of stories here. Maybe the best story, though, the story Tim knew she'd find the most interesting, was the one being told by Gus Duncan. Only slightly thinner but more jolly than sloppy, a big cigar chomped in his teeth with his huge arms fanned out embracing two smiling, fresh-faced kids in their twenties, thirties at most. Gus, wearing the same gray fedora Jane now wore on her head, looked like he was giving the world to these two young people who were happy to get it. The smiling man and woman, snugly wrapped in Gus Duncan's large embrace, were looking straight into the camera. Jane pushed the hat back on her head with one finger to the brim and let out a low whistle: Don and Nellie.

16

Don and Nellie never *went out*. They lived their daily lives *out*. Morning until night, they worked at the EZ Way Inn, a destination spot for many who wanted to go *out*. After work, when one of their erratic employees consented to show up for work at six—"Bartending doesn't exactly attract the most reliably career minded," Don had reminded Jane when she'd wept over their late arrivals, often nonarrivals, at school events—they'd stopped for dinner at a casual restaurant. That was not going *out* to dinner though; that was just getting something to eat on the way home.

They didn't attend movies or plays, go to concerts or art openings. They had no friends who asked them over for dinner or card games. Their euchre-playing friends were with them at the EZ Way every day. When they grabbed dinner at cafés where they knew the owners, who often sat down with them and joined them over coffee and pie, it was as close to a dinner party as they got. By the time Don and Nellie got home in the evening, their social energy was spent. They had smiled and laughed and kidded and prodded and coaxed and listened and advised quite enough, thank you. Don usually managed to read a section or two of the paper and exchange some "How was school?" niceties with Jane and Michael before he fell sound asleep in his recliner, blanketed with the sports pages.

Nellie, an undiagnosed manic-manic, managed to find laundry, dusting, and sweeping to do. Regularly, on a Tuesday or Wednesday night, while Don slept through the ten o'clock news, Jane would find her cleaning out the refrigerator, wiping shelves, and Windexing surfaces. Nothing was ever clean enough, finished enough for Nellie. Mornings she waited outside bedroom doors for all of them to hand her their pajamas so she could throw them in the washing machine before they all left the house for work and school. When Don, Jane, and Michael were all cigarette smokers, Nellie, an emphatic nonsmoker always, ran herself ragged emptying three separate ashtrays after each flick of a Tareyton, Marlboro, or Kent.

For all of their years in the saloon business, Don and Nellie had followed the same pattern. Work hard all day, come home and find comfort in quiet routine: Don in his recliner, Nellie running from corner to corner with a broom. So now, when Jane returned to her parents' home at six-thirty, she was shocked to find a note in Don's beautiful penmanship.

Janie, we've gone out. Be home around eleven.

Jane felt the up-to-the-minute frustration of cellular technology. It was the age of always being in touch. She had promised Nick she would always have her phone, turned on and at the ready, so if he needed her, she, or at least her voice, was available. Nick would always have that safety net. Jane, on the other hand, was in the transitional generation.

Always worried that she would forget her phone and disappoint her son, always anxiety driven by her own parents who refused to get one. She could not reach them where they had gone *out* because they did not tell her where that might be; and since they did not ever go *out*, she could hardly make any sensible guesses. She could not call them on their cell phone because they believed that cell phones were a passing fad, a dangerous, expensive gimmick.

Where in God's name *were* they? Jane had spent time studying the photograph under Tim's gazillion-watt lightbulb and now badly wanted to turn that lamp on Don and Nellie and ask them what the hell was going on. Don had taught her to hate no one, to be kind to all, except for Gus Duncan. He had taught her that Gus Duncan was an enemy of the family, an evil, small toad of a man whom she and her brother, right along with Don and Nellie, could despise. It was one of their few family activities, this Gus Duncan hating, and now her completely dysfunctional family minus one function—the family hating of Gus Duncan—was revealed as a sham. They were completely dysfunctional because their family hatefest was based on a lie.

Where were they?

Jane, fuming, opened a can of soup and poured it into a pan. As she adjusted the low flame, she realized that Nick would starve to death in his grandparents' house. He and his friends were the soup-to-bowl-to-microwave generation. The small saucepan had been bypassed several years ago. Nellie believed microwaves were a fad, a gimmick just like cell phones and compact discs. Jane hadn't even broached the subject of DVD.

Would Charley's professional heirs dig around a Don

and Nellie site someday and hold a battered saucepan, waving it in the air speculating on its use? Too small for the cassoulet and bouillabaisse that archived, turn-of-the-century *Gourmet* magazines would suggest home cooks were preparing. Jane tasted the minestrone and wondered for the thousandth time how her parents could tolerate oversalted canned soups at home when Nellie had made giant pots of perfectly seasoned chowders and soups from scratch at the tavern. Jane, since childhood, had asked why "home cooking" was reserved for the EZ Way Inn. Nellie, having suffered from irony deficiency since birth, suggested Jane try one of the many frozen dinners she and Don squirreled away if she did not want canned soup.

Jane ate her dinner out of the pan, standing at the sink, listening for a car, a groan of the garage door being raised, but all was quiet. Don's note had said eleven, but still, she listened. The kitchen clock, a nonvintage, boring eighties, serviceable tool hummed as the second hand circled. Nellie's African violets were blooming, as usual, on the windowsill. Nellie had always claimed that she did nothing special, but somehow these plants always performed magnificently for her. Jane noticed that Nellie had elevated two of the small plastic pots on a brick, a soft dark red with rounded corners. Jane picked it up and read, KINGSLEY PAVERS. Must have been a company here in town or nearby because she had seen a pile of the same old bricks in back of 801 Linnet Street, piled by the crumbling back porch.

Where were Don and Nellie?

Jane had promised Tim she'd meet him at the Gerber place. She already had the pantry "wallpaper" packed in her car. It would be such a lovely surprise for Tim. Even though he would redo most of the decor she and others brought to the McFlea, she had a feeling he would love the pantry.

A pile of bricks? A brick in the window?

"A brick through the window," Jane said, finding the right preposition. "Damn it."

Don and Nellie had gotten used to paying off Gus, their neighborhood blackmailer. They accepted being blackmailed as if it was some kind of penance they were supposed to pay. Aggravating, annoying, but harmless in any real sense. What if someone, a new generation of blackmailer, had decided he could take over Gus's business and make it more lucrative? Maybe this wouldn't be your run-of-the-mill Kankakee entrepreneur like Gus, but someone who could be harmful? Someone who threw bricks through windows? Someone who murdered Gus and tried to cut off his finger?

Where were her parents?

Jane opened her notebook. She flipped through her lists for estate sales, her "Lucky Fives," the shopping game she had invented for herself, and looked at her list of phone numbers and calls she had to return.

She dialed Oh's number from memory and wasn't surprised to get his voice mail. If he were available, she was sure he would have called her back by now. As she was trying to compose a concise message, she was surprised by a hesitation after the rote "Please leave a message," and then, "If this is Mrs. Wheel calling . . . I am at work in your area and will contact you. I have news about your . . . um . . . canned goods."

* * *

And what is my *area*? Jane asked herself. The land of conjecture and guesswork? Oh remembered that she couldn't retrieve her cell phone voice mail, bless his heart, but he still hadn't totally given up on her. He was even rather poetic and diplomatic in referring to her noncase. Jane's "canned goods" did not refer to the soup, she knew, but to Bateman's finger. She had not forgotten about it, sloshing away in her glove compartment. Perhaps Oh had finally found some kind of assault complaint, something that would link . . . Link what? Did Jane really think Bateman's finger would point to Gus Duncan's murderer? No, of course not. Bateman's finger was a curiosity—something that stirred her interest in finding the whole story. Duncan's hacked finger was something else—a message that signaled that his heart didn't just stop on its own. So if nothing linked them, why couldn't Jane shake the feeling that Bateman and Gus were somehow tied together? What was this brotherhood that Jane felt but couldn't prove?

Jane drove to the McFlea and unpacked everything she needed to start on the pantry. She left her phone within three feet of where she was working, since she had left a message in large block letters for her parents to call her as soon as they arrived home. Detective Oh had received the same message from her on his machine, "Please call me immediately."

Jane had already asked the painters to prep the built-in pantry shelves, which they had done beautifully. They had expected her to stencil or sponge on a design, possibly do a trompe l'oeil of canned goods and boxes on the back of one of the shelves à la *Home & Garden Television* do-it-yourselfer shows. "It was all the rage," they had told her. She only smiled at their guesses and warned Tim that he could not see it until it was finished.

She unpacked the boxes of fragile yellow-and-cream sheets of paper. She put Elmira Selfridge's schoolwork, her spelling tests and history notes, into one pile. She hadn't been able to answer anyone before about why she'd bought them, but now she knew.

Wallpaper. The childish block printing and the cursive handwriting practice sheets created spectacular graphics. Elmira's report cards and drawings told a child-size life story.

Jane made another pile with papers from the Shangri-La. She had left the bound ledgers for her dad to study and exclaim over, but there had been boxes of loose sheets, lists of names, customers' tabs, receipts, whiskey orders. Although all the pages were intact, they were aged just enough. Old typewriter fonts made, not by a computer program, but by a quirky old manual Smith Corona, the letters signed in Bateman's spidery handwriting. Some loose labels and paper coasters. The old letterheads and logos had a kind of simple beauty that thrilled Jane, though she couldn't explain why.

She had the box and bags from Gus Duncan's basement that Tim had been ready to toss out. Loose pages that Gus had scribbled names and numbers on mixed with the old newpaper clippings of public property auctions. These had all been in a moldy Monopoly game box they had opened in the basement. Tim had thrown it in with the box of spent punchboards that he figured had little value to anyone except Jane. Tim wanted hers, the boards she had found intact at Bateman's. The papers were dry enough to use, and Jane fanned them out looking for some bits and pieces that would go into her collage. The cookie fortunes were especially charming. She tried to imagine Gus holding, "You will soon be crossing the great waters" in his meaty paws. Jane wondered if that fortune had been recent. Gus had certainly crossed over. Could he have prevented it if he had taken this little slip with its micelike typewriting seriously? Gus had tiny handwriting, too, Jane noticed, looking at some of the other scraps in the bag. "Meeting at 2. Bring title." These little messages would fit neatly inside cookies, too.

Jane had a box of handwritten recipe cards that she had bought in a wooden box from the estate of an elderly Margaret Mann. Margaret had scribbled lovely notations in the margins about who had liked the confetti Jell-O salad and how many helpings of creamed peas Elmer had eaten over his potatoes. Jane had actually tried some of Margaret's more outrageous recipes, the mock apple pie out of Ritz crackers and the chicken à la king. Nick and Charley had asked for seconds, but when Jane, in her excitement, showed them the actual recipe card and Margaret's notes about who had attended her luncheon, they both lost their appetites.

"A whole stick of butter?" Charley asked, clutching his chest.

"What's heavy cream?" wailed health-conscious Nick.

They failed to see the poetry of Margaret's guest list, nor did they appreciate the historical significance of high-fat cooking.

Jane had promised to finish the pantry and kitchen in two days, which would have been impossible if she hadn't had all the makings of the room waiting in bags and boxes. The Buffalo China she had been collecting would look great on these open shelves. An old toaster and fifties blender . . . an original with the ribbed-glass container and one speed, the only one necessary to make creamy, chocolate milkshakes. She had packed up all her doubles of colorful Hall ball jugs that would line up across the top of the hutch. Her only task besides unpacking and arranging, most of which she had already finished in her head, was to decoupage these shelves.

She spread the tacky glue and began slapping up the scraps of handwriting, the formal letterheads with their deco graphics. She worked quickly, trying not to take too seriously the order of words, the non-sense she was making. Later she would go over it and find the coincidental jokes that the overlapping pages made, the profound absurdities that the disjointed words created.

Tim was going to work at the shanties until late, waiting for her before he went through all the boxes. He had promised. Now she was torn. Should she go back to Linnet Street and lose herself in the disparate boxes Gus had accumulated? Or should she be at home waiting for her parents, sitting with the photograph in her lap, waiting for them to break down and confess . . . confess what?

Jane slapped her final coat of sealer over the collage she had created, then stepped back to admire it. The art and work of Elmira and Gus and Margaret and Bateman intersected and melded into a wallpaper of words and graphics, a grid of Palmer Method cursive and Royal Typewriter letters and hand colored United States maps. Next to a pale pink

Tennessee was a recipe for grasshopper pie that was so scrumptious, Margaret noted in the margin, that she had seen Leo lick his plate when he thought she wasn't looking. Diagonally placed across an aqua Texas was a fortune that read "Happy thoughts will never slow you down." Jane wiped the glue off her hands with a rag from Tim's neatly packed and stored box of cleaning supplies and nodded in satisfaction. Every time Tim came to the pantry to fetch a tin of McCann's oatmeal or to get an extra water pitcher, he would read something fresh, read a new spelling word from one of Elmira's lists, find out what Bateman had paid for a case of Seagram's, or what Gus's fortune cookie had cautioned. Maybe he would even try Margaret's version of chipped beef on toast.

Jane checked her watch and was delighted to find it was only ten. She could rush over to Linnet Street and unpack a box or two, just to clear her head, before she talked to Don and Nellie. Packing up her supplies, she noticed she had hauled in the box with the used punchboards and flipped through them. The usual suspects, lots of cigarette boards and colorful prize boards that didn't name the specific prize. A few of them had their keys retaped to the back, but all were partially punched. She set out a few of them along the window ledge of the pantry and decided to leave them there until she saw them in daylight. Maybe she would get rid of them. Punched out they were worthless to collectors. Then again, punched out only meant that someone, maybe Jane herself, had gotten the thrills and chills of winning a box of chocolate-covered cherries off of that very board. Didn't they have an even richer story if they were used?

Jane found all the lights on at 801 Linnet, but nobody home. Tim's car wasn't out front, but the wooden shoeshine caddy that he used to carry rags and markers, sale tags, and inventory supplies still sat on the kitchen table. He had also begun to clean the kitchen, Jane noticed. At least now surfaces were wiped down, so they could lay out glasses, dishes, and knickknacks and check for cracks, crazing, and chipped rims.

Ten o'clock was right around Tim's dinnertime. He liked to keep a "European lifestyle" he'd told Jane in order to soften the corners of his "Kankakeean address." Jane hoped he'd bring back enough for her. The canned soup was ages ago. She found Duncan's fedora that she had worn earlier and put it on to keep the dust out of her hair.

She slit open the tape on a box marked "variety store invent." Inside were packages of paper coasters. Dainty little white paper circles rimmed in pink-and-gold scallops. Sealed packages of matching guest towels: a dozen in pink and gold, a dozen more in turquoise and gold. *Perfect for baby showers*, Jane thought, *but do people do baby shower decorations in vintage?* Of course they do, she could hear Miriam saying; they do everything . . .

Jane stopped and held her breath. Was that something in the basement? She heard it again, but this time it sounded like it was coming from the roof. Hail? She looked out the front door. Evenings were just beginning to get cool enough for jackets and sweaters. Tonight, with the breeze, she realized there was almost a shiver in the air. The old oak in the front yard swayed again in the sudden gust, and she heard the knocking, hard on the roof. Of course, it was midwestern September hail . . . acorns. They came down hard and clattered over the roof. Jane went back to the next box with the variety store marking. She wanted to find that Bakelite Tim had described. This carton, though, had old tape that had been in place so long, it had fused to the cardboard. She remembered that Tim had his box cutter in the basement and headed downstairs.

Jane had read enough Nancy Drew mysteries and seen enough of the scary movies that Charley and Nick loved to know she shouldn't go down into a dark, abandoned basement alone. This particular basement, though, was illuminated like a movie set, with Tim's brilliant work lights trained on every surface, lighting up every corner. He was no fan of spiders and critters himself, and they had long ago agreed not to tease each other about hearing mice or feeling something crawly. That's why Jane blithely ran down the steps and walked right over to the workshop table where she had last seen Tim ripping through cardboard. His cutter was right where he'd left it. Jane carefully retracted the blade, slipped the box cutter into her jean jacket pocket, and, out of habit, did the left-to-right, top-to-bottom scan of the basement room.

It was small, not nearly the nooks and crannies that had presented themselves to Jane in most of the smaller Chicago estate sales she liked. Those little bungalows had deceptively large and full basements. This one was small and stacked with boxes, fairly well marked as Tim had said. On the floor was a packet of handwritten letters. Ten, maybe twelve were tied together, with a few that had come loose splayed out. Which box had they fallen from? Jane wanted to keep these things together—maybe she'd find a whole box of correspondence that she could take home and read in bed. First she had to figure out which carton they belonged in. She stuck the letters in the pocket of her overalls while she studied the storage area.

Reading left to right, she recognized a lot of the markings on the boxes as tavern suppliers, the boxes probably coming intact from underneath one of the businesses Gus had snatched up when it failed. Across the empty cartons that Gus had reused for packing papers and books and pots and pans, Jane read a history of bottled beer: Pabst, Drewery's, Schlitz, Hamm's, Lilly.

Lilly. She was sitting on a stack of three boxes, her head against the wall. Another full box was on her lap. It held her there, seated among the carefully packed and taped cartons. Poor Lilly. Right in the middle of all this dead guy stuff, a dead girl.

17

"Stop scowling at me."

"I'm not scowling," Tim said. He wrinkled his forehead and scrunched up his eyes.

"You are most definitely scowling," Jane said

"No, I am not." He concentrated on furrowing his brow. He willed the corners of his mouth to turn down.

"But . . ." he said, ordering his entire face to give in to gravity.

"What?" Jane asked. "It's not my fault."

"Oh no, it's not your fault. Not at all," Tim said, walking away from her, then turning back. "I call you in as a partner on one of the most interesting sales I've had in months. Oddly enough, the last time you found a body for me at my workplace, I lost a little business; and now, when people are starting to forget, I get two housefuls of untouched buried treasure and you come along and find Lilly Duff dead with a box of Bakelite on her lap. A box of Bakelite, I might add, that we can no longer touch."

"I was your partner on this?" Jane asked, her eyes wide.

"You've been trying to turn the shanties into a crime scene for days," Tim said, boiling over. "Are you happy now?"

Detective Munson stepped in front of Jane and Tim

with what might or might not be a smile on his face. It was one of those all-purpose expressions, a kind of do-it-yourself grin-grimace that allowed a great deal of range in the interpretation.

"Why would anyone be happy to see a pretty young woman murdered, Mr. Lowry?" Munson asked.

Jane knew that even though Munson didn't exactly emphasize the word *woman*, Tim would hear it that way, interpret it as a vague accusation, as if any time a *woman* was a victim, a gay man might be the logical suspect. She wanted to jump in, but Tim beat her by a mile.

"Look, Detective, I am very upset. Lilly Duff was a friend of mine. She and I were working together on our high school fund-raiser together. I am upset that she is dead. I'm also upset that she is dead here, on my work site," Tim said. He took a breath, which made him sound almost apologetic. "I made that sarcastic, rude, and thoughtless comment about being happy to Jane because . . ." Tim stopped and considered. "Because it's always been very hard for me to admit to my friend, Jane, that she was right and I was wrong."

Jane put her arms around Tim, and they held on to each other tightly while Munson tried to get their full attention.

"Right and wrong?"

"Jane said all along that Gus Duncan was murdered, and none of us would believe her," Tim said. "I'm sorry, dear," he whispered to Jane.

"I forgive you, partner," Jane whispered back.

Tim winced. He knew he would pay dearly for letting that "partner" remark slip.

"We're investigating Lilly Duff right now, not Duncan," Munson said. When both Jane and Tim began to speak at once, he added, "Not yet, anyway."

Jane gave her statement. She'd thought she had heard something somewhere in the house, dismissed it, and gone on working. When she heard acorns on the roof, she was sure that they accounted for the noise and thought nothing of going into the basement to fetch Tim's box cutter. She did tell the police her first impression of the shanties from the afternoon—that she had thought that 801 and 803 had been searched, at least cursorily, because a few of the boxes were unsealed, she could see paths cut through the dust, but . . .

"What, Mrs. Wheel?" Munson had prompted, sounding interested for the first time.

"I'm not sure there was any rhyme or reason to what Gus saved or kept, and he could have scuffled around through the dirt himself looking for things. The place didn't look ransacked, more like, I don't know . . . ," Jane said, "like whoever searched didn't know what he or she was looking for. Or even if . . ."

"If?" Munson and Tim both asked.

"If they knew there *was* something to find. It was more like someone was just looking around, casually, maybe," Jane said.

"Just browsing, perhaps?"

Munson and Tim looked past Jane in surprise at the questioner. Jane turned around, quite pleased to see former detective Bruce Oh.

"Yes, Detective Oh, just browsing," Jane said.

Munson glared at the uniformed officer stationed at the door, hoping that his cold-eyed stare would convey the message that Oh should not have been permitted into the house. This particular house on Linnet, 801 Linnet, to be precise, was now taped off, officially an investigation site, and Bruce Oh was no longer an official investigator. Munson had gone along with his request to revisit the Duncan house out of a kind of collegiality; but since Oh was no longer a member of any police department, Munson felt his collegiality did not have to extend very far. In fact, he decided, it was over.

"You're going to have to wait out there, Oh, behind the lines."

"Of course," Oh said, evenly and cordially. Jane watched him glide out the door, thinking that if he had been wearing a hat, he would have tipped it.

Jane, she realized several minutes later, was herself still wearing the hat she had found in the house. Tim asked her about it as they walked toward the street where Bruce Oh stood between their parked cars. He neither leaned nor slouched, and Jane found herself admiring his posture. She, on the other hand, could not stand straight. She leaned against Tim as they walked out, overcome with fatigue. She was so tired, in fact, that she forgot to ask Detective Oh—retired he may be, but he would remain detective to her—what he was doing long past midnight on Linnet Street in Kankakee, Illinois.

"Is there a restaurant open where we might have coffee or tea, Mrs. Wheel?" asked Oh. "You, too, Mr. Lowry, if you're free."

Jane stood straighter. Coffee would revive her. She had, after all, just found the body of a murdered woman, a woman she had known since their high school days. She really didn't want to go home to Don and Nellie's quite yet.

"Pinks," Tim and Jane both said at once.

Jane and Tim were of one mind on many things. They agreed that really good American art pottery was best displayed one piece at a time. A simple, dark green arts and crafts vase, alone on a mantel, could tell you the story of the house as soon as you walked into the room. The cheap stuff, the colorful flowerpots that were bought by the boatload at five-and-ten-cent stores in the thirties and forties, looked best huddled together in groups, holding on tightly to their sweet nostalgia by clustering. They agreed that boxes sealed in an attic were better than boxes sealed in a basement, although treasures and duds could be found in both. They usually preferred red wine to white, but always preferred vodka to wine. They differed strongly, however, on the matter of what to order at Pinks.

Pinks Café was in a ramshackle building perched on the bank of the Kankakee River, nestled close to the Schuyler Avenue Bridge. The back of the tiny restaurant was supported, one hoped, by a kind of stilt arrangement that made the floor almost even, although if you walked in the front door you stayed on level ground, and if you exited through the back, you climbed down thirty stairs. The original Mr. Pink, who had passed into legend years ago, was rumored to ask first-time customers whom he disliked for one reason or another to please exit by the back door because he was locking up the front. Then he and the waitress, Aggie, and any other regulars left in the joint listened to hear if they clattered and bounced down the wooden steps and stopped before rolling into the Kankakee River. Don and Nellie loved to tell Mr. Pink stories, Nellie with a kind of gleeful malice, and Don with a rueful longing for less litigious days.

"They'd sue him now," Don always added at the end of a Mr. Pink tale, as if that were the only problematic aspect to the story.

Tim insisted that the only thing to order at Pinks was coffee and pastries. He did not trust the grill, the pans, the refrigeration, or the food purveyors. Jane checked her concerned-mother-nutrition-label-reading self at the door and recommended the American fries.

"If you have any of the 'messes,' which are just scrambled omelets, you get the potatoes and heavenly buttered toast," Jane said, feeling guilty about being hungry—*hadn't she just found Lilly after all*—but being ravenous nonetheless.

"I'm surprised you have, here in Kankakee, a restaurant that stays open so late," said Detective Oh.

"That's the beauty of Pinks," said Jane. "It just opened."

"It's an all-night diner," Tim explained, "but just all night."

"Midnight to 8:00 A.M. or so," said Jane.

Pinks had been a godsend to high schoolers for years. In a town where "There's nothing to do" is the nightly battle cry, Pinks was the place to be. After movies, parties, late-night golf course drinking bouts, illicit road trips, and romantic rendezvous at the boat docks, everyone showed up at Pinks. There, the teenagers mingled with representatives of every stratification of Kankakee society. The late-shift factory workers, the drunken bar closers, the bartenders who had overserved them, the businessmen who had worked overtime to avoid their families. Those nighttimers arrived late and tired, but just hungry enough to brave a Pinks Mess, three eggs scrambled with cheese and whatever vegetables, fruit, condiments the cook felt like adding. Cries of, "I got olives!" were usually echoed by someone else at another booth, "I got raisins," who was answered with, "You'd better hope they're raisins," which grossed everybody out for about a second before they continued shoveling in eggs and bacon and buttered white toast.

"Yeah?" asked Bonnie, Aggie's granddaughter, as she held her pencil poised over pad and listened to Detective Oh order whole wheat toast and a cup of tea.

"That's all," he answered.

"Yeah?" she answered again, shaking her head at Tim and Jane.

"She'll bring you white toast and coffee," Tim said. "Don't take it personally."

Jane found it charming that Detective Oh built a small tower with shrink-wrapped jelly containers as he told them what had brought him to Kankakee.

"I visited Mrs. Bateman," he began, but Jane interrupted him. She put her hand over Tim's and nodded toward the door. Tim turned to look and whistled softly.

Lilly Duff's brother, Bobby, had just walked in the door with two other men. Jane thought they looked familiar and realized they were probably Bobby's friends from high school, guys she'd probably known back then, too. None of them had aged well. They all seemed to have had more than a few drinks, and they kept bumping up against each other as they staked out a table of high school girls, preparing to intimidate them and get their booth before the girls were even served their food. It was an old Pinks routine—the pecking order of customers—and no one in management interfered. "If you can't stand the grease fire get out of the kitchen" was their motto. High schoolers were lousy tippers anyway, and drunken factory workers often mistook twenties for tens.

Bobby leered over the shoulder of one of the girls, mumbling and making small talk. It didn't take long before the blonde across the table stood up and told the others they were welcome to stay, but she was taking her car and leaving. They followed like lambs, passengers after driver, and exited. Remarkably, Bobby and his friends grew immediately sober and less clumsy and took over the table. Jane spotted one of them grab the five-dollar bill that one of the girls had thrown down in guilty haste as they left.

"He can't possibly know," Tim said.

Jane shook her head. She found herself completely detached from Lilly Duff and her apparent murder. She was thinking of it now as information, something she knew that thirty-seven-year-old Bobby Duff didn't know, would soon be told, and that would change his life forever. She remembered Lilly and Bobby as kids, the other saloon keeper children at her school. Bobby was wild, just as Lilly had been, but they were always sweet together. Jane could remember Lilly threatening some boy in Jane's class, two years older, who had made fun of Bobby tagging along behind her. They were scrappy and loyal. Bobby, Tim had told Jane, was helping Lilly run their folks' place. He, too, had gone into debt to buy it from Gus Duncan. He, too, had been stood up like

Don and Nellie on the day of the "final paperwork." Perhaps, he, too, was being blackmailed. Jane realized, in those few seconds as she watched Bobby's face, two things: One, having the kind of power she had now over Bobby, her knowledge that his sister was dead, murdered in a basement on Linnet Street—knowledge that would change his life, would gray his hair, would line his handsome face—felt like the opposite of power, and two, Bobby would be asked if he had an alibi for the time of his sister's death. Jane no longer felt like she could eat a Pinks Special Mess.

There were only so many places people could be late at night in Kankakee if they weren't in their own homes and the bars were closed: the police station, the emergency room, and Pinks. Jane saw the police car park outside the front window. One uniformed officer, about the same age as Bobby Duff, came in and went straight to him, squeezed into the booth, and whispered something in his ear. Bobby got up immediately and left, clutching the cop's elbow.

Jane turned away from the window, thinking she didn't want to see the moment in the parking lot when the cop told Bobby, then turned back, surprised to find that she did want to see it, wanted to verify Bobby's expression, wanted to make sure she saw genuine grief and shock, and spotted no false horror, no faked sobs. But when she turned back, the police car was pulling onto the street with Bobby in the backseat.

Jane picked at her American fries, but felt squeamish about exploring her "mess." Tim raised an "I told you so eyebrow" but mercifully didn't tease her. She wanted to move beyond the almost-crying stage every time she discussed a case with Detective Oh.

Detective Oh was puzzling over his coffee cup. Aggie's granddaughter had brought him coffee as Tim had predicted but had also placed a generic-brand tea bag on the saucer.

"I can't imagine how this would taste, but I somehow want to use it to show my appreciation," said Oh. "What can that possibly mean?"

"You've become a Kankakeean, Oh," said Tim. "Confused because, like, 'What am I doing here?' is the main thought that buzzes through your head. Guilty because the second most common thought is 'I could be doing something better with my life.' Third and most important, grateful that you're in a place where, screwy as it might be, people try to do the right thing, try to make you as happy as they think you should be."

Jane had taken out her small notepad, the one where she kept her Lucky Fives along with her notes from Miriam. She wanted to clear her head by making a list; she just wasn't sure what information she could codify.

"There was no blood," she said, closing her eyes, imagining the scene in the shanty basement. "Her face was contorted, twisted, turned away, like she had looked at something she didn't want to see. I knew Lilly was dead right away," Jane said.

"It's really quite clear, the difference between life and death. Breath animates, doesn't just make the chest rise and fall. It quivers the eyelids, it pulses under the skin, it warms a body, all things visible to those with eyes that see. Your eyes, Mrs. Wheel. I'm sorry to remind you, also, that this isn't your first dead body."

"So how will we find out cause of death? Wait for the papers? Munson won't be calling us with news we can use," said Tim.

"I'll make a few calls," said Oh.

"Mrs. Bateman? Mary?" Jane asked. "You started to say . . ."

"I went to see her, told her I was working privately on an old case, and wondered if she remembered or could supply me with any information about Mr. Bateman's gambling charge," Oh said. "Strictly confidential, of course."

"She was quite forthcoming and yet . . ." Oh stopped, and tapped his finger against the thick rim of his coffee cup.

"Yes?" Jane asked.

"I felt like she wanted me to walk away and think exactly that. That she was forthcoming. I realized, as I drove away, that I'd gained no new knowledge from our conversation," Oh said. "For example, she told me that Bateman had been in jail for only a few months, then got released because of a loophole his lawyer had found in the case. When I asked if he was guilty of running gambling, she said Bateman did the same things that all the other saloon keepers did, he was just honest about it."

"I like an honest gambler," said Tim. "Honest, crooked."

"Better than crooked, crooked," said Jane.

Their waitress came and refilled their cups, hesitating a moment as she held the pot over Oh's cup with the unwrapped, but unused, tea bag on the saucer. He shook his head and covered the cup with his hand. She nodded, seeming to indicate that an understanding had been reached.

"So what did you learn?" asked Jane.

"Hey, Nancy Drew, you're not listening. The good detective said he didn't learn anything from Mary Bateman," said Tim, yawning and stretching.

"Learned nothing *from the conversation*," Jane said. "You must have learned something, Detective Oh. The leaves are beautiful along the Kankakee River in the fall, but peak color comes in a few weeks. Pinks is a quaint and unusual restaurant, but it hasn't been reviewed favorably in a Chicago paper. And the McFlea Showhouse doesn't open until Sunday, so . . ."

"It was the way the women all sat and held their hands when we talked. I remember learning long ago that children of a certain era who went to parish schools, Catholic schools, often formed the habit of folding their hands when sitting and listening because the nuns had taught them to do it at their desks from an early age. Like you are doing, Mrs. Wheel," Oh said.

Jane leaned forward over her folded hands and nodded. Tim smirked and shook his head slightly, quietly unfolding his own hands that were resting just like Jane's in his lap under the table.

"The women . . . Dot and Ollie were there?" asked Jane. Oh nodded.

"And as we chatted, all three of the women sat with their hands held just so," Oh said, demonstrating. He held his hands in front of him, palms facing up, his right hand on top of the left. He wrapped the fingers of his left hand around his right pointer, holding on to it for dear life. "They held their hands so, and Mary and Dorothy, Dot, rocked back and forth slightly, like this." Oh rocked back and forth almost imperceptibly, the barest of movements.

Jane and Tim both imitated the position and began rocking.

"Protecting those hands, those fingers," Tim said.

"Yes," said Jane, "but from whom?"

10

Jane tiptoed through the dining room and into the kitchen. She had seen Nellie's shoes placed in their usual spot by the door, Don's hat hung on a peg inside the coat closet. They had returned from wherever they had been, their mysterious evening "out."

On the kitchen table, the group photograph taken in front of the EZ Way Inn was still propped against the wall. Nothing was disturbed around the picture. The basket heaped with plastic flowers and fruit was still dead center, the cloth still smooth and unlined covering the round, wooden table. A nightlight was plugged in over the kitchen counter that gave off just enough glow to show Jane that the room remained untouched. But was it untouched? Or had it been Nellified?

Nellie had the ghostly knack of living and working on the surface of a space. She walked through a room and ashtrays were emptied, candy in dishes rearranged to look untouched, pictures were straightened on walls, the nap of a carpet lay redirected and aligned. She left the neat and clean aura of the unlived-in. Years ago when Jane came home alone to an empty perfect house after school, she could calm her fears by standing stone still inside the front door, sweeping the room with her eyes, making sure nothing was out of place. That would mean she was alone—no mysterious strangers lurked behind curtains or closet doors.

Nellification gave Jane a measure by which to assess her safety, her security in a space, but it also rendered the same room sterile, untouched, lonely. Jane remembered too many after-school hours sitting perfectly still, trying not to disturb the objects in the living room. The television tuned to something noisy, a Three Stooges rerun or a loud cartoon, for company, for the sound of voices, even if they belonged to Moe and Curly or a jabbering rabbit and duck. Jane read books and did her homework in her dad's recliner, parked in front of the television, the lamp turned on to its brightest setting, a frivolous 75 watts that Don demanded for reading the newspaper, and Nellie grudgingly allowed. Before her parents picked her up for dinner, Jane repacked her books, smoothed out the pillow in her dad's chair, and straightened the throw rug by the door. Still, she had left a trail. A napkin she had used to clean her glasses was half out of the garbage can, the dishtowel she had dried her juice glass with was unevenly folded. The drawn curtains were slightly in disarray where Jane had pinched them back to peek out at the world.

Nellie walked in the house and went right to the offending objects, straightening, smoothing, stowing, and poof! The room, the house, within five minutes of her arrival, was Nellified.

Is that what happened this night? Had Don and Nellie come into the kitchen, gasped at the photograph, sat and studied it, wringing their hands? Had Don called for a pot of coffee and a cookie to dunk in it while he sat and named all the people? Had Nellie pointed to a few figures herself, spoken disparagingly of whomever she recognized?

Then, after yawning and surmising that Jane would be back late, imagining her lost digging through dusty boxes with Tim, they would rise to go to bed. Nellie would clean their fingerprints off the glass of the photo and replace it just so. She'd wipe Don's cookie crumbs off the table, smooth the heavy plastic tablecloth. She'd clean and put away their dishes, then fill the coffeemaker's reservoir with water for the morning. All would be tidied and untouched—Nellified so Jane would not know if her parents had walked straight through the kitchen and to the bedroom or if they had played out the late-night scenario she had just imagined.

Jane slept badly. She barely dozed, then woke every thirty or forty minutes to remember Lilly, sitting on top of the boxes in the basement. *She wants to tell me something,* Jane thought, the way one thinks in a dream . . . absolute clarity one second, a fuzzy haze the next. Lilly seemed to beckon with one hand, point to something. What she pointed to was unclear. The box? Something inside the box that held her body against the wall? At 5:30 A.M., Jane gave up. She rose and wrapped herself in her mother's old chenille robe. In the kitchen, she pushed the button on the coffeemaker and sat down with pencil and paper, ready to make a list, take notes. Anything to clear her mind.

Had Lilly visited her in the night because Jane had put the discovery of her body on some kind of time delay? She couldn't think about it when it happened; her brain was already in the process of filing away too many pieces of information, too many disconnected images, literally. Bateman's severed finger, Duncan's body with another *almost* severed finger, and now, poor Lilly. Jane, with her fuzzy morning brain, tried to organize her thoughts but kept coming back to the same paradox. The two men with their unconnected fingers were connected in their disconnection. Lilly, on the other hand, *no pun intended*, Jane silently told herself, was intact. Dead, yes. Had she been hit in the head? No blood that Jane saw, but she thought she had heard one of the police officers speculating. No mutilation of the body though, no mangling of hands or fingers.

Lilly had probably been dead less than an hour, perhaps less than thirty minutes, according to the eavesdropping Jane had done at the scene.

"Whoever killed Lilly," Jane said aloud, drawing on her notepad, "was in the basement when I came in the house." She held her pen poised over the face of the dog she had just sketched. "The noise was the murderer ... maybe propping her up then leaving by the basement door."

She remembered that pile of bricks by the door. They would have been in the way. As the door opened, it would have moved them, pushed them aside. One might have tumbled down from the top of the stack. Jane wrote down Lilly's name and underneath, printed, BRICKS? The one thrown through the EZ Way Inn was a Kingsley Paver. That was the name stamped on its face. She would check the bricks in the basement of 801 today. If she could get into the basement. If not, would her parents report their act of vandalism so she could get Munson to recognize the importance of connecting those bricks? She would also find out what caused Lilly's death. One of those bricks? —

"You sick?"

Jane jumped in her chair and stifled a scream.

Nellie had been sneaking up behind her for over forty years, and yet it still spooked her. Her mother was as silent as a baby breathing, and when she appeared at your side or behind your back, she always spoke as if you had been enmeshed in conversation for hours. "In medias Nellie," she and her brother, Michael, had always said. Every conversation with their mother began somewhere in the middle.

"You scared me, Mom," Jane said.

"Yeah?" asked Nellie, sounding not at all displeased.

Nellie poured Jane and herself a cup of coffee. She opened a package of chocolate doughnuts, the kind Jane knew Don and Nellie sold off the bread rack at the EZ Way Inn, the kind that were encased in a hard shell of chocolate, the kind that no one she knew ate anymore. They were the vintage items of the breakfast pastry world. Jane selected one from the box and dunked it in her coffee. It was as different from a bakery croissant, a fancy food store muffin, or a meltingly delicious Krispy Kreme as it could be. It was high in fat (and all the wrong kinds of fat, too), full of chemical preservatives (that gave it a shelf life akin to a Twinkie), and unappetizing in its hard, brown shell (surely containing more carnuba wax than chocolate).

Jane ate her first one in three bites and took a second.

"Where were you last night?"

"Out," Nellie said.

"Yeah?" Jane asked, trying to match her mother in minimalism and attitude.

"We had a meeting, that's all," Nellie said. "What about you? You and Tim find any good junk?"

Nellie had tipped her hand. It had only happened a few times in Jane's company in Jane's lifetime. If Nellie asked her a question, tried to change the subject, deflect her daughter's inquiries, Jane was as close to breaking into the vault of Nellie's memories and secrets as she had ever been.

"I'm going to get to the bottom of all of this, Mom," Jane said softly. "Why don't you tell me about it yourself?"

"I already told you I killed Gus Duncan. Isn't confessing to murder enough for you?"

"Mom," Jane said, "you know . . ."

"I know, I know. Just because I want to be the one who killed him, doesn't mean I get the title."

"Well, Nellie, maybe not the title you wanted, but if you mean literally, we got that. The title to the building, I mean," Don said, padding into the kitchen dressed in a plaid wool robe and brown, fur-lined slippers. "Morning, honey. Save me a doughnut?"

Jane waited until her father had gotten his coffee and sat down at the round table with them. Nellie started to jump up and get a rag to wipe up the small circle of liquid that had splashed out when Don set his cup and saucer down, but he put his hand over her arm.

"Let it go, Nellie."

Nellie grunted and gave in. At least for the moment. She did take a paper napkin from its holder and mop up around his cup, but she remained seated.

Don gestured to the photograph with his doughnut. The three of them were seated in a half circle around it. Since the round table was pushed up against the wall to fit in this small square kitchen space, the picture was propped up like a fourth guest at breakfast.

"Find this in Duncan's house?" Don asked.

Jane thought it sounded like a statement rather than a question, and she nodded.

"We should have told you a long time ago," Don said, looking directly into his daughter's eyes. "It wasn't fair to keep . . ."

"Why the hell wasn't it fair?" Nellie asked, her own eyes blazing. "Kids got to know everything their parents do? Even when their parents do something stupid? I thought the point of raising kids was to make them smarter and better. Isn't that what you always said? Educate them and send them off into the world? Jane and Michael didn't need to carry this," she said. "We made *our* bed," Nellie added, hitting the *our* hard, "not theirs."

Don patted Nellie's arm. Jane noticed that he had kept it there when he restrained her from jumping up to clean. He took a deep breath and shook his head at Nellie and smiled slightly.

"But a picture's worth a thousand words, hon," he said gently. "We got to give Jane a few of our own words before she makes up her own."

Don began his story, punctuated by a few snorts and curse words from Nellie, while Jane kept eating doughnuts. She doodled through her entire scratch pad. It wasn't a shocking story, nor was it a particularly surprising one. It all made sense. Sort of. In a Kankakee, Don and Nellie kind of way.

Don had worked as a milkman, a railroad signalman, a farmhand, and a printer's assistant all before the age of twenty to help support his mother and an invalid stepfather who had lost everything in the Depression. Jane knew most of that part of her father's history. He had told her about the dogs who had chased him when he delivered the milk, about the empty bottle he kept in his back pocket as a weapon if he was attacked. As a little girl, she had traced the outline of the large, jagged scar on his ankle. It had been the illustration to the lecture on why she could not have a puppy. Rita, Jane's adopted German shepherd, was the first dog Don had allowed in his house, the first dog, he told Jane, he had ever viewed as a man's potential acquaintance. He would never admit to the possibility of a canine best friend.

Don's dreams of college and a professional life flew out the window when he had to quit high school to support his family, so he modified the dream. "If I could be my own boss," he always told Jane and Michael, "I knew I'd be a happy man." It didn't matter how hard he had to work, how many hours he had to put in, as long as at the end of the day, he had ownership.

"Gus came up to me at the bar of the Brown Jug, used to be over on East Avenue, one night and told me I could buy a tavern and have my own business," Don said. "Told me he could fix it for me."

"Just like that?" Jane asked. "How did you know him?"

"Everybody knew him," Don said. "I don't know how.

He was just one of those guys who knew everybody and owned property and always had the money to buy a drink for himself and everybody else. I think he started in the candy and cigarette business, had a piece of the vending delivery service, something like that. Something that got him into every tavern and on the listening end of every conversation when somebody was in trouble or couldn't pay off a note. Gus was there to help or to lend or to give advice. Pretty soon after that, he'd be there to buy or to foreclose."

Don took out his pipe from the pocket of his robe. He had quit smoking cigarettes and tried to keep from lighting up anything in the house; but occasionally, Jane knew, he still indulged. Now he used the stem as a pointer, gesturing to the photograph.

"When that picture was taken, we had just signed the lease on the EZ Way Inn. Your mother and I had been married a few years and saved enough for that little house over on Calista. We put a down payment on that in the spring and by fall, Gus had found an opportunity for me, the EZ Way Inn. I'd own the business, but he'd keep the building. I'd pay him rent, but I'd be my own boss."

"Yeah," Nellie said, "'Cause a landlord never has any boss power over you."

"You liked the idea at the time, Nellie," Don said, without any anger or recrimination in his voice.

He was staring at the photograph, at their young images, full of hope and smiles, and seemed wistful but not bitter. None of this, Jane noticed, was being told in the hard voice he usually reserved for conversations about Gus Duncan.

"So what happened?" Jane asked.

"Gus had set up a lot of people, given them good deals on places. Some made it; some didn't. We made it," Don said.

"Most of them drank themselves into early graves," Nellie said, "thought the tavern business meant that they could drink all day for free. Nothing free about it."

"We did okay, and so did Duff. The ones who could add two and two and could hang back on the bottle. Larry, Jack, and old Pink. They all held on and built up their businesses. During the war, everybody made money. Nick did great with that little fried chicken place on the river," Don said.

"Duff," Jane said aloud, thinking to herself, *They don't know about Lilly. I'm going to have to tell them.*

"Bill Duff had the place down the road from us. You know the one. Lilly and her brother are running it," Don said. "Anyway, Gus just kept his eyes and ears open all the time until he got something on you."

"Got something?" Jane asked.

"Got something, made up something," Nellie said.

"Let me tell it, Nellie."

The phone rang and he patted Nellie's arm to keep her still and got up to answer it.

Jane could tell by the look on Don's face and the one-syllable expressions that he let escape that she wouldn't have to tell him about Lilly. Someone was filling him in right now. When he hung up, he came over and stood behind Nellie and put his hands on her shoulders. It was more physical contact between them than Jane had seen in thirty years.

"Lilly Duff is dead," Jane said.

Nellie stared at Jane for a moment, then stood up, pushing away Don's hands.

"The old bastard kills people from the grave," she said, clearing away the coffee things and doughnut crumbs.

"Son-of-a-bitch won't stay dead," Don said. Jane saw tears in his eyes. "That Lilly was shaping up into a fine saloon keeper, too."

"Who called?" Jane asked.

It was Benny, an old pal of her dad's who tended bar for Lilly part-time. Benny had served a drink at almost every bar in town at one time or another. He had a terrible stutter and preferred not to talk at all, which made him the perfect bartender. He was a born listener. Don told Nellie and Jane that he'd been crying when he called. Hadn't been able to find Bobby and was afraid of what he'd do when he found out.

Jane told her parents that she had seen Bobby leave Pinks with the police last night.

"Poor kid," said Don. "He was one step out of trouble anyway, and now with Lilly gone . . ."

"Did Benny say anything about how it happened?"

"I suppose he thought you'd fill me in," Don said.

"What? Why should she . . . ? Oh, shit," said Nellie, "you weren't the one who found her, were you?" Nellie went to the sink and washed her hands. "What's wrong with you anyway, getting mixed up with dead people all the time?"

"Don't look at me that way. I didn't kill Gus, did I?" Jane stood up, too. She wanted to keep asking about Duncan, about what had made everything turn out so badly, so wrong for everyone. What did he have on everybody? What did he have on Don and Nellie?

Her dad, though, couldn't finish his story now. Jane would have to wait until later. He had promised Benny he'd make some calls, and her mother was already planning on the food she'd bring over to Lilly's brother. "Somebody's going to have to help that one. He isn't worth a damn as a worker, and Lilly was the only thing that stood between him and jail most of the time," Nellie said. "I'll make him a ham."

Jane had a million questions and had to start finding answers. Bruce Oh had never even gotten to why he had come to Kankakee last night, not the details. He had told her they'd talk about it today. Maybe if she started with him, she could follow some kind of Bateman to Duncan to Lilly trail. Jane dialed the cell phone number that Oh had given her last night. It wasn't quite 8:00 A.M., but she was sure he'd be awake.

Oh was ready to meet with Jane, but the last thing she wanted was to bring Oh and Nellie into the same room. She gave him directions from his motel to the McFlea house. She had planned to finish the kitchen this morning so she would be able to work with Tim over on Linnet Street. That was probably out of the question now. She figured the shanties would be off-limits for a while.

Jane's old room was just off the kitchen. She put on her overalls again. If she was going to work on the McFlea, she might as well start out dirty and paint spattered. She stuck her hands into the deep front pockets to straighten the pants and felt a thick wad of paper. Pulling out the packet of letters, she remembered. They were on the basement floor. Maybe that's what Lilly was trying to point to in Jane's dream. Maybe she wanted Jane to read them. Sitting on the edge of her bed, Jane pulled out the first in the packet and unfolded the yellow sheet covered in small flowery script.

Trying to decipher the handwriting in the low light of

her bedroom, Jane heard her parents talking about the people in the photo. It sounded to Jane like a morbid listing of everyone who was dead, followed by how and when they had died. Were her parents the only ones left? She thought she heard them talking about Lilly's father and called in to ask them the how and when on him.

"Couldn't handle things after her mother died. Year or so later, must have been, he took the same way out," Don called in to her.

Jane came back in the kitchen. "Suicide?"

"Yep. Louella cut her wrists in the bathtub one night, and Duff came home and found her. Ruined the man," Don said. "One day he went out and started his car in the garage but forgot to go anywhere. That's why Benny's so upset. He found him and then had to go in the house and tell Bobby."

"Where was Lilly?" Jane asked.

"Last year of nursing school," Don said. "She came home and took care of everything, and Gus told her she could have the same deal if she wanted to run the business. She was doing okay, too."

"When was all this?"

"I'm not sure, maybe ten years ago? Fifteen? Lilly was always going back and forth to school. She'd work for a while, then go back to school, then be back here working some more. Thought she'd stick with nursing though; she seemed to like it, Duff told me. After he died though, she just decided to run the saloon. I figured she did it to give Bobby a home and something to do. He was always drifting from one thing to another."

"Lilly was a hard worker," Nellie said, bestowing her supreme compliment. "Who killed her?"

210

Nellie asked this question as if Jane, as the one who'd discovered the body, would have all the pertinent information. But before she could answer her mother, Don chimed in.

"Nobody. Did it herself. Must run deep in that family."

"What are you talking about?" Jane asked. She thought maybe her father had misheard or that she was dreaming again, so she pinched herself hard while she waited for her dad to set the record straight.

"Pills, she took something, but nobody knows why she was down there in that shanty basement."

"What about . . . I heard them say they thought she had been hit in the head," Jane said, beginning to get agitated. First Gus, now Lilly. Didn't anybody believe that people could get murdered on Linnet Street?

An hour later Jane was unpacking boxes at the McFlea. She had brought some of her favorite linens from home—dish towels embroidered with dancing silverware and hand-crocheted pot holders that were shaped like little dresses and hats. She decided to set the table. She chose Harlequin plates, not as pricey or popular as Fiestaware, but just as honest and strong on the table. She used some of her mismatched Bakelite-handled flatware and drew solid red napkins through thick, butterscotch, grooved napkin rings to tie it all together.

On an open shelf over the sink, she carefully set out ten clear juice glasses, none of them exactly the same. They were all Hazel Atlas with the cute little H and A mark on the bottom, each in a different pattern but just close enough to be sparkling variations on a theme. She jotted down a reminder to get flowers for Sunday, so she could put tiny bunches of fresh daisies, stems trimmed down to size, in each Hazel Atlas, so there would be a row of flower-filled glasses over the sink. She was picturing it and humming to herself when Oh tapped at the back door.

"How does someone commit suicide, then set herself up like that? Do you mean to tell me that she picked up that box and held it on her lap while she died?" Jane asked, not wasting anytime with small talk. She had put the shiny chrome kettle that she had just unpacked on to boil, hoping Oh didn't require tea more exotic than the Constant Comment that she had in her shopping bag.

"I spoke with one of my new friends at the police department this morning," Oh said, accepting the tea gratefully. "Lilly Duff took several doses of penicillin, as much as she could get down, before she went into anaphylactic shock. She was highly allergic and knew it. She had made a phone call on her cell phone. Probably just before taking the pills."

"But she was moved? I mean, someone set her up like that, with the box on her lap."

"No. She probably sat down on one box and put the other one on her lap to hold herself there. Maybe she wanted something to hold onto?"

"It seems odd, doesn't it?" Jane asked.

Oh nodded. "But the police don't question the suicide. The phone call she made was to her brother. It was still on his machine when the police brought him home last night. She sounded distraught, said that she had found out something terrible. She said she couldn't live knowing it was true." Oh stopped to sip his tea and take a breath. "She told her brother she was so sorry to have to leave him alone."

"But I heard the police talking about her head—trauma?"

"Speculation at the scene. She had hit her head against the wall, sitting there, a kind of choking spasm, but it had nothing to do with the cause of death."

"Are you satisfied with their explanation?" Jane asked. She found she needed to keep busy while she discussed this or she would keep seeing Lilly sitting up on that box, trying to tell her something, and she wouldn't be able to listen to what Oh was telling her.

Earlier she had strung a small piece of clothesline across the top of the small window in the pantry and the matching window on the same wall outside of the pantry, opposite the kitchen table. She took out a shirt box and opened it, revealing colorful handkerchiefs, some trimmed in hand crochet, some embroidered, all relics of a day when every lady carried a hanky or two in her pocketbook. Jane selected handkerchiefs seemingly at random and, folding a small triangle of cloth at the corner over the line, she attached them one by one with time-worn wooden clothespins. They made a triangle valence across the top of the window, adding color and movement to that side of the room.

"Charming," Oh said, shaking his head in a kind of wonderment.

Jane faced Oh, and he remembered that she had asked him a question. Was he satisfied with the police explanation? The first answer that came to mind was *no* since he was never satisfied with anyone's explanation except his own, and he hadn't been allowed to get close enough here to reach the explanation stage. However, he reminded himself, he was no longer a police officer. He was a consultant, a private investigator of sorts, and with the information he had gotten this morning, he was satisfied with the facts of Lilly Duff's death.

"I believe she died as a result of an allergic reaction. I believe she took the penicillin voluntarily. Yes, I believe she committed suicide."

"It's the way she was sitting that bothers me. Like she was using that box for a table. Or a lap desk ..." Jane touched the letters still unread in her pocket. "Like a lap desk so she could read ..."

"Hey, Lucy, I'm home," Tim called out, as he entered the house through the front door. Jane had made him promise not to come in through the kitchen so the room would be a surprise. Other McFlea workers would be coming in and out all day putting the finishing touches on their rooms, readying the house for the opening. Jane wanted to hold onto the kitchen for as long as she could.

"Don't come in; we'll come out," Jane said.

"Lucy, what are you and Ethel up to in there?"

Jane looked at Oh, who looked thoroughly puzzled.

"It's from a television show," Jane explained, "Lucy and Ethel ..."

"Yes, *I Love Lucy*. I know. I was thinking about Lilly Duff's message to her brother. What evidence might she have found in the basement? Did Mr. Duncan have any files or records, anything in which she might have discovered ... anything? Accounting books, records, old ledgers?"

"Yes, there were boxes of that stuff. Duncan had records from old buildings he took over. Came from all over town."

"Is that Detective Oh I hear in there?"

"Yes, Timmy, we'll be out there in a minute," Jane said. She picked up the last of her empty boxes and stuck them on the back porch.

Jane and Oh went into the living room. Two wing chairs had been placed by the fireplace, and Tim had piled one of them with slipcovers and hand-knit throws. Jane eyed a beautiful green chenille that was just one of the pieces Tim had told her Karen Hack, the woman in charge of the living room, had gotten at a rummage sale for end-of-the-day prices. She had filled a plastic garbage bag during the last hour at Saint Stan's and paid two dollars for the entire stack on the chair. She had laundered them and ironed the slipcovers and now was ready to remake the ten-dollar chairs. Jane was mightily impressed. The room wasn't necessarily her taste—a little too symmetrical and traditional—but it was clean and comfortable and fairly chic. The oak-framed mirror over the old sofa was a great touch. Karen had also found some great vases that she was planning to fill with flowers, and Jane knew the room would look like it had cost a fortune. The flowers, purchased from Tim's store, would be the most expensive accessories in the whole space.

"What was in the boxes in the basement, Tim, where Lilly . . . you heard, right?"

"Suicide? Yes, I heard. Bobby called me this morning. Wanted to know if I knew what the status of the house was, whether or not I'd be going back in today."

Jane checked her watch and realized that she needed to

call Evanston and leave a message on the machine for Nick. She wanted to wish him good luck in the soccer tournament and hadn't gotten home to her parents' last night in time to do it. What was she supposed to say? Mom meant to call, but another one of those pesky dead bodies turned up. She should fill Charley in, too, but she was feeling guilty somehow, like she was responsible for Lilly. *Maybe,* she thought, *when you find a body, it makes you the one who's supposed to discover the truth about what happened. Like if you saved a life, you were responsible for the person.* God, she was starting to think like one of the fortune cookies she had used to paper the pantry wall last night. Jane left her message, then sat down with Oh and Tim to go over what she didn't know about the crimes that hadn't been committed.

"If the police think Lilly committed suicide, they'll never reopen their investigation of Gus Duncan's death. We're back to square one on that."

Tim looked at her, his face expressionless. "We? Who's we?"

"You said last night that you believed me, that I was right all along about Gus."

"I thought Lilly had been murdered. That made me believe that Gus had been, too. You know it follows you around in multiples, so I figured those little crime-dog instincts that you've been honing were right on. But now . . ." Tim let his voice trail off.

"You don't want to believe anybody's been murdered so you can get back into those shanties and inventory the stuff," Jane said.

"I believe that Gus Duncan's death was . . . ," Oh hesitated, choosing his words carefully, "more complicated."

Jane tried not to let her delight show. It was, after all, murder they were discussing on this lovely autumn morning. But she had to know what had persuaded Detective Oh that Duncan might not have died of natural causes.

"It's my experience that when someone hires an investigator to look into the circumstances of someone's death, there's a good reason to believe that there are, or were, *circumstances*," said Oh. "And I have been hired."

A tinny cellular ring sounded. Not "La Cucaracha," so it wasn't Jane's phone. Not "Hernando's Hideaway," so it wasn't Tim's. A straightforward two-note ring. Detective Oh nodded and looked at his watch. His client, he explained, was most punctual and had told him to expect a call that morning. He pulled the phone from his pocket and answered on the second ring.

Oh spoke only a few words. His client was doing most of the talking. Jane didn't think she would normally have pried into anyone's private phone conversation, but things were getting curiouser and curiouser around here, so she stood up to shake out one of the slipcovers and pretended to take a look at its condition. She stepped behind the couch where Oh was seated. In doing so, she couldn't help but notice as he tilted the phone away from his ear slightly to reach for a pencil on the coffee table that the caller number was still displayed. Jane might not have even registered that she was taking note of the number if it hadn't been such a familiar one. Kankakee area code, then the number. One she had dialed almost every day of her life.

The EZ Way Inn.

10

Jane knew that the EZ Way Inn was not officially open. The grand reopening was scheduled to take place in a few days. That didn't mean, however, that Francis, the bread delivery man, and Gil, the retired Roper Stove foreman, weren't sitting at the bar right now having a late breakfast glass of beer. It also did not mean that any number of regulars and irregulars could not be sipping coffee or having a wake-up shot while Don and Nellie continued to scrub and polish and set up for their Monday opening. Jane's parents wouldn't think of actually closing the bar while the bar was closed.

Even on Christmas and Thanksgiving, Don found a way to cajole Nellie into spending at least a few hours at the EZ Way Inn so Barney and Vince and Carp and Chef would have somewhere to go. One Thanksgiving, they actually brought Barney and Vince with them to Grandma's for dinner because Don and Nellie knew they had nowhere to eat turkey and watch a football game. Nellie's mother and father, Lithuanian immigrants whose hearts were much bigger than their house, did not seem to find it odd that Don and Nellie had brought in a few extras. More card players for after the meal; more hungry eaters to appreciate the Kugela.

Because she knew there would be a few customers seated around the bar, because she knew anyone who walked in the front door of the tavern could round the corner into the dining room where the pay phone hung on the wall in the corner, Jane knew that seeing the EZ Way number displayed did not mean that Don and/or Nellie had hired Detective Oh.

But wouldn't it be a huge stretch of even Jane's elastic imagination to believe it was someone else who had just happened to wander into the tavern to make a phone call?

How would she approach the question with Oh? Was the relationship between a detective and client as inviolate as that of a doctor-patient, priest-confessor? She did not want to jeopardize the quasi-professional, almost friendship she was developing with Oh, but she had to know. As she was composing the question in her mind, delicate yet detailed, Tim spoke up.

"So who's your client?" he asked, as Oh slipped his phone back into his pocket.

"Bill Crandall, the nephew of Gus Duncan, the only relative," Oh said, turning to Jane. "He was calling from the EZ Way Inn. Says it's very near the shanties? Where we were last night? He wanted to know if I could expedite matters with the police. If he could get into the houses today."

"Good question," said Tim. "I was wondering the same thing."

Oh didn't think there would be any reason that the middle house, 803, would be closed off. He wasn't even sure

801 or 805 would be off-limits. Although technically suicide was a crime, the police probably finished there last night. But 803 would be open for sure. No dead body had turned up in that house.

"Janie, maybe you ought to stay out of that one," said Tim.

Jane gave him a frosty smile. She spoke, however, to Oh. "How did Bill Crandall know to hire you?"

"I asked the same. He said he had known someone who had taken a course from me and also recognized my name from a story his uncle had sent him about the murder at Mr. Lowry's flower shop."

"Yeah, what a marketing brainstorm that was. The bouquet business just boomed after that," Tim said. "Glad it worked for you, too."

"One little quote in the paper hardly seems like a ringing endorsement for a private investigator, and you weren't even in business then," said Jane.

"Yes," said Oh, "it seemed off to me. I did check out his friend's name, the one who took my class. There was such a person signed up for a summer seminar. He only came once or twice. I might have mentioned that I was thinking about beginning a consulting business."

"Really odd. A long shot that he even knew you were taking private clients, and," Jane said, her voice a shade higher, "why would he hire someone in the first place? Gus Duncan died of natural causes; that's what everyone keeps telling me anyway."

Jane's phone began playing, and Tim snapped his fingers as if he held castanets.

"Did you tell Nick to do this?" Jane said. "You know I don't know how to change it back to a normal ring."

Charley's voice was calm, but Jane could tell by the way he began the call that something was wrong. He said her name twice, in that reassuring tone that he used to calm her whenever he had bad news.

"Nick? What's happened to Nick?" Jane asked.

"Nothing. He was at school; he doesn't even know what happened, and he's off to his soccer tournament and everything's fine with him."

"You, Charley, are you okay? What's wrong?"

"Fine, everybody's fine. It's just that someone broke in," Charley said. "We had a burglary."

"Oh, no," said Jane. "Did they get . . ." Jane hesitated. Everything in her house was valuable to her, but what would a burglar see as a moneymaker? Could you fence hand-crocheted linens for enough to buy a fix? How much did mismatched Russell Wright cups and saucers fetch on the street? Bakelite bracelets, that's what they'd take. Those things went for a fortune on Ebay. Did burglars know how much they could get on Ebay? Did burglars own scanners?

"They didn't touch my research, thank god. None of the samples from the dig were touched; none of my rare fossils in the bookcase. Not interested in my hard drive or disks at all," said Charley.

"Of course . . . ," Jane had been about to say, "not" but caught herself in time, "they wouldn't be smart enough to realize what you had there, Charley. Thank god for that."

"But your stuff, Janie . . ."

"The Bakelite, isn't it? Oh shit. I'm wearing my carved

ring, and I have my red hoops in my suitcase, but they got the scalloped, butterscotch bracelets, didn't they? Oh god, the buttons. Did they get that wooden sewing box with the little Bakelite sewing kit and all the carved buttons? And the cookies? Oh god, I had at least two dozen big Bakelite cookies in there. And those two little carved acorns that were so sweet. And I had stuck that little candy tin with the realistics in it in that box, too. Why did I keep them all in one place? Damn, damn, damn!"

Tim had jumped up and was standing next to Jane, his arm around her, trying to get the phone out of her hand. Oh looked from Jane to Tim, hopeful that one of them might soon remember to translate for him.

Tim had taken the phone and was talking to Charley, while Jane held her head in her hands. Oh offered to make tea and she nodded, saying only that the house had been robbed and shaking her head.

Tim grinned and told Charley he'd tell her, then rang off.

Jane reached for the phone. "Wait! Why'd he hang up? What did he say? Why, in god's name, are you laughing?" Jane said, furious.

"First of all, your buttons are fine. No jewelry taken, no buttons, no sewing paraphernalia from the guest room. It's just that everything downstairs and in the garage got thrown around. All the boxes in the garage that were packed up for Miriam, everything on the shelves marked "current" got unpacked. A few pieces of pottery broke, but nothing too valuable by what Charley described to me. And it was all stuff you were sending, all garage stuff. It's just that everything's such a mess. All your suitcases, with the photographs, were emptied on the floor," Tim said, then started laughing. "I'm sorry, honey, I really am, but it sounds like your stuff really pissed them off."

"What do you mean?"

"No silver, no good electronics, no paintings, nothing really valuable," Tim said, then added, "At least, nothing of immediate recognizable value to the kind of jerks who would rob your house."

"Why are you laughing at this?" Jane said, hurt, accepting a cup of tea from Oh.

"I am truly sorry, but Charley said you sounded like Leo Liebling all over again."

Jane tried to stay outraged and wounded, which she surely was, but when she heard the name Leo Liebling she couldn't stop herself from smiling.

"Charley said to call him back in an hour or so, and he'd give you details; but in the meantime he was going to clean up as best he could, leave the true inventory of the garage to you, but I was supposed to just say 'Leo Liebling' everytime you started to get upset."

"Liebling?" asked Oh.

"When Charley and I were first married, I was in graduate school. I had gotten into this poetry seminar taught by this really famous professor, Leo Liebling, an authority on the romantic poets. He had written eight or nine books, scholarly books on the subject, and I thought it was really a big deal to be in Leo Liebling's course. Then one night," Jane struggled not to laugh, "I was in the bathroom, brushing my teeth, and I heard a news bulletin come on the television, and I thought I heard them say that Leo Liebling had died. I came rushing out all upset and saying how terrible it was and what a tragedy it was, and I realized Charley was just staring at me.

I asked him what was wrong, and he said it was clear to him that I was way too immersed in school and my own little world if I thought Leo Liebling, who might be a great guy and a fine teacher, was really the kind of national public figure whose death would prompt NBC to interrupt *Johnny Carson*.

"We must have laughed for hours. 'Leo Liebling' became our buzzword for when one of us got a little self-important," Jane said. Charley's invocation of the name brought Charley's presence into the room. She could feel him, knew he'd take care of business at the house, just like he always did. *Good husband*, Jane thought. *That's what it would say under Charley's picture. Good husband*, Jane thought, *how underrated is that?*

"I know Leo Liebling," Oh said.

"How's his health?" Tim asked.

"Perfect."

"Thank god," said Jane. "I couldn't take another shock."

"Interesting that your burglars were interested in your current packages, the things you had recently packed to ship," said Oh. "Not even the television or VCR?" he asked Tim, who shook his head. "I'll call a friend at the police department in Evanston and find out what they know."

Jane stuck her hand in her back pocket to find the notes she had started to take while talking to her parents but pulled out instead a leftover fortune from one of the Duncan boxes.

Never allow perfect to be the enemy of good.

"I love that," Jane said, handing it to Tim.

"So fix things up with Charley, sweetheart. You accept

that nothing you find in all this treasure hunting is going to be perfect. You love all the dings and chips and flakes that make stuff used and familiar anyway. Marriages get dinged and chipped and flaked, too. Take the *good*, honey, and leave all the bitching about *perfect* to me." Tim ruffled her short hair as if she were a small child.

"Maybe you've got . . ."

"Mrs. Wheel?" Oh asked, "I'm sorry to interrupt, but I promised to go to the EZ Way Inn and meet Mr. Crandall. Would you like to go with me? I could introduce you as one of my associates, and perhaps we could find out exactly what he hopes to find out."

Jane jumped at the chance. Last night Tim had called her a partner, now Oh was naming her an associate. She knew Charley would take care of the mess at home—it seemed like more of a mess than a tragedy—and she needed to clear up some of the messiness around here. After all, she still had a displaced finger floating in her glove compartment trying to point her in some direction.

Tim promised Jane that he wouldn't peek at the kitchen; he would make the living room the base of operations for the volunteer decorators and alums who would be coming to put the finishing touches on the McFlea. The show house, opening this weekend, would welcome visitors for three weekends with a single admission charge of five dollars; a McFlea show pass for unlimited visits was fifteen—Tim's idea. The grand finale would be the McFlea Gala, held in three weeks when the show house closed. Tim had encouraged attendees who would be paying fifty dollars per ticket to wear vintage party clothes—their prom attire from the year they graduated was one of the invitation suggestions—and to bring their checkbooks, since the committee was planning to auction most of the furniture and decorative items that had been scrounged for the house.

Tim had his eye on several pieces that he would bid on himself, they seemed so at home here in his new place. What a perfect marriage of charity and desire. Tim and the committee would raise more money for his old high school than any previous fund-raiser, plus he would have first pick of so many found and scavenged pieces already dusted and carried into his house and up the stairs. And since he knew the taste of almost everyone who would be coming to the gala, he knew he would have few alums bidding against him.

Unless, of course . . . how would he keep Jane away on auction night?

As his only competition for the items they would both recognize as more than the usual scavenged flea market finds, she would drive the bidding sky high. He knew she would find the signed sweetgrass baskets Becky had used in the upstairs bathroom irresistible. The hand-stitched wool coverlets piled in the guest room were exactly her cup of tea. She'd be waving her auction paddle like crazy to get that old cedar-lined trunk in the master bedroom. Yes, he would need to find a compelling reason for Jane to avoid the gala.

Unless, of course . . . he did make her his partner.

He needed some help. He was quick, he was nimble, he had an impeccable eye and unparalleled discipline, but even he, Tim Lowry, purveyor extraordinaire of the fine, the rare, and the cherished, could not be in two places at once. An elegant estate sale in Lake Forest held at the same time as a promising barn sale downstate presented him with a terrible dilemma. Jane had a great eye, although he tried his best not to let her know he thought so. He loved her, he liked her, he trusted her, and, most important, he could train her. *I can get her off the junk—the flowerpots and the buttons—I know I can*, he told himself with the zeal of an AA sponser. He had decided. He'd make a formal offer just before the gala and take her out of the bidding and into his logo.

Tim surveyed the basement recreation room and smiled. It was a teenager's dream. Comfy couches and big floor pillows he had covered with rug scraps, pieces of good Tibetan carpet from an estate sale attic that had been too damaged to salvage for the floor. Lots of low tables and a sweet little refrigerator tucked into the corner stocked with sodas and snacks. This *family* half of the large main room was arranged for cozy viewing and popcorn munching.

Turning into the L-shape that made up the other half of the basement, one entered a time-warped combination of swinging sixties bachelor pad, a wet bar worthy of at least half the rat pack—Sinatra, Martin, and Sammy, not Lawford, Bishop, and MacClaine—and a Las Vegas backroom complete with old felt-covered poker table under a green, glass-shaded, hanging light fixture. Cards were dealt out for six hands of draw poker, and Bakelite chips spilled out of their red-marbled holders.

Jane had left the punchboards Tim had coveted, and he'd hung them over the bar. Chase chrome cocktail shakers, trays with luscious butterscotch handles were piled with bartending guides and canapé recipe books. Glass shelves hung on a mirrored backsplash that held every size and shape of cocktail glass. An oversized deco chrome ice bucket with matching ice tongs and a chrome divided dish that begged to be filled with olives, lemon twists, and cocktail onions sat on the bar. Bakelite dice cups held the usual suspects in Bakelite and bone and specialized game cubes—Put-N-Take and poker dice. A square silver plate held cards printed with HORSE RACE, a bar game where four people picked a different horse pictured and named on the heavy stock, then the bottom half of the paper was dipped in water to "magically" reveal the win, place, and show. Loser paid for that round of drinks.

An ivory-colored plastic box with WHAT'S YOURS? etched on the cover sat open to reveal small, round, colored drink markers to assist the waiter. Roaming through the crowd with his tray, he might encounter a doe-eyed blonde who asked for a rye and soda. Waiter would drop onto the tray a blue disc with rye and soda marked on it. Doing the same for the orders of scotch and soda and bourbon and water, he returned to the bar and the bartender made the drinks to order, clipping the appropriate marker to each glass rim. *Great invention or too much leisure time on someone's hands?* Tim asked himself.

He hit the play button on the CD player, hidden behind a turquoise-and-white late fifties portable hi-fi. Bobby Darrin's voice filled the basement with "Beyond the Sea" and Tim nodded, dimming the overhead fixtures and flicking another switch that turned on the white twinkling bar lights.

"Eat your heart out, people," Tim said aloud. "This party palace is mine."

The doorbell chimed and Tim, for a moment, was ready to go greet a guest and offer a Gibson straight up and pass the cheese puffs. He had regained sense of time and place by the time he got to the front door. A man stood on the porch, one hand in his pocket, the other fingering the ornate brass cover over the mail slot. He was tall, with dark hair and dark eyes. Tim prided himself on being able to guess ages, but this man stumped him. Could be forty, with a few strands of gray and smooth boyish skin. Could be sixty by the way he slouched and selected his clothes. He wore a tan cotton, zip-front jacket and loose, creased pants. His shoes were black and well polished. Tim thought his late fifties, early sixties retro look was impeccable and would have complimented him on it if he had been certain that the stranger was intentionally affecting a retro look.

"I saw the sign," the man said, gesturing toward the McFlea banner hung from the porch roof.

"Sorry, I just hung that and haven't posted the hours yet. They're over there," Tim said, pointing to a wooden sign that would be placed just to the right of the front door. "We're not open until Sunday."

"House for sale?"

"No, it's just been decorated as a show house, for people to walk through, you know, and get decorating ideas," Tim said, feeling pretty certain that this gentleman did *not know*.

"Free?"

"Five dollars."

"Who gets the money?" the man asked, leaning against the doorframe.

"Bishop McNamara High School . . . their scholarship fund," Tim said.

"Be a good moneymaker for you, if you got it," the visitor said.

"Yes. Well, I don't," Tim said. The man seemed in no hurry, content to stay and chat, and Tim was formulating his excuse for closing the door when the visitor straightened, checked his watch, and nodded.

"Thanks, buddy, good luck," he said, and waving goodbye, he got behind the wheel of one of the biggest cars Tim had ever seen outside of his parents' Florida retirement community. There was a university of something decal on the rear window, but Tim couldn't make out the name as the car sped away and careened around the corner.

"Now *that* was odd," Tim said aloud.

As he closed the door, he heard a rattle and crash at the kitchen door. A pot or pan had fallen in the pantry, maybe? Tim wasn't supposed to look at the kitchen yet, but what if something spilled or had been damaged. Jane would want him to investigate, wouldn't she?

At the back door, there was a small entryway they were calling the mud room, although it didn't have the contemporary tract home size or utility. It was a five by seven space where pegs could hold coats and a storage bench would fit to keep boots. Jane had left some of her boxes and bags on the bench earlier, but Tim noticed that they were gone. She must have taken them when she left with Oh. A broom, bucket, and dustpan had fallen down behind the door, accounting for the noise he had heard. Picking up Jane's quaint broom and dustpan, he noticed the Fuller Brush signature on them.

"Nice touch," he said aloud, making a mental note to tell her how much he appreciated the authenticity, and said again, "Nice, nice touch, partner."

If Jane was going to be introduced as Oh's partner, or "associate," as he called it, she worried that her blue jean overalls might not be quite the professional touch.

"Not to worry," said Oh, "look at my tie."

Oh's wife, Claire, was an antique dealer who rented a stall in a highly regarded Chicago mall. At their first meeting, Oh had told Jane that his wife was responsible for the ties. *They were stunning,* Jane thought, *real finds.* There were many hand-painted whimsies with figures and objects from the forties and fifties, but there were also vintage prints that had eye-popping art deco geometry and color combinations. Today's tie might have been titled "Square Pegs in Round Holes," since that was the repeating design in red and black.

"It's elegant," Jane said. "Your wife has an excellent eye."

Jane wondered if she had ever encountered Claire. Was she the heavyset woman with a ponytail who was always a few places ahead of her in line, carrying two folded canvas bags and smiling at everyone? Or was she the skinny blonde who always piled her stuff under tables and barked at anyone who came near, "That's sold, babe, that's mine. Put it down, sweetie. I bought that." No, Jane refused to believe that Oh's wife fit any of the typical dealer profiles. She was probably one of the more elegant professionals who was called in before the public, found her inventory at the presales that the people in the Friday and Saturday lines always complained about. "Yeah, this place is probably fished out," the grizzled old men and women who wore their oldest clothes and gloves with fingers cut out to ward off the early morning frost, complained to each other. Jane never knew how many presales actually took place. She suspected that some of the grumbling was just part of the ritual of waiting in line. It might scare away some of the amateurs, and it made for good posturing to explain why they might not find anything after waiting so long. They could do the old "I told you so" later as they walked out with their empty bags and boxes and raced to the next address on their lists, rehearsing in the car their bitching about how bad that sale was to discourage everyone waiting at the next.

"When Bill Crandall hired you, did he say why he suspected Duncan's death was anything more than a heart attack?"

"No. He says he has no real reason to doubt the cause of death being natural. That isn't what he wanted me to investigate. He thinks his uncle's property might have been tampered with. Some of it stolen, perhaps, and he wanted me to find out who had come to see him over the last few days he was alive. He seemed to think that his uncle's recent property transactions, like his sale of your parents' tavern, might have prompted some 'funny business,' as he called it," said Oh.

"I can tell you some of the people who visited him on the night he died," said Jane. "My mother, my father, Lilly Duff, the Chinese takeout guy . . . I think he had a whole parade in and out of there."

"Crandall said he has all the books, the accounts and ledgers, but valuable business papers are missing. That's what he thinks someone took."

"I have some stuff. Back at the McFlea. Scraps of papers and old looseleaf notebooks. Mostly torn-out pages and writing on empty matchbooks. Stuff that looks like sacks of garbage that didn't make it out to the alley. When Tim and I were cleaning, he let me take it with the old, used punchboards and old cardboard coasters and junk," said Jane. "But there was nothing coherent in there, nothing that could be read as business records."

"My wife has taught me never to ask this question when she comes home from a sale, but here I feel I have to," said Oh. "Why? Why would you want what you describe as sacks of garbage?"

"Are you allowed to ask how much?" Jane asked.

Oh shook his head.

"Well, I collect handwriting," said Jane. "It's not as popular as Bakelite bracelets or darning eggs or McCoy cookie jars, but there's something about it I like. I mean, I mostly like written things that make sense, you know, to other people, like recipe boxes filled with handwritten cards or autograph books from the early 1900s, the kind where Alvah wrote to Jessie, 'One if by land/two if by sea/where ere you travel/remember me' stuff like that. Those things I keep intact.

"But I've bought, or sometimes been thanked for taking, boxes of schoolwork that was saved for fifty years in a trunk, old spelling tests and stuff. Once," Jane said, her face flushing with excitement at the memory, "I was at a convent sale. The building had been sold. The nuns had boxed up tons of stuff, just emptied desk drawers and briefcases into boxes and taped the tops over with plastic wrap, then stuck a dollar or two price tag on them. It was heaven. Boxes had old mechanical advertising pencils and key rings and holy cards and letters and notes . . . all mixed together. One box had a book of lettering styles and a handbook of *Palmer Method Handwriting* exercises with practice pages. Just old fragile notebook sheets with capital Fs flowing over the page. I still get light-headed when I look through the box."

Jane stopped for breath and to peek at Oh to see if he was looking at her strangely. His wife had taught him well. His expression remained one of polite curiosity, which encouraged her to continue.

"I like the handwriting because it's all that's left of some people. All they left behind of themselves. It's so personal—more than photographs, I think. Anyway, I like the way it looks. As art. Or as a graphic design element. I use it on walls sometimes. I love individual letters. Typewriter keys. I have a collection of name pins—you know, mother of pearl pins from the forties that say JANICE or MAY—just because I love writing. The actual words, names, letters written over and over." Jane smiled. "If you come to the McFlea, you'll see it in the pantry. I used all kinds of ephemera, paper and writing stuff, as wallpaper and shelf paper."

"Maybe," Oh began, but Jane shook her head.

"I really didn't see anything that could be put together as business records. Unless he kept notes on the backs of his cookie fortunes. I have some letters I have to read," Jane said, patting her pocket, "but they look like personal correspondence."

Jane was not surprised to find the EZ Way Inn parking lot almost full. Her parents seemed to have more customers when they were closed than when they were open. She smiled at all the big boats parked there. Most of her parents' friends still drove throwbacks, large comfortable four doors, the kind she and all her friends learned to drive when they were kids. Nicky kept telling her she'd better not have a minivan when he was sixteen or he'd never learn to park, but Jane knew better. The family cars when she was a teenager were as big and heavy as today's omnipresent SUVs. Pulling into her parents' garage at curfew, she always thought, must qualify her to dock the *Queen Mary*.

Nellie watched Jane pull into the parking lot. Someone with her, too. Probably Tim with more junk to hang on the walls or stack on the shelves she kept hanging up in the dining room. It wasn't that she didn't appreciate the effort—god knows Nellie liked the place to look nice, too—but jeez, the trash that girl could find. Souvenir plates from 1908 with pictures of the Kankakee River on them. Who the hell cared about that old junk? They were penny souvenirs then and were worth less than that now, if you asked her. Of course, Jane wasn't asking her. When was the last time that her smarty-pants daughter asked her opinion on anything? And the old photographs she brought home where she didn't even know the people. What the hell was that about?

Of course, the photograph sitting at the kitchen table was different. Jane recognized people in that one, all right. Nellie and Don, just children, smiling away like it was Christmas morning and Gus Duncan was Santa Claus. *Well, he was Santa Claus to us,* Nellie thought. Giving us a start in the business, making it easy for us to make money and make our way. When he offered extras to make a little more money on the side, how were we going to say no? Little gambling games here and there, numbers and punchboards. The slot machine they kept in the backroom for a while. She had known that slots were trouble, too big, too noisy, and too many people had to be paid off to make any profit anyway. What Nellie didn't know back then, at the beginning of it all, was how deep Gus had sucked Don and the rest of them in.

First, he'd get them to run a little game, harmless enough. Then he was moving them into something else, hinting that if they said no, the wrong people might find out about that little harmless game from a few months back. Nellie never knew who they were supposed to be afraid of—the police or the boys Gus talked about that he was working for.

She remembered the first time she heard Gus say to Don when he collected the rent, "Be a shame to lose your liquor license over that little numbers game." Hell, by then, they had a house and a car they were paying on. They wanted to have kids and raise them with more hopes and dreams than the two of them had ever . . . *Oh shit*, thought Nellie, *what was the point of all this thinking?* Jane was coming through the door with some strange guy in a goofy tie. Probably one of Tim's antique dealer buddies who wanted to offer them twenty bucks for the old Slim Jim rack. Tim or one of his pals was always wanting to buy some old piece of scrap right out from under them.

Nellie waited in the kitchen until she heard Jane introduce her friend to Don and then watched the two of them sit down next to Crandall. Duncan's nephew was the one who'd thrown the brick, probably. Had to be. Probably inherited the blackmailing business along with the shanties. Well, it didn't matter anymore. She'd told Don that morning that it was over. What the hell were they afraid of anyway? The gambling all stopped when the government took over. Lottery, Lotto, that had set them free. Nobody could make any money once it was all legal, so Gus had just stopped the games, just kept charging them a little extra to keep quiet about it all. They wouldn't want their kids to know, right? Wasn't their son, Michael, a lawyer out in California? Didn't Don say Michael might be a judge someday? Shame if he heard all kinds of bad stuff about where his fancy college tuition money had come from.

Don knew it was all a bluff. Gus was as guilty as everybody else, wasn't he? But still, Don didn't want to take a chance, didn't want his name in the paper, didn't want Jane and Michael to know how he had gotten drawn in. Well, it had been forty damn years, and she'd had enough. She had seen it on an old *Law and Order* rerun last night, what she needed. And she had told Don in the car that morning.

"There's a statue of limitations," said Nellie, "and we're going to get one."

"Statute, Nellie," said Don, smiling.

"Whatever the hell it is. We're getting one and finishing this business."

Don had asked what about Jane and Michael, and Nellie had told him that they were grown-ups now, making their own damn mistakes. They weren't going to give a damn about what Don and Nellie had done forty or fifty years ago.

"Besides," Nellie had added, "that little private-eye

daughter of ours is going to take a good look at that photograph and keep asking questions anyway. She won't care about running numbers, but she'll be all weepy that we haven't told her the truth."

Kids, Nellie thought, *you feed them, you clothe them, you educate them, and still, they want you to tell them the goddamn truth, too.*

"We owe them the truth, Nellie, you're right," Don had said.

Nellie heard the rain before she looked out and saw it, big drops that were going to start coming down hard and fast in a minute. She saw Jane's windows rolled down and grabbed the big navy blue raincoat they always had hanging on a nail by the back door. Whoever had to haul out the garbage or run out and down the cellar steps used the coat whenever it rained. She wrapped it around her tiny frame, put the hood up, and ran out to Jane's car. In the driver's seat she cranked up the window, wondering how much Jane and Charley had saved by not getting power windows.

"Probably thinks these are more goddamn vintage," she mumbled, as she leaned over to roll up the passenger side. The driver's side door opened, and Nellie didn't even look up.

"I already got the windows; just get a rag to wipe the seat before you go," Nellie said.

"Shove over, Mrs. Wheel. I'll drive."

A clean-shaven man, forty something, with a short ponytail—god, how Nellie hated to see a man with a ponytail—had gotten into the car and shoved her over into the passenger seat. He took a ring with at least forty keys on it out of the pocket of his tan cotton jacket, chose the right one without a problem, and started the engine. The back door opened and someone else got in, grumbling about all the bags on the backseat. The driver backed the car out of the space and sped out of the parking lot, sending up a spray of gravel.

From behind, the man in the backseat tied a scarf around Nellie's eyes without removing the hood of the raincoat.

"I'm not tying your hands, Mrs. Wheel, not yet; but I've got a gun and if you go for the steering wheel or a cell phone or try to roll down the window and yell, I'll use it, you understand?"

Nellie nodded. She didn't know how to drive, didn't own a cell phone, and she had just rolled up the damn window because it was raining cats and dogs. She had lived through the Depression and the war years and cared for both her parents as they'd wasted away from age and cancer. She had had two miscarriages and broken her toe a year ago when she dropped a fifty-pound sack of onions on her foot. She had been in the tavern business for fifty years and cleaned up the men's bathroom every morning for all fifty of them. What was so damn scary about a gun?

20

Bruce Oh was still more public servant than private eye, Jane decided. He was too open, too forthcoming. He needed to incorporate more suspicion and paranoia into his conversation. He needed to be less *blanc*, more *noir*. He needed, Jane decided, her as his associate.

"Mr. Crandall," Jane asked, "I'm not clear on what you're looking for. What was so important about these papers? How would we know if we found them?"

"Good questions," he said. "My uncle was kind of mysterious about them. He said he was leaving me everything; and when he died, I should go through his stuff carefully because if I was smart enough, I'd find my fortune and have a steady income for life."

"Why papers, though?" asked Jane. "What made you think business records?"

Crandall scratched his ear and pointed to his glass. Jane noticed Don was ignoring him, giving him the same treatment he always gave Gus Duncan when he came in for the monthly rent.

"Don't know. I just figured it had to do with his property, his leases and stuff. Then when I saw all the junk in the shanties, I hired Lowry and you to inventory and price the stuff. Thought maybe my fortune was in those boxes."

Oh had been listening and tapping his finger softly on the bar. "Have all the property transfers gone through? All the sales Mr. Duncan arranged before his death?"

Crandall nodded and handed Oh a sheet of paper.

"This is the list you asked for," he said. "The only thing Gus kept was the shanties. How about it, Mrs. Wheel? Anything worth a fortune down there?"

"The stuff I've seen will make a great sale. I mean, you'll make money, and people who come to buy will find great stuff; but I haven't found anything yet that suggests you should quit your day job."

Crandall nodded and craned his neck to get Don's attention.

"Which is?" Jane asked.

"What?"

"Your job? What do you do?"

"Little of this, little of that. I own some apartment buildings downstate, Urbana-Champaign. Rent to university students. They don't ask for much."

An academic slumlord, Jane thought. *Despicable as his uncle.*

"Seen your mother?" Don asked.

"Can I have . . . ?" Crandall asked, but Don glided away to the other side of the bar as soon as he saw Jane shake her head.

"If I can get back in the house today, I can go through the boxes fairly quickly. Tim and I have an overview, and we can list contents pretty fast; but . . . you said you already have the business ledgers and formal books. Are you sure you haven't missed anything there?" Jane asked.

"I couldn't find anything other than the rents collected, improvement costs, tax information. No figures that weren't connected to what they referred to, no initials or names that seemed like codes or anything. EZ Way was written as EZ Way, Duffs as Duffs, Pinks as Pinks, and all the others the same. He collected his rents on the first or second of every month, listed them, and wrote down any notes from the tenants," said Crandall.

"One of the notes I remember reading when you showed me the book was to fix the pipes in the cellar of the EZ Way. That was just two months ago, before the sale," said Oh. He had seen Don leaning on the bar to his left, close enough to listen, and he turned to him. "Did Mr. Duncan fix the pipes?"

Don shook his head. "He always wrote down what I told him; then I didn't see him again until the next month."

"So you told him about the pipes; they were really leaking?" Jane asked.

"Sure," said Don.

"Just checking," Jane said. "I thought that could be some kind of code for something."

Don reached under the bar and pulled out the brick that had been thrown through their now-repaired front window. *That Jimmy from the glass company is a quick fixer,* thought Jane, not registering at first how strange that Don palmed the brick and hefted it, as if testing its weight. That's why she was just as startled as Francis and the other morning regulars when Don slammed the brick down in front of Crandall, making his empty glass jump.

"Here's your code; your gift from Uncle Gus." Don spoke very quietly, but Jane heard the steel in his voice. "Duncan was a liar, a crook, a blackmailer." With each title he gave Gus, Don poked his finger at the brick. "He left you a pile of bricks, and you knew whose windows to throw them through. You were with him often enough in the car when he came and collected. You know what he left you all right, a list of willing suckers who would pay you every month to keep your mouth shut."

Crandall smiled. Jane was surprised to see how unpleasant a smile could be. He pulled his head back, then brought it forward again, reminding her of a snake about to strike. Don's hand was still on the brick. Bruce Oh gave Jane the quickest look, his eyes directing her to her father's hands on the brick, then back to studying the two men. Jane laid her hand over her father's. She felt Don relax his hold on the brick. She kept her hand on his just the same, a gentle pressure.

"There's more to this, Don. I need that information. There are other people who . . ." Crandall let his voice trail off, and Jane realized his head resembled not so much a snake as a turtle. He was thrusting his head forward in a kind of feigned boldness, but he was ready to withdraw it and hide at any moment.

"Where'd Nellie go for that pie?" asked Francis. "Chicago Heights?"

All eyes turned to Francis, who was stirring his coffee, nursing it along until Nellie found him something sweet to go with it.

"What the hell are you talking about, Francis?" Don asked.

"I asked her if there was any pie in the kitchen and she said no, but she thought she might have some coffee cake that you guys brought in yesterday while you was working. Then I saw her leave and I thought maybe she went to pick up a pie down at Connie's; but she's been gone longer than that'd take, so I just said where'd Nellie go for that pie . . ."

Francis might have gone on to explain the story in a kind of circular manner that could have taken up the rest of the day. Most of his conversation worked in a kind of tape loop that would just go around and around until someone stopped him.

"What do you mean leave? What did you see?" Jane asked.

Francis gestured out the window next to him. "Saw her get in your car, Janie; then I saw her back out and leave."

Don straightened and Jane hopped down off the bar stool. She ran to the window and looked out where Francis had pointed.

"My car's gone."

"Jeez, Francis, why didn't you say something? You know Nellie can't drive!" Don shouted.

Francis shrugged. "You don't need to drive very far to get to Connie's and I thought maybe she'd just gone there because when I asked if she had any pie . . ."

"Call the police, Dad," Jane said.

Don walked over to the pay phone and dropped in coins. He called Jane over to give the information on her car, license plate number, and detailed description.

"Your wife, Nellie, would not under any circumstances drive your daughter's car?"

"She doesn't even know how to start the engine," Don said.

"I've got the keys, anyway," Jane said. "Who could have driven it away?"

Crandall sat quietly, his hands spread in front of him at the bar. Jane noticed the pinky ring again and leaned toward him. "Who took my mother?"

"Some guys have been following me. Maybe . . ."

Don slammed the brick down on the bar again.

"They're guys from Chicago who Gus worked with sometimes. I don't know them, but they've been following me. They been following you, too, Mrs. Wheel. I heard them say you must have the books because you got the dead guy's stuff," Crandall said.

"I don't have Gus Duncan's stuff," Jane said. "Some of his trash, but there's no accounting or . . ."

"Not Gus—not *just* Gus anyway—the other dead guy," said Crandall, his lip starting to twitch as he watched Don pick up the brick.

Jane reviewed her latest sales and pictured the stacks of boxes in her garage. *Which dead guy?* She had so much waiting to send to Miriam . . .

"My house was ransacked. Charley thought they were looking for something in my new stuff in the garage. It's about Bateman, and Bateman's stuff, too." Jane looked at Crandall. "What about Oscar Bateman?"

"I don't know any Bateman. The guy with the ponytail told me they wanted to keep doing business. I said sure, you know, like I knew what they were talking about, but I don't. Now they think I'm holding out on them. Told me I could keep collecting, but they needed some stuff from me," Crandall said. "I told them okay, but I was faking it. I don't have the books; I don't have anything. I thought it might be in the basement. I thought you and Lowry could find it for me."

"'Collecting'?" said Jane.

Don looked at his daughter. "Collection business, Jane. Blackmail. Gus had us all by the . . . years ago. Gus had us all running gambling for him. Numbers and punchboards at the bars. Backroom games at Pinks and some of the other places. Slot machines here and there. Lottery came along and dried up a lot of the numbers games, and Gus lost all his people in high places. Don't know if everyone got honest, or if Gus finally wore out his welcome. After that, he just settled for a small monthly fee to keep quiet, not release all his records," Don said.

"Wouldn't his records make him just as guilty?" Oh asked.

"Yeah, but he didn't have a family or anything. He said he had ways of keeping himself out of it since he was just the middle guy and nobody cared about the middle guy. I asked him why anyone cared about the bottom guy, which is what all of us were—just rinky-dink nickel dimers . . ."

"What'd he say, Dad?" Jane asked.

"Said our problem was that we all cared, cared about our reputations and our families and what everyone would think of us," Don said. "He was right. None of us wanted our names in the paper."

A police officer Jane recognized from last night at the shanty came in the front door and Oh conferred with him, filling him in on what was going on, or what everybody thought was going on. Jane heard Francis begin to talk about pie again.

"What about Bill Duff? What happened to him and his wife? I mean what could Lilly have found that would make her . . ." Jane let her question hang, thinking that if she could keep asking questions she could stop her father and herself from growing frantic about Nellie.

"Dad?" Jane asked. "What did you say Lilly's mother's name was?"

"Louella," said Don. "Why?"

Jane shook her head. She took out the thirty-year-old letters and started scanning them as her father talked.

"Duff was going to quit, stand up to Duncan," Don said. "Told everybody. Duncan warned him that he had bosses who would do terrible things. There was bad blood between Duncan and everybody, but it was worse with him and Duff. See, I think whoever ran things out of Chicago just gave us to Duncan. Gus wasn't that greedy, didn't want much except some of us guys in his pocket. Didn't make a fortune off of us, but it was enough. He had all the records on us, everything we ever signed for, agreed to. Every payoff we made that we thought went to him, he had made it so it looked like it went to cops. We'd not only be the ones who'd take the fall legally, we'd take the lumps from all the illegals. Dirty cops would want to keep us quiet. The Chicago gamblers who Gus answered to would want us quiet. So when Duff started saying he was going to sing out the story . . ."

"They threatened Louella?" Jane asked, her finger holding her place in one of the letters.

"Cops said it was suicide. I think it was. I think the big boys just told her they were going to let Duff take the fall.

She wouldn't have been able to handle it if it had been in the paper and all. Her parents were rich; dad was a doctor. Never wanted her to marry Duff. And there was Lilly and Bobby. I don't know if Louella could take it, that's all. Maybe Gus had all that stuff written down and Lilly found it. Since she and Bobby were running the bar, she had been paying him off, so she knew part of it. Maybe knowing that her father was responsible for her mother . . ."

Jane held up her hand. "Is that the phone in the backroom?"

After thirty years of one phone line, the pay phone, Don and Nellie had finally installed a private line in the backroom of the EZ Way Inn. They didn't tell anyone about it because they knew everyone would want to use it instead of the pay phone. Since they didn't want anyone to know about it, they didn't use it to call out and they didn't want it to ring. Consequently, the only people who knew the number besides Don and Nellie were Jane and her brother.

"Make sure Crandall doesn't slip out the door," Jane said to Oh, as she ran to the backroom.

How long were they going to take before they answered the damn phone? Nellie shook her head in disgust and wonderment, mixed in equal parts. Something big finally happens to her and she can't even get anybody to pick up the phone so she can tell them about it.

"The hell with them," she said out loud and hung up. "I'll just stay kidnapped awhile longer."

Mel looked at Frank, who looked at Stuart. Stuart would never let them kill an old lady, would he? It wasn't as if he didn't believe in killing people on the other side. That's how he always explained it. "There are two sides to everything, boys, and if someone is on the other side, they have to go." It made it all simple, organized. They had rules, and they followed them. But no rule covered this old lady who was not really on any side that they could tell. They had grabbed the wrong lady. She had been wearing a rain poncho for god's sake, and who could tell who anybody was in a rain poncho? She was at the right place at the right time to be Jane Wheel, but she wasn't Jane Wheel. They'd only seen Wheel up close a couple of times. They'd followed her home from the Bateman housesale and turned around in her driveway, but that didn't mean they could tell her from some old woman wearing a rain poncho. Wasn't their fault. Unless Stuart said it was, and Stuart hadn't said anything much yet.

Stuart had told Nellie to call the tavern and tell everybody she was okay and that they shouldn't call the police, they should just sit tight and wait for instructions. Mel wondered what those instructions were going to be since he didn't want to have anything more to do with this old lady, who had been dusting and wiping and folding and yapping since they had gotten to the apartment. She reminded him of his grandmother, who never shut up either. She hadn't said a word in the car, no tip-off that she wasn't Jane Wheel, but now she was going full speed, hadn't stopped since they got here.

Frank is going to blame it on me, Mel thought. Frank was

always quick with the excuses and somehow grabbing this old lady was going to end up, according to Frank, being all Mel's fault.

"Got any food here? Want me to fix lunch?" Nellie asked, wandering around the small apartment. She had been able to see through the flimsy scarf they'd tied around her eyes, and she knew exactly where she was. There was a barnlike auction house just west of town, and a three-car garage adjoined the property. They were in an apartment over the garage. Pretty nice, too. *Three bedrooms and two full baths*, Nellie thought, even though she had only seen one of the bathrooms. It wasn't messy enough for all three of them to be using it though. Two at most had thrown towels around and brushed their teeth and combed their hair without so much as a tissue wipe up to make the sink look decent.

What was wrong with people that they didn't know that just a little effort, just a little commonsense wipe up after they'd used something, would save them time and energy later. No pride in their surroundings; no care for what people thought of them after they left. Nellie had stayed in motels only a handful of times in her life, but she was proud to say that the maids wouldn't have had a lick of work to do when they came in after her. Nellie had made sure the room looked just as spic and span when they left as when they had come. Truth be told, the rooms were *spiccer* and *spanner* after she had Nellified them.

This garage apartment had been one of Gus Duncan's rentals, she knew. Had to be since it was part of Amos Auction House, and she was sure Gus owned that building until Amos signed the papers last week and bought it, just like she and Don now owned the EZ Way Inn. Big deal, those papers. Meant something to Don, maybe, but not to her. Paper wasn't what made anyone own anything; she knew that. It was taking care of it for thirty years, that's what made something belong to somebody. Did Don really think that the big old iron stove in the kitchen where she cooked fifty hamburgers every Monday through Friday could belong to someone else? That grill she cleaned, scraped with a razor blade every day wasn't hers until they legally owned the building and its fixtures? She knew where to put the meat when she needed it to cook fast and where she could count on food to just stay warm. She knew the temperature of every square inch of that goddamn grill, and that's what made it hers and nobody else's.

What about the back screen door? Nobody had been able to fix the hinge on it so it would stay fixed, and Gus wouldn't buy them a new one, so she had taken a pair of old pantyhose and woven them in and out of the spring and tied it off so the door had enough bounce to work. That made it *her* door, didn't it? Let Don and all the rest of them sign their papers and stick their deeds in a vault. She owned plenty. All the property she could handle belonged to her.

Now she had to figure out what these three bozos wanted, and she might as well start by cooking bacon. She didn't wait for any of them to give her an okay, she just started looking through the grocery bags and refrigerator and came up with eggs and bacon and potatoes and onions. Nellie checked the cupboard. Someone who had stayed here liked to cook. There was quite an assortment of spices and condiments.

She'd make a Pinks mess à la Nellie and get them all filled up and cozy. They had told her to call and get her daughter on the line, but it might be better if she could take a little more time with them. Maybe she could keep Jane out of this altogether.

Stuart stood up and looked into the kitchen. Nellie was using a small paring knife but didn't seem to have any ideas about fighting them. There didn't seem to be anything larger in there that she might use as a weapon; and as far as he could tell, she had no idea where she was or why she was there. Might as well let her cook for them. He was so tired of fast food.

Life on the road played havoc with your gut. He was sucking down Pepcids like candy. He could carry a hundred concealed weapons and use ninety-nine of them in a fight, but the thing that was going to do him in was the damn acid reflux. And Mel and Frank were no help. They just wanted McDonalds three times a day to keep them happy. He watched Nellie put bread in the toaster and check the refrigerator for butter. They stayed in this apartment fairly regularly, and he tried to keep it stocked with some healthy food, but it wasn't easy.

"Were you planning on frying those eggs in the bacon grease?" Stuart asked.

Nellie looked him in the eye, then gave him the once-over.

"How about I poach them for you, put a couple on toast? The bacon won't hurt you the way I do it, cook it slow until it's well done, then drain it really good."

Stuart nodded. The old lady could stay until after lunch, then they'd have to get her to call Jane Wheel and dump her somewhere. They could scare her into not identifying them. She wouldn't want her family hurt. This would be easy. Maybe they could even get Jane Wheel to say over the phone what she had done with the dead guy's stuff.

Jane sat by the phone in the backroom, waiting for it to ring again. She had screwed the hundred-watt bulb in again and could now see the letters clearly. She spread them out on the desk and read carefully. It made a difference, she realized, spreading one of the letters out flat on a smooth surface under a bright light. It must have made a difference to Lilly, too, holding onto that box, reading each letter carefully, using the box as a lap desk. Jane pictured her holding on for dear life as she read these thirty-year-old passionate love letters, filled with promises and pleas and desperation, addressed to "Dearest Gus" and signed from "his darling Lou."

Lilly hadn't found the stuff Crandall had been talking about. There weren't any payoff dates or dollar amounts or names in these letters. There was just the awful truth about her mother and Gus Duncan, the man everyone in town loved to hate. Lilly, alone in that shanty basement, finding out the truth about her depressed mother and the despised Gus and her baby brother, her sweet Bobby, whom she had come home to bail out of trouble over and over again, Bobby, who couldn't seem to get a break, who had depended on Lilly for everything. Jane tried to imagine what it must have felt like to find out that Gus was Bobby's father—and Gus knew it. He had read these letters and saved them along with all the other debris from his years as a despised slumlord. And even though he knew Bobby was his own son, he kept collecting the blackmail money every month from Lilly and Bobby, screwing them just the same as he screwed everyone else in town.

Lilly must have read the letters, put them back in their envelopes, and taken the penicillin out of her pocket. She was allergic to it, she had told Jane in the kitchen of the McFlea. She knew exactly what it would do to her. She carried it in with her because she knew that if she found what she was looking for, she wouldn't want to go on anymore. Jane folded up the letters and put them back in her pocket.

These guys who had been following Crandall and following her, who had grabbed Nellie, who were they? Ponytail. Hadn't she just seen a guy in a ponytail? What was she thinking? Half the guys at sales had ponytails. Old hippies in blue jeans and dirty sweatshirts. How would she notice one more?

Jane stood up and looked out the back door. Three police cars were parked among the big old sedans that her dad's customers still drove. She smiled, thinking about how uncomfortable her dad was with smaller foreign cars and how hypocritical he thought the big SUVs were. His Buick, he'd always told her, was no more a gas guzzler than those . . .

Jane remembered. A big old dad car that had turned into her driveway the day she'd bought out so much of Bateman's stuff. They had asked her if she was having a sale. The driver had a ponytail.

Jane wanted to slap somebody, anybody, to jump-start someone with authority so they would head out, sirens blaring, and find her mother. Four local police officers talking quietly to the denizens of the EZ Way Inn was not what she considered action.

Pacing back and forth in the kitchen, Jane saw the photograph from Duncan's house. It was out of the frame, lying on the cutting board in the kitchen. She hadn't noticed her parents take it with them that morning. She waved it at her father, who was listening to the officer try to get Francis off pie and back to the men who had climbed into Jane's car after Nellie.

"Why'd you take it out of the frame?" she asked.

Don shook his head. "We didn't. That's our copy. Your mother dug it out of the backroom this morning."

Jane brought it into the barroom and studied it. Without the glare of the glass, Jane could see it much better. She held it close. That was Duff and Louella in the corner. Old Pink was holding up both hands, making Vs for victory, Jane figured, not flashing the peace sign in this crowd in that year. Don and Nellie looked so young, so attractive. Her mother was really spectacular: great figure, thick curly hair, a smile like a model. Those forties fashions didn't hurt either: peplum jackets with shoulder pads really flattered. In this photo of at least fifty people, Nellie was definitely the best-looking woman in the picture. Except for that blonde in the back. She'd give Nellie a run for her money. That slouch and the way she held the cigarette, her hair practically draped over one eye. Who did she aspire to be? Veronica Lake? Lauren Bacall? Mary Bateman?

Mary and Oscar Bateman, second row from the top, center.

Jane brought it to her father and pointed.

"Bateman and Mary," Don said. "Mary sure was a beauty, a beautiful woman."

"Didn't I tell you all this stuff I brought was from the Shangri-La? From Bateman's tavern in Chicago? Why didn't you tell me you knew him?"

Don shook his head. "I'm sorry, Jane. We didn't want to open up all the old stuff, so we just . . . I'm sorry. I have been wrong about all this from the get go."

Jane studied Bateman's pose. His arm was around Mary, but he seemed to have Gus Duncan in his sight. Their eyes were definitely engaged, and they were both smiling broadly. Both had cigars clenched in their teeth.

"They were partners, weren't they? Gus and Bateman?" Jane asked. She could see it all now. Gus didn't come up with all the gambling for the saloon keepers here; he was getting everything from Chicago. He was getting it from Bateman. That's why Don was so spooked by the punchboards from the Shangri-La; they were ghost objects.

"Detective Oh," Jane called him over. "If Bateman went to jail on some gambling charges, then threatened to name names—you know, higher-ups—would that be enough to make someone lose some paperwork? I mean if they couldn't make an open deal, do you think that would be enough to get him out of prison?"

"Possibly," said Oh. "Even more possible if he could name names of police or judges who had participated in the gambling."

"What would give him leverage? I mean, he was

already in jail. They could leave him there and lose the key. Or kill him?" Jane said.

Oh looked over to where Crandall still sat at the bar.

"Records. Bateman and Duncan both protected themselves by hiding records," Jane whispered.

The phone rang again in the backroom. This time, Jane bolted for it and caught it on the third ring.

"Mom?"

"Took you long enough," said Nellie. "Now, listen to me. I got two of these boys to sleep, but I don't know how long it'll last. One of them went out to do something and took the car, and I fed the other two enough Valium to get them napping."

"You take Valium?" Jane asked, shocked. Uppers, maybe, but nothing had ever chemically slowed down her mother.

"Oh, for crying out loud, use your head," said Nellie.

"Do you know where you are?" Jane asked.

"Of course I do," said Nellie. "Now do you have anything in your car that they want?"

"I don't think so. Have they said what they're looking for? Exactly?"

"Duncan's list of names and dates, his blackmail files. And Bateman's stuff, too. I'll explain about that later, but . . ."

"I know, I know, but I haven't seen what they're looking for," said Jane, "at least I don't think I have."

"Where in hellfire is she?" Don shouted. The police came crowding into the door of the backroom.

"What's he want? Does the bar need washing?"

"Mom, where are you?"

"Shit . . . ," Nellie said and the phone went dead.

Jane immediately dialed *69, and handed the phone to one of the policeman to take the number.

"They can find out the address from the phone number, can't they?" Jane asked Oh. He nodded. He was holding the list of buildings that Gus had sold. Jane reached out her hand.

"May I?" She scanned the names of the tenant/purchasers and the addresses and phone numbers of the businesses. The policeman handed her the phone number he had taken down. It didn't match any on the list. "This might be a private line because I'm sure they're at one of Duncan's places. Push Crandall on this. They've been following him; they would have told him how to get in touch."

When Jane looked back in the barroom to where Crandall had been sitting, she was surprised to see he had changed his shirt. She blinked, squinted, and looked again. No, it was now Bobby Duff sitting there.

"Where'd Crandall go?" Jane asked.

One of the police officers gestured toward the men's room.

Jane went over to Bobby Duff, not knowing what she was going to say, even when she opened her mouth.

"Lilly . . . I'm so sorry. I wish she could have waited . . . ," Jane stammered.

"Waited for what?" asked Bobby.

"For us to find out who killed Duncan and took his records. We're going to make all of this stop," Jane said.

The brick that Don had used to punctuate his conversation with Crandall still sat on the bar. Bobby picked it up and turned it over in his hand. It began to hit him, hard, that his sister was gone. She wasn't going to get him out of trouble this time. He knew Jane Wheel was still standing there, maybe waiting for him to say something. He hadn't blackmailed anybody yet; he had just thrown a few bricks. It wasn't too late to get out of all this.

"I'm sorry about the window. Lilly told me not to do it," Bobby said.

"Do what?" Jane asked.

"I thought I could take over the blackmail. I knew your dad and mom and lots of people went to see Duncan the night he died. Me and Lilly, too. We didn't kill him," Bobby said. "I wanted to help him with the business. I thought I could collect for him and stuff. He laughed and said anybody could have these suckers. Nobody would find his records, he said. So I got to thinking I could pretend to have the records. Who would know? Everybody'd been paying the bastard for so long without any proof. . . . It was stupid. I took the bricks out of the basement and tossed them because Don and Nellie had called that meeting about not paying anybody anymore. It was so stupid. Lilly told me it was."

Jane couldn't stand how young Bobby looked, how his hair fell into his eyes. He sounded no older than Nick. She looked at his hands, now stroking the rough brick and, without thinking, asked the question that had just popped into her head.

"When your dad died, when he committed suicide, Bobby, who found him?"

"Benny," said Bobby. "He tended bar for us sometimes. Came over a lot and cooked for us, hung out and watched television with me sometimes. Told me my dad had asked him to look out for me if anything ever happened to him."

"Was your dad depressed, you know, before?"

"Drinking more. Sad. Kept saying he didn't care about anything in the world except my mom; and if she was gone, why shouldn't he give it all up."

Oh had come over to listen.

"Give it all up? What did he mean?" asked Jane.

Bobby shrugged. "Kill himself, I guess."

"Did you see him?"

"Benny wouldn't let me. Said there was too much blood, and I should remember him alive, not like that."

"Blood? Didn't he asphyxiate himself?" Jane asked, forgetting that she should be sparing Bobby the memory.

"Yeah, but he had cut himself trying to attach a hose to the tailpipe. Benny said . . ."

"Yes?" Oh asked, fully engaged.

"Benny said he had cut his finger clear off," Bobby said, shuddering. "Said it was a wonder he could get back into the car and turn it on since he was practically bleeding to death."

21

Don called Jane and Oh over and gestured to the list of Duncan properties. He pointed to the Amos Auction House and said they had found the garage apartment had an unlisted number that matched the number from where Nellie had called.

"It's only about ten blocks west of here," Jane explained to Oh.

"How do you plan on going in there?" asked Don. "You're not using sirens and all? They could get scared and . . ."

"We've got an unmarked car on the way," said one of the Kankakee officers who had given up on questioning customers. "We're heading over for backup."

Don shook his head as they went out the front door. "Francis, tend bar for me. I'll be right back."

"No, Dad, we'll go," Jane said.

Detective Oh was standing next to the men's room. When he pushed the door open, hard enough to break through the flimsy lock, Francis jumped.

"What the hell's going on in here, Don?"

The window was wide open, the screen lay on the floor.

"Mr. Crandall decided to leave us," Oh said, looking out the window.

"Stay by the phone, Dad. Mom might call again. Call my cell phone with anything you hear." Jane hugged her father. "And keep Bobby Duff here. I don't think he has anywhere to go, but it won't hurt to keep his glass filled."

Jane and Oh went out the back door, but Jane stopped short.

"They took my car," she said. "I'll get my dad's keys.

Before she could reenter the EZ Way Inn, Tim pulled into the lot. If they had rehearsed the pickup, it couldn't have worked better. Oh slipped into the backseat, Jane into the front.

"Amos Auction House, Tim. They took Nellie."

"Who took Nellie?" asked Tim, already backing out of the parking lot.

Jane looked at Oh, who held his palms up. "I don't have names, I'm afraid."

"The bad guys," Jane said.

"Of all the times I imagined myself in a detective movie," Tim said, "all the chase scenes I pictured myself in, all the secret missions where I played hero, I never once imagined rescuing Nellie from the bad guys. This scene will not be appearing in my fantasy, I'll tell you that."

Tim spent almost every weekend scouring Amos Auction House for bargains. He knew about the apartment over the garage and also knew there was an access road behind the main auction hall. As they approached the property, Oh pointed out the unmarked police cars parked on the road, watching and waiting. No one was rushing into anything, since the Kankakee police didn't know exactly what the kidnappers wanted from Nellie or had wanted from Jane. On the way, Tim told Jane and Oh about his visitor at the McFlea.

"At first, I didn't think it was that suspicious—you know, somebody just checking out the banner and all—but the noise at the kitchen door, the broom falling . . . I checked around the back porch and saw a cigarette butt thrown down, still lit, fresh. So I figured someone had been in the back while Mr. Curious talked to me at the front door."

"Was he driving a big car?" Jane asked.

"Pale yellow yacht. You know, he was one of those retro-looking guys who isn't really retro. Skinny tie with a windbreaker type."

"They were looking for the stuff I brought from Duncan's—and Bateman's for that matter. There were no *records* in the *records,* so they think there's something valuable in all the paper scraps," Jane said.

"Wasn't there anything that could be a file on someone? You'd want initials, maybe. Dates? Amounts of money?" asked Oh.

"Nothing," said Jane. "The only things remotely mysterious were the fortunes from fortune cookies. It just seemed odd that he'd save those."

"Some kind of code?" Tim asked.

"Totally random," Jane said. "Factory printed with no notations on them."

Tim drove past the main driveway into the auction house and circled around the back, parking behind the large garage and storage area. There were outside stairs leading to the apartment over the garage space. Jane's car was nowhere in sight, but they all knew it could be parked inside one of the three garage bays.

The realization that Nellie was being held by the bad guys was starting to sink in. Jane had managed to deny the worry and fear in order to function efficiently, but now the repression of those fears was turning into anger. Who were these guys—these gamblers or collectors or whatever they were—to come down to her town and grab her mother?

Jane started to get out of the car, but both men protested.

"You can't just waltz up the stairs," said Tim. "You're Nancy Drew, not Rambo."

"He's right, Mrs. Wheel," said Oh.

"Is there a way into the apartment through the auction house?" asked Jane. "That back door is wide open."

A truck driver was wheeling crates on a dolly into the wide back doors of the Amos Auction House. They had driven past the sign when they were turning into the access road. SALE ON SUNDAY NOON—PREVIEW 9:00 A.M. DAY OF SALE. The merchandise was arriving.

"There are inside stairs right next to Amos's office. They must go up to the apartment or to the hall right outside of it," Tim said.

Jane was out of the car before either man could stop her. She walked in alongside the ramp from the truck to the doorway. Tim and Oh rushed to catch up.

Jane wasn't quite sure her plan would work. Actually, she wasn't quite sure she had a plan. Her mother certainly hadn't sounded scared on the phone; but then again, she wouldn't. Did it mean they didn't have guns, weren't threatening? Not necessarily. It would just take more than kidnappers to ruffle Nellie. Her fearlessness might work to her advantage, or, Jane thought, it could really piss these guys off. Didn't bad guys become bad guys so people would take them seriously? These were men who probably worked as enforcers for Chicago gamblers, who, if they hadn't killed before, at least had hacked off fingers. Jane crossed her own and hoped that a plan would materialize as soon as she saw her mother, as soon as she saw that Nellie was all right.

Nellie was more than all right. Nellie was on top of the world. She had found a roll of duct tape in a kitchen drawer and, after rinsing all the lunch dishes and wiping off the stove, she took the tape and scissors over to the couch where Mel and Frank slept like bad guy babies.

It hadn't been that hard to put these two to sleep, not for someone who watched as many cops and robbers shows as Nellie. She'd found a prescription bottle of Valium in the bathroom cabinet, crushed the tablets into the scrambled eggs, making sure she had loaded the mess with plenty of fried onions and bacon to mask what she assumed would be a medicinal flavor. She sautéed mushrooms she had found in the refrigerator and splashed in as much wine from an opened bottle on the counter as she dared to boost the pills. She wasn't sure exactly what Valium did, but she had watched enough episodes and reruns of *Dallas*, *Dynasty*, and *Melrose Place* to recognize the name of a downer when she saw it. She also figured if these guys had been snooping around town on some kind of job, they probably weren't sleeping that much. They asked her to make coffee, and she found a bag of decaf in the freezer and used that instead of the can of regular on the counter. She had always believed, and told the EZ Way customers, that if real coffee woke you up, decaf must put you to sleep.

Stuart had put Mel and Frank in charge while he went down to the garage to search Jane Wheel's car. They had thrown into the trunk the bags of Duncan's stuff from the McFlea that Frank had snagged while Mel kept the pretty boy busy, plus there were boxes Jane had been driving around with. Maybe something of Bateman's was in there, Stuart had told them. Nellie knew it was just luck that Stuart wanted to do the searching himself since she hadn't been able to slip anything into his poached eggs. He was hurting, Nellie could tell that. She found Mylanta in the bathroom, and thought about emptying a few Valium capsules into it, but realized if she offered him something for his heartburn, he might realize she had looked in the medicine chest and put two and two together. No wonder Jane had such a glow lately . . . this detecting stuff was okay.

Mel and Frank were happy to relax on the couch while Nellie tidied up. Asleep two minutes after Stuart went out the door, Nellie gave them five more minutes, then approached with tape and scissors.

Feet together first, she figured. Even if they woke up, they'd fall if they tried to get her, so that was the best place to start. She taped their ankles as tightly as she dared, then for good measure, taped each pair of feet to a leg of the couch. She taped Frank's hands next. Easy, they were folded together in his lap. Just for fun Nellie made a final loop that went around his neck, picturing him yanking his hands and nodding like a rocking horse.

Mel's arms were spread out wide, one hand fallen off

the back of the couch and the other on his knee. She studied him and decided it would be safest not to try to get them together. She wound duct tape around each hand, making big steel gray paws. Couldn't do much without fingers and thumbs working, could he? The paws still seemed potentially dangerous, so she connected each hand to his head, figuring that pulling on his hair would hurt enough to at least slow him down. A final duct tape square over the gaping mouths, and her work was done.

She called Don and whispered that Stuart was down in the garage and he had a gun, but Mel and Frank were taken care of.

"Nellie, get the hell out of there!" Don shouted, adding, "And be careful."

"Yeah, yeah."

Outside the door, Jane whispered to Tim, who swallowed and nodded. Oh watched the stairs behind them. Jane knocked boldly and gestured to Tim to start talking.

"Mr. Amos, where do you want those armoires unloaded? And how about that Empire chest?" Tim said, in a voice an octave below his normal register.

"Shush," said Nellie, opening the door, "you'll wake up the dead."

"Mom, you didn't . . ." Jane said rushing in, trying to hug her mother who ducked away, "you didn't kill these guys, did you?"

"Could have," Nellie said. "Let's go. Your dad's about to blow a gasket."

Oh got on his phone to the police downstairs. Nellie gave him a description of Stuart, right down to his navy blue jacket and polished black loafers.

"Walks bent over a little, like he's got a stomachache," Nellie said.

"Did you poison him, Nellie?" asked Tim.

"Could have," Nellie said. "Didn't need to though, with you coming to rescue me and all." Nellie narrowed her eyes, looking at Tim. "Think you could have gotten those bruisers tied up like that?"

"I am great with duct tape, Nellie," Tim said, trying to put his arm around her and guide her down the stairs.

"What's the plan? You in charge?" Nellie asked Oh.

"Not really," Oh said, "but I think if we go down this way, through the auction house, we won't run into Stuart. He'll go back up through the backstairs, from the garage."

Jane introduced her mother to Detective Oh as they hurried down. When they entered the showroom, they saw six police officers, guns drawn and pointed at them. Amos, owner of the auction house, was peeking out of the window of his office, the delivery men crouching next to him.

"Upstairs," Jane said, "that's where the kidnappers are. But those two aren't going anywhere. The one in the garage is . . ."

Munson slammed the door on his way in.

"Gone. The one in the garage is gone," said Munson. "He either made the unmarked cars parked out on the road or . . . ," he turned to Oh, "he made the little civilian posse tiptoeing up the inside stairs."

"You know he didn't, Munson, 'cause he wouldn't know that his two lugnuts up there weren't in control of the situation," said Jane's mother, picking a piece of lint off the sleeve of Jane's shirt.

"Glad to see you're okay, Nellie. Don's fit to be tied,"

said Munson. "I'll have someone drive you all back to the EZ Way Inn. We're going to hang on to your car for a bit, Mrs. Wheel, see if we can pick up prints and find out more about this guy. Stuart, Nellie? That his name?"

Jane listened to her mother describe Stuart and his stomachache for a minute, then stepped into the garage area to look at her car. She put her hands behind her back so she wouldn't inadvertently touch anything and peered into the backseat. Elmira's schoolwork and all the other leftovers from her pantry project at the McFlea were dumped on the floor. The trunk was open, and Jane saw more papers dumped out. She thought one or two brown paper bags might be missing. She couldn't remember how much of Bateman's or Duncan's stuff she'd still had in the car that morning.

"Your prints will, of course, be on your car anyway," said Oh. She hadn't heard him come up behind her. He could give Nellie a run for her money in the silent sneak competition.

"I don't want to mess up anything they might be able to find. Especially since we don't know what it is we're looking for. But if you think . . . ?" Jane asked Oh.

Oh reached into his pocket and brought out a pair of disposable plastic gloves. He handed them to Jane with a small shoulder movement, an "any-Boy-Scout-could-tell-you-it-never-hurts-to-be-prepared" kind of shrug.

Jane put on the gloves and opened the door quickly and quietly since she didn't want Munson and his officers swarming. She unlocked the glove compartment, and from behind the owner's manual and box of Kleenex, she took out Bateman's finger. She was unreasonably happy to see it, delighted that Stuart had not even bothered with the most obvious storage area for valuables in the car. She gave it a little slosh, the way a snow globe collector must greet her favorites when she rearranges them on a shelf.

Jane slipped the jar into her pocket and peeled off the gloves.

"What is it you think we're looking for?" Jane asked.

"It's usually a notebook with names and dates. Amounts of money paid off? Bookkeeping done in some novel way, I suppose," said Oh. "In a case I worked on years ago, a man had one of his assistants tattooed with the name of the man who had hired him to commit a crime."

"Why would that be proof of anything? I could get Tim's name tattooed on my . . . somewhere . . . and say that he did something, but it wouldn't prove anything, would it?" Jane asked.

"But how embarrassing for Mr. Lowry to have to deny it," said Oh. "And if he did do it, it certainly makes everyone look in his direction. When he makes a slip, everyone is watching."

"Seems ridiculous, if you ask me," said Tim, who had come in behind them. "All of these businesses in Kankakee, these taverns and restaurants . . . Who cared if they ran a little gambling thirty or forty years ago?"

Jane looked into the showroom where Nellie was lecturing Munson about how to be a decent cop. Oh's and Tim's eyes followed hers.

"People like my mother and father and all the rest here didn't want their names dragged through the mud. They didn't realize at first it was going to tie them up for all this time. Gus was smart. He played the right people, knew he could count on them to stay quiet to protect their families."

Munson waved the three of them in and pushed them along with Nellie toward a uniformed officer to whom he gave instructions to drive them back to the EZ Way Inn.

"How does Munson know you, Mom?" Jane asked. "He called you Nellie."

"Everybody calls me Nellie. We know all the cops. We've been robbed about twenty times. Besides," Nellie said, "your dad always said we should know the cops and stay on their good side because sooner or later one of them would be the chief and sooner or later he might run for mayor. Back when we got our liquor license, it paid to know how to stay on everybody's good side."

"That's right. Dad always had matchbooks that supported the democratic candidates on the bar right next to the matchbooks for the republicans," Jane said.

"Have to treat them all the same," Don said, when they got back to the EZ Way Inn and Jane pointed out pamphlets on the bar from two opposing candidates for county sheriff. Jane laughed at the way Nellie almost let Don hug her. It reminded Jane of the way Nick avoided the appearance of family human contact.

"You had to support all the candidates because you didn't know who was going to win. Saloon keepers always want to be on the side of the winner. That way, if you were a little late closing on a Saturday night, you could catch a break. Course, it doesn't matter anymore. Our customers are all too old to stay up past ten, so we close well before legal hours now," Don said. "Unless a ball game on the West Coast goes into extra innings, everybody's home safe in bed by eleven."

Munson had been talking to Bobby Duff, whose head could not hang any lower on his neck. When Munson stood up and gave him a slap on the back, Bobby nearly pitched forward into his glass of beer.

"That is a sad case, everybody in his family gone, all committed suicide."

"Not his father," Jane said, not ready to reveal any new information, she added, "Not Duff."

Munson groaned. "Another murder, Mrs. Wheel?"

"Yup. Someone hacked off his finger, then set him up in the car to make it look like a suicide," Jane said. "And I'm beginning to think I know who."

"Will we be sharing today?" asked Munson.

"Couldn't have been Stuart or his clowns," Nellie said. "Too young."

"If Detective Oh can get some information, I think we can figure out who Stuart and the duct tape twins work for," said Jane. "If there were any young cops or lawyers working on the Bateman case or at the time of the Bateman case who went on to higher things—elected to office in the city, someone now a judge or something—I think we could find some connections."

"How did you come up with that?" Tim asked.

"It's what Mom said about Dad. Got to be nice to all the cops because they all end up moving up. Once you get 'up' you got something to lose. You said part of it, too, Tim. Who cares about all the nickel-dime gambling that went on

272

years ago? Unless you were a part of it forty years ago and now you want to keep a judgeship or vote against more riverboat gambling in Chicago?"

"May I get some change for the pay phone?" Oh asked. "I don't want to use my cell phone for this call."

Nellie shook her head and took him by the arm.

"I'll be damned," said Don, "she's showing him the private phone. I've never seen her do that for anyone."

"You have a private line here?" Tim asked.

"See?" said Don.

"Detective Munson," said Jane, "I know it's a hassle to open up cases, but I think Duff was murdered because he was going to talk. When his wife committed suicide, he decided to give up the information he had. Whoever killed him cut off his finger as a warning to the other saloon keepers."

Jane looked at her father, who had been watching her with wonder and admiration.

"No one ever knew for sure. The finger seemed like a message, but no one knew for sure whether it was a rumor or it had really happened. The kids, you know," Don cocked his head in the direction of Bobby Duff. "He was young, still in high school, and Lilly, well, it seemed like Lilly might be able to escape it all, but she came back."

Jane was close to saying something about what Lilly had found in the shanty basement. She'd wait. Maybe what Lilly had found out wasn't really anybody else's business. Bobby hadn't read the letters yet, but he had said something that led Jane to her conviction that Duff was murdered. "He said he wanted to give it all up," Bobby had remembered. He didn't mean give up on living, he meant giving up information. Duff's mistake was drinking too much and talking about doing it for too long. Someone got to him before he could name names.

Since the EZ Way Inn wasn't officially open, it wasn't really a problem to shoo out the regulars who were drawn like magnets when word got out that something was going on at Don and Nellie's. There were, after all, police cars parked in the lot, and customers felt it was their duty to come over and find out what was going on.

Francis, who felt like he had been in on everything from the beginning, although he had no idea what was going on, what beginning he witnessed or how whatever he didn't know could possibly end, took charge, ushering folks out the door, saying in his best television cop voice, "Show's over. Let's go."

Don himself escorted Francis to the door, thanking him for all of his help, his steady support in a crisis. He turned to Nellie as he left, "Are you going to have pie tomorrow?"

"Don't you think maybe we ought to quit before all our customers are as senile as Francis?" Nellie asked Don.

Munson finished with his questions and notes. He shifted his weight back and forth, left foot to right, and finally took Jane by the arm and led her away from her parents.

"My dad was a cop back then. He's dead now, gone ten years, but he kept a diary. Sometimes I read in it, you know, just to feel closer. He didn't like the investigation on Duff. I remember he said that Duff wouldn't have done that. Half-ass drunk, maybe, he'd say, but he wouldn't have left his kids that way." Munson paused. "He was Catholic, you know."

Jane nodded, waiting for Munson to continue, not wanting to say anything that might break the spell of him trusting her with what seemed to be a great confidence.

"When Louella killed herself, Duff couldn't get the old priest that was at Saint Pat's to bury her in the church. It just about killed him. He wouldn't have committed suicide is what my dad always said."

"It might make a lot of difference to Bobby Duff if he knew that his dad didn't really want to leave him," Jane said.

Munson nodded and clapped a paw on her shoulder. He even nodded to Oh, who came out of the backroom reading over the notes he had taken while using the backroom phone.

"I've just got phone numbers to call back later when people have had time to check some names and dates," said Oh.

Don suggested that they all go to the house, have some lunch, and give Nellie some time to recover from her ordeal, which everyone knew meant that Don needed a nap. Nellie was glowing with vim and vigor, as if she had found the secret to the fountain of youth—doping and duct-taping thugs who were dumb enough to mess with her.

Tim shook his head. The McFlea, he reminded everyone, opened tomorrow, and he needed to make sure everything was in order. He was going back to his shop to pick up all the flowers the amateur decorators had ordered for their rooms and stop at the Jewel to pick up a frozen apple pie.

"You and Francis and your pies," said Nellie.

"Not for dessert, Nellie, for perfume," Tim said. "At one o'clock when the McFlea opens, that fresh-baked apple pie aroma will put an already sure hit over the moon."

"Just goes to show you," Nellie said, as she watched Tim leave, "you don't have to be as old as Francis to be senile."

22

Autumn in New York. April in Paris. Moonlight in Vermont. Everyone knew there were seasons, times that matched romantically with geography. Songwriters crowned these places, these months, these times of day in their lyrics, and they stuck as the memories that launched a thousand nostalgic flights of fancy. No one yet had written the Ballad of Illinois in September, the definitive tribute to the turning leaves and their crunch underfoot, the drumbeat of acorns, the crisp cut of light through a window, the whiff of smoke and frost in the clear air.

Autumn in Kankakee was not memorialized, not a song destined to be sung. If Jane could compose, she decided, as she lay awake in her childhood bedroom in her parents' house, she would make her signature song "September in Kankakee." It was her favorite place to be—for a day or two anyway—in her favorite month—all thirty days that it hath. Part of it, she knew, was the memory of sharpened pencils and knee socks, the joy of going back to school after a muggy summer spent lying on the floor holding down the pages of comic books with both hands in front of the oscillating fan, waiting for August to end.

September. Crack open the seal on a brand-new

crayon box, inhale the magical bouquet, and spill out the burnt umber and goldenrod and raw sienna and ochre—all the colors that they wore down to a nub on Fridays in Sister Ann Elizabeth's second-grade room recreating the September to October trees outside their windows. Memorize the answer to "Why did God make me?" for catechism class. Look out the window, Sister. God made me to see this.

Jane reached for the phone and dialed Tim's number. He answered with a sound somewhere between hello, what, and go away.

"Huway."

"Can you see out your window from bed?"

"Huway."

"Has there ever been a song written about Kankakee?"

"Kan-ko-kee, ke-ko-can-who-can-we-can-kan-ko-kee-can."

"That's a football cheer."

"It's 7:39 A.M. My repertoire isn't fully downloaded and operational," Tim said.

"Shouldn't you be up basting turkeys and baking pies to perfume the McFlea?" asked Jane.

"I've got everything timed. Grand opening's at one. Everybody coming?"

"That's the plan."

Nellie was sliding eggs onto Don's plate when Jane joined them in the kitchen. Nellie still tied an apron over her clothes when she cooked, even though the sweet shirtwaist dresses Jane remembered her wearing had given way to jogging pants and sweatshirts. Don had the *Kankakee Sun-*

day Journal spread out in front of him. Nellie shuffled the pages aside as she placed two slices of toast next to the bacon and eggs.

"How do you want yours?" Nellie asked, already holding an egg over the pan.

"Just toast," Jane said, brushing her hand over the top of her dad's steel gray crewcut as she passed by his chair on her way to the toaster.

"It's Sunday," Nellie said.

Her mother had always spoken her own language in her own rhythm. To be conversant in Nellish, one had to be proficient in a kind of mental leapfrog. Nellie never bothered to fill in the gaps between her comments. You either followed along or you didn't. Some people might say Nellie didn't listen, but Jane knew that wasn't true. She filed away everything everyone had ever said. If pink was your favorite color when you were five, you would be reminded, as you rejected a rose-colored prom dress, that "Pink is your favorite color"; and, in your forties, when you came around to the flattering glow that wearing pink cast, Nellie was right there behind you in the fitting room saying, "Pink was always your favorite color." Nellie listened all right. It was just that in the land where Nellish was spoken, she didn't answer, respond, or recognize any words that weren't part of her own agenda for the day, the week, the rest of your life.

Jane knew, that in Nellish, what her mother meant, what another mother might say, was, "I know you don't normally eat a big breakfast, dear. Nor do we. On Sundays, though, it is our habit to cook a big hot breakfast, which might consist of eggs, bacon, potatoes, and not have another meal until dinner. Wouldn't you like to join us in our hearty, delicious, and special occasion meal?"

Maybe no mother would say exactly that, thought Jane, but somewhere between Nellie's grunts and non sequiturs and Jane's fantasy mother who was always gracious, articulate, and affectionate, there had to be a happy medium. Would Nick think she had landed there? In that happy medium of motherhood between one's own parents' shortcomings and fifties television perfection?

Jane shook her head again and put two pieces of bread into the toaster.

"Are you two ready for the McFlea today?"

"I'm not sure your mother should go," Don said. "What if that Stuart decides to show up and get even with her for capturing his friends?"

"He doesn't give a rat's ass," Nellie said. "Those guys were losers, and he's better off without them. He knows that. They're probably what gave him reflux."

"Did you give Tim all the ledgers and account books?"

"Everything you gave me is over there," Don said. "Munson called while you were in the shower. They picked up Crandall last night at his motel. Didn't say why he bolted yesterday. Said he panicked, has a history of claustrophobia and anxiety. Gave Munson the name of his doctor to verify and offered to pay me twice what the bathroom window would cost to repair."

"What did Munson do with him?"

"He had nothing to hold him on really, besides the damage to the EZ Way," said Don.

"What about blackmail?" Jane asked.

"Who's he blackmailed? He might have planned on

carrying on the family business, but he hasn't done anything yet."

"How about our front window?" Nellie asked.

Don and Jane both looked at her.

"He's willing to pay for the bathroom window, but what about the front window? The brick?"

"That was Bobby," Don said.

Nellie and Jane looked at him.

"How did you know that, Dad?" Jane asked, trying to remember if she had mentioned it to her father last night when they had all been working out their plans and roles for today's McFlea McSting, as Tim had named it.

"While you were off taping up the bad guys, Bobby started crying in his beer and apologizing. He thought he'd be able to take over the blackmailing business. Poor sap."

"Dad, how much do you figure the total take of the blackmailing business was? I mean how much was everyone paying? Total?"

"I added it up. Altogether it was $875 a month until last June. Old Pink was paying $150 of it. When he died, Pink Junior said he didn't give a damn if his dad had run roulette on the front lawn, he wasn't paying Duncan any more than the rent listed on the lease."

"How'd Duncan take it?" Jane asked, half listening. She was thinking about how much chaos $875 a month had caused. Did any of them realize what a paltry sum they were fighting over?

"Told Pink to expect a grease fire within the year, then just laughed," Don said. "No one knew if he was serious or not. Pink told us at the meeting we had the other night that he just laughed right back at him and said he was insured,

Duncan could do whatever he wanted; it was his building. Come to think of it, maybe that's why he was selling them all to us; maybe he was going to torch everything."

Jane reminded Don and Nellie to be at the McFlea by noon. At one, the school bus would start dropping off paying visitors who were parking at the high school. Jane was certain they could accomplish what they needed to in an hour. She packed her car and headed off to the McFlea, formerly the Gerber house, future Tim Lowry casa.

It was a glorious day, sunny and golden. Jane longed to roll down the windows and sing that September in Illinois song, if only someone would write it. She parked next to Tim's mustang in back and went in through the open kitchen door. Tim was studying the kitchen left to right, east to west, top to bottom.

"Beautiful job, Janie," Tim said. "I didn't really pay too much attention yesterday when I came through and checked after the duct tape twins were here. You did good."

"Will you keep it like this?" Jane asked.

"It's a little fabric-y for me," Tim said. "I'm not sure what I'd get rid of, though. Love the hanky curtains, love the pot holders. Tell you what, how about doing a kind of display with some of this stuff down at the store. I'm taking over the frame shop next door, and I'll have my own little antique mall. You and me, okay?"

Bruce Oh came in on the last sentence, putting his wallet away and shaking his head. "Inexpensive taxis here in Kankakee. I'm sorry, Mr. Lowry, I think Mrs. Wheel is going to be my business partner, yes?" he asked.

"What? Selling vintage neckwear?" Tim asked, sounding defensive, but in reality, admiring today's tie with its pattern of question marks and exclamation points within diamonds and squares. Where did Oh's wife find them?

"Mrs. Wheel is not only a picker of things, Mr. Lowry, she seems to spot motives and murderers, too," Oh said. "I'm hoping she might agree to join my consulting business."

"A detective? A PI? Jane Wheel, girl sleuth?" Tim said. "No way."

"Don't fight over me, boys, let's just see if this plan works today," Jane said.

The plan, she had explained to Oh, Tim, Don, and Nellie last night, was simple. Every bit of Bateman and Duncan's stuff that might hold the key to the blackmail would be set out as part of a tableau somewhere in the house. Since none of them knew what to look for, what these alleged records looked like, they'd let everyone else have a go at it. Someone would lead them to the blackmail records and the murderer.

"If there was a murderer," Tim reminded Jane. "No weapon, no evidence, no reason for anyone to believe Duncan was murdered. Heart failure, right?"

"We're baiting traps," Nellie had said, nodding her approval. Nellie heartily approved of snapping the heads off rodents.

"Yes," said Oh. "There might be a few people who thought the blackmail money that Duncan collected would make a nice income. Bobby Duff and Bill Crandall, for example. But if someone killed Duncan, if someone caused that heart to fail," he said, looking at Tim, "if someone killed Duff Senior for that matter, there was more to those records than a small monthly income."

"People don't want their names in the papers," Don said, "not respectable people."

"Or *disrespectable* people, Daddy," Jane said. "That's the key here. Somebody whom Duncan and maybe Bateman had something on had more to lose than $150 a month."

"Not Bateman," said Nellie, using a paper towel to wipe a fingerprint off the jar that held Oscar's finger. "If Bateman was in on it all, why's his finger in here?"

No one answered. Bateman's finger rolled gently in the jar, participating in the discussion as best it could until it slowed and pointed at Jane. You'll find out, it seemed to say, you'll find out.

Jane, Tim, and Oh finished arranging flowers and baking apple pie and walked through the house, trying to imagine it as paying visitors. Each volunteer designer had printed display cards for their room, listing their finds, where they'd got them, and how much they'd spent.

The downstairs powder room was a riot of pastel poodles. A pink, crocheted poodle toilet paper cover, a collection of three paint-by-number Fifis placed on the wall opposite the mirror. When you checked your lipstick or hair in the mirror, poodles were standing on your head. Tim planned on paving this room over first after the McFlea. "I mean," he said to Jane, "could we be more obvious? A florist with a poodle motif? Please!"

The bedrooms were fabulous. One had a scrounged set of almost-matching thirties wood furniture painted to look like tiger eye maple. The faux finished dresser and chest were from the same set, and the double bed, the almost match, had been found taken apart in the basement of a house sale in Limestone, a few miles west of Kankakee. The pieced wool coverlets piled on the bed had been purchased at a church rummage sale for ten dollars each. Every square was hand embroidered with a name. In the corner, someone had stitched "1967." Not exactly antique, but distinctive and warm and just the right finishing touch for this room.

Another bedroom was a little girl's fantasy. Tim had told his decorators to envision a family of four, a son and a daughter, and to plan accordingly. He would be redoing anyway. This hideaway was so perfect, Jane hoped Tim would leave it long enough for her to use it once as his house guest. Gauze fabric, yards and yards of it picked up at a rummage sale, was draped over the window alcove. Inexpensive Christmas lights had been layered in the fabric and when turned on by a simple added floor switch, the window seat became a fairyland retreat. Starlit fabric was hung over the bed as well, a wooden platform put together by Marla Dorndon and her husband, who had collaborated on the "girl's room" and were sure to get the most oohs and aahs on the tour.

The hall was a large room in and of itself, and one of the teachers from McNamara had offered to tackle it. She had found an old desk at a yard sale with matching rolling wooden chair and put it in the corner of the large square space. The desk was almost square itself with a kind of rail around it. Jane went over and sat. A lift on the blotter area revealed a flip-up manual typewriter built into the desk.

"Will this be auctioned, Tim?" Jane asked, feeling herself go weak in the knees as she touched the old typewriter keys and pushed the carriage return.

"We'll see," said Tim.

Jane returned the typewriter to its hidden spot and turned on the green metal desk lamp. She took out the ledgers and account books from Bateman's and placed them on the desk, opening the largest book to a center page. Jane took out a Bakelite mechanical pencil that advertised the SHANGRI-LA and, under that, OSCAR BATEMAN, PROPRIETOR. Jane set it next to the account book. Baited.

The hall was well lit, with brass sconces in each corner and next to each bedroom door that opened off of it. They turned on all the lights and hung some of the photographs they had brought along.

"I'll hang the rest in the basement," said Oh, "if you think that's where they fit?"

Tim nodded. "On the wall opposite the poker table," he said.

When he was finished setting the music for each room, lighting a candle here and there for scent and atmosphere, and scanning each room for anything out of place, Tim took Jane's hand and they walked together down into the kitchen.

"I'm not kidding about you as a partner, Jane. You could handle the Chicago sales—well, most of them," Tim said. "You have a great eye."

Jane smiled. She couldn't remember when she had felt so wanted and needed. Oh seemed serious about her becoming an investigator, now Tim wanted her as a partner, Miriam had loved every shipment she had "picked" and sent off to Ohio this summer. Three months ago she had been out of work and at ends as loose as they get. Now everybody wanted a piece of her.

"I'm so flattered," Jane said, "but I'm . . ."

"I'll get you a truck," said Tim.

"A truck? So tempting, but it's . . ."

"Your own flatbed with a ramp and dolly, babe."

"Tim, it's . . ."

"What?"

"Charley!" Jane said.

"Well, of course it is. And he'd rather have you be my partner than a detective, for god's sake."

"Would you, Charley?" Jane asked with a smile.

"Maybe. But it's going to be your choice that counts, isn't it?" said Charley.

Tim whirled around to find Charley at the top of the steps, nodding approvingly at the well-appointed hallway. Charley gave him a hug, watching Jane over Tim's shoulder. Her smile was one he hadn't seen in a while. Welcoming. Or had he been missing it?

When he hugged her, she rested her head on his shoulder, in no hurry to pull away.

"Thanks for taking care of business at the house, Charley. I think I know who our burglars were."

"Yeah, your dad told me Nellie duct taped a couple of guys who sounded like they might have been the ones who didn't appreciate your Bakelite buttons."

"Or your T. Rex teeth. Nick with you?"

"Downstairs with Oh. They made it to the semifinals. He played great," Charley said.

"You went? I thought . . ."

"I went to the early game this morning, which they lost. They were out of it, so we drove straight to Don and Nellie's. We couldn't miss the McFlea, could we?"

Jane didn't get much of a play-by-play from Nick, but

he managed to provide just enough description of the soccer tournament and the motel he had stayed in last night to make her feel that he sort of cared that she had at least asked the questions.

They all spread out through the house, preparing for the earliest visitors. They had invited all of the new property owners in Kankakee who had recently done business with Gus Duncan. Pink Junior arrived first, then Bobby Duff, looking hungover and confused. It appeared to have sunk in that Lilly was gone. He looked lost, deserted, and a little angry that anyone expected him to do something as silly as walk though somebody else's house and look at furniture.

Crandall arrived, apologetic about leaving the EZ Way Inn via a window rather than a door. Don introduced three tavern owners to Jane. She remembered them from her childhood and wondered why they looked so much older until she realized that she must look like a giant to them. They had last seen her when she was six and seemed to think she was the one who had aged.

Tim was walking visitors through the rooms quickly, hurrying them down to the basement, where he could show off his party room. Nick planted himself on a bar stool and watched in disbelief as the parade of visitors nodded and smiled and snapped their fingers to Bobby Darin, another name from the past that his mother would lecture him on if he forgot himself and asked about him on the way home.

The tavern owners congregated in front of some of the group photographs and more than one finger pointed to

Gus Duncan in front of the EZ Way Inn and called him a son-of-a-bitch.

"Oh he was all right," drawled a sultry voice behind the knot of saloon keepers. "I mean, he was all right for a son-of-bitch."

Pink Junior turned around.

"Mrs. Bateman?" he said. "You haven't changed a bit."

"Liar just like your father, Junior," said Mary. "And you *have* changed. Used to be a dashing young man, now you look just like Old Pink."

Mary had discarded the walker altogether and carried a cane. It appeared to be more prop than aid, and she used it to part the crowd, clearing a path to Don and Nellie who had drifted to their positions of comfort behind the small wet bar.

"Donald," Mary said, "has Nellie thrown you out yet so I could have you?"

"Take him," said Nellie, pouring out a Sprite for Nick and sticking some of Tim's prop marachino cherries on a toothpick and dropping them into the glass. "Dot and Ollie here?"

"Parking the car. They dropped me off in front. Nellie, being mean has kept you young and fit."

"You look all right, too, Mary," said Nellie.

"You sure do," said Don.

Jane watched her mother slice open her father with a look and nudged Tim.

"Are you Jane?"

A young woman with long blond hair clipped back with a barrette held out her hand. Jane knew by her blue eyes she had to be Susan, Oscar and Mary's granddaughter. When she shook Jane's hand, she held on tightly for that extra moment, the telling moment when someone wants to convey something without words. In this case she seemed genuinely grateful to be invited, and Jane was uncomfortable with that, not sure the spider was supposed to accept gratitude from any of the flies she'd invited for dinner. Jane avoided her blue eyes and looked instead at her hand. Clean and cool. Nails spotless, clipped short, straight across. A strong, capable hand. A nurse's hand. Jane looked up, startled. That was it. She had to find Oh and tell him.

"Thank you so much for inviting us to this opening. Grandma and Aunt Dot and Aunt Ollie were so excited. When they realized that the person who bought my grandparent's stuff was someone they knew, or rather whose parents they knew, they were thrilled to death," Susan said. "To tell the truth, I regretted rushing in and selling it all without, you know, going through things more carefully, but I had to do it when Grandma was still a little groggy from her accident because I didn't want her to talk me out of it. I just want to thank you so much for the pictures," she said.

That's why she was clinging to Jane's hand. She had gotten the packet of family pictures. Jane hoped she wouldn't notice the photocopies of the vintage shots that Jane had framed and hung all over the house. Might take the shine off the gift. Jane made an excuse and went off to find Oh to tell him what she had figured out.

"I smell pie," said Hunter Smith, new owner of the Brown Jug, a tavern he had run for thirty-five years. "Serving any food here?"

Nellie shook her head. "No food, Hunter, this is just to give you ideas about furniture." Nellie winked at Nick.

"Furniture? What the hell do I care about furniture?"

Jane found Oh and Tim following visitors around, answering questions when they could, explaining the premise of the fund-raiser when asked, but mostly just listening to people talk about what they recognized and what they saw that they remembered throwing away.

Everyone, it seemed, had thrown out old Bentwood chairs like the ones that sat around the oak pedestal table in the dining room. And everyone's mother had thrown out a table like that, too. The tabletop on this one had been completely ruined—warped and splintered by water damage—and one of the Grant boys had hauled it home from an alley. Their family had offered to decorate the McFlea dining room and, to salvage the table, they paid for a piece of glass to be fitted for the top. It was their only expense, since they scrounged old menus and illustrations from vintage cookbooks and shelter magazines, set them "under glass," and had a beautiful easy-care dining room table at an extraordinary price. It was changeable, too, they explained on their description card—you could put holiday pictures, family photos, Christmas cards, whatever, to fit whatever kind of gathering you were planning.

"So clever," Susan said. "I really shouldn't have been so quick to get Grandma to sell all her stuff. Is most of it here in the house?"

"Some," said Jane, reminding her that she had bought almost all tavern memorabilia.

Dot and Ollie were reminiscing with Nellie about basketball when Jane walked over to listen. Apparently, they had faced each other on the court in the thirties or forties, when women's basketball had been big entertainment.

"Yeah," Hunter said, "remember when some girl'd break her bra strap and have to call time out? That was worth the price of . . ."

"Quiet," said Don, nodding his head in his grandson's direction.

"Grandpa, I know what a bra is for Pete's sake," said Nick.

"No, you don't," said Jane, from behind him.

"You always fouled out, Nellie," said Dot. "Remember, Ollie, how Nellie always fouled out?"

"Remember? She yanked out a handful of my hair once," said Ollie. "You were dirty as heck, Nellie."

"I hustled," Nellie said. She looked at her grandson. "It's important to hustle."

Jane looked at her watch. People had been milling around a long time in the basement. Tim's party room was such a success, people didn't want to leave it. Saloon keepers, Jane figured, all comfortable at the bar.

She walked upstairs to the second floor and took a moment to turn on the lights in the girl's bedroom. Jane knew they would have their best effect at night, right after the reading light was dimmed, when the magic lights would illuminate dreams, but they were lovely in daytime, too. Jane curled up in the window seat to get the full effect and loosened some of the gauze so she could have the full tent-like experience.

When they peeked into the room, they didn't see Jane behind the fabric, but she saw them. She listened to them whispering, standing at the desk right outside the bedroom.

"There's nothing in these books. This is just the Shangri-La stuff, the day-to-day."

"You don't know what to look for."

"I suppose you do."

Jane came out of her lair and stood in the doorway and watched Dot and Ollie turn the pages of Bateman's ledger, shaking their heads and squinting over the figures.

"If you had known what to look for, you could have just gotten it at the sale or asked Susan not to sell it in the first place," said Ollie.

"Is that what happened?" asked Jane. "Did Susan arrange to have the sale without asking Mary?"

"Oh, lord," said Ollie, "don't sneak up on old ladies, dear."

"We're liable to shoot you," said Dot.

"I'm sorry," said Jane, coming out into the hall. "Can I help you find anything?"

"I doubt it. Mary's so distraught. She thinks Bateman left some message or something for her in the things you bought. That's why she was so keen on coming back to Kankakee. Thought we'd just find it."

"Any idea what it was?"

Jane had her back to the stairs, but she could tell by the sounds on the stairs that other people were coming. The step, step, click rhythm told her it was Mary Bateman. Someone was with her.

Bingo, Jane thought when she turned around. It was Susan. She hoped Tim hadn't gotten so enmeshed in throwing his little basement party that he had forgotten to cordon off the steps after he saw them come up. Jane would need a few minutes alone with them if she was going to get any information.

"I'll tell you what I want," said Mary, "besides not needing this cane and not being an old lady, I would like to have anything written on Shangri-La paper before 1958."

Mary walked over to the desk and held up the advertising pencil Jane had placed in the ledger. "See this pencil? This was a little Christmas giveaway from Bateman. He always gave the customers some little thing at Christmas, a pen or a coin purse or maybe something for the ladies like those little plastic rain bonnets."

"I enjoyed those rain bonnets," said Ollie.

"But this pen is from after 1958. Know how I can tell?" asked Mary, not waiting for an answer. "Because it says that the proprietor of the Shangri-La is Oscar Bateman. It doesn't say Bateman and Duncan, like everything did before 1958."

"They were partners," Jane said.

"And best friends until"—Mary stopped to think— "until they became worst enemies."

"Grandma?"

"Hush, Susan, you don't know anything about this," Mary said.

"Sure she does," said Jane. This part of the plan was new. When she told Oh what she thought had happened, he'd told her to go after Susan, not to let up. This was going to be difficult. Jane took a deep breath.

"She knew enough to come down to Kankakee and kill Gus Duncan before he could tell anybody anything. Stop him from blackmailing you after she realized your stuff, all the dirt you had on him that protected you from him, had been sold at your house sale."

Jane hadn't moved from the doorway, hadn't approached any of the women, but she saw now that Dot and Ollie had both backed up, retreated into separate corners of the hall. Jane glimpsed, out of the corner of her eye, some one or two or three standing on the stairs. She wasn't sure who they were, but they were standing still and silent.

Susan inhaled sharply and made a choking sound. "Killed who? I killed who?"

"Hush, Susan. You didn't kill anybody," said Mary, smiling at Jane.

"Gus Duncan had high blood pressure. He took medication. Sometimes. When he wasn't too hungover to remember. He was a heart attack waiting to happen. When he did take his medicine, he took potassium, too. Which is why the police wouldn't think it was odd that his potassium level was elevated. He had both bottles of medication on his kitchen counter," said Jane.

Mary sat down in the desk chair and looked down at the ledger. When she raised her eyes, she saw the jar and smiled. She picked up Bateman's finger and held it up to eye level.

"There you are, you rascal."

"Susan, you're a visiting nurse with access to supplies. If you injected Duncan with potassium, his heart attack waiting to happen would happen," Jane said.

"I have a gun in my purse, Mary. I could just shoot her," Dot said. "I bought it when I turned seventy, for protection," she explained to Jane.

Jane looked at Dot and saw she was reaching into her

bag. *What a loyal friend*, Jane thought, as she watched Dot pull out the gun and point it at her.

"Put it away, Dot, nobody's killing anybody. Not today. If Duncan was killed with potassium, the police would find an injection site, and nobody found an injection site, did they, Jane?" asked Mary, holding the jar with Bateman's finger up to her cheek.

The last piece of the puzzle clicked into place. Everyone in the hall watched Mary slosh Bateman's finger to and fro in the jar. Jane had thought the police hadn't found an injection site because they hadn't looked hard enough. She knew now that they hadn't found a site because the site had been sliced away when the murderer cut off or tried to cut off Duncan's finger.

What had Oh told her? If you want Mary to talk, keep directing the questions toward Susan. Accuse Susan.

"You must have had small needles? The kind you could stick between his fingers. I mean, anybody who watches television knows that junkies run out of veins and they use the places between their toes, their fingers. He wouldn't be expecting it, and you could just stroke his hand and boom, he's stuck."

Susan looked like she was going to be sick. Jane wasn't sure she liked this part of detective work.

"Leave my granddaughter out of this, doll. She didn't do a thing," Mary said.

"I'm a nurse, I wouldn't . . . ," Susan said.

"A nurse would know how to do it," said Jane.

"I'm a nurse," said Mary, smiling.

"So am I; so is Dot," said Ollie.

Jane hadn't expected that. Was it going to be like that

movie when the whole village stood up and admitted killing the bad guy? Nellie had already confessed and might pop up any minute wanting credit again. Pretty soon they'd have the whole womens' basketball league shooting free throws for the title of Duncan's killer.

"And I have access to my granddaughter's supplies . . ."

"We all met in nursing school," said Ollie.

Jane nodded.

"I am eighty goddamn years old. A man everybody in this town hated is dead, a heart attack waiting to happen. And I am a poor old woman whose husband had his finger cut off by that bastard, Gus Duncan. You know why? Because he thought Bateman made a deal to get out of jail. Thought he gave up names. Oscar never gave up anybody in his life. He got out." Mary hesitated, but only for a second. "He got out because I had friends, made friends in high places." Mary looked like she wanted to spit. "Duncan and his names, his famous record keeping, and his claim to having the goods on everybody. Plenty of people wanted to kill him. Because of Duncan and his bragging, people thought Bateman knew stuff, too. Kept records. Me, too.

"That's why, when my daughter and her husband borrowed my car one night when theirs was in the shop and they got hit and run off the road by a driver who left the scene, I knew it wasn't just a drunk driver; I knew it was somebody supposed to . . ."

Mary stopped. She wasn't out of control; she wasn't weeping. She was, however, watching her granddaughter's eyes grow wide. This wasn't the way to explain the way of the world to your granddaughter, Mary knew, but it looked like the kid was going to find out anyway.

"When Gus Duncan and Oscar Bateman were partners, they ran a little gambling. They bribed a few cops, a few judges. Oscar handed an envelope to the wrong guy one night and ended up doing time and never turned anybody, even though people thought he did when he got out so soon. People thought he had things he never had. Duncan claimed to have records of everything: every payoff, every dirty cop, and every ward boss. Nobody ever saw them. I don't even think they exist."

"But you killed him anyway," Jane said softly.

"I am eighty years old. I live in an assisted-living residence. I have neighbors who think they played euchre with me when Duncan was killed. Whenever that might have been," Mary said. "In fact, my euchre partner, Leonard, will sign any statement about my whereabouts. And he will be believed, you know. Important man. Used to be alderman of our ward. Then judge. His son's running for reelection in the state senate. Leonard and I are very old friends," Mary said, and for the first time turning away from her granddaughter. "We became close when Oscar was in jail."

Bruce Oh strolled out from the bedroom across the hall, as casually as if he had just awakened from a nap.

"Mrs. Bateman, I know Detective Munson will want you to make a statement. Would you like me to drive you down to see him now?"

"My pleasure," Mary said.

"Grandma?" Susan sounded like a ten-year-old girl. Dot and Ollie came over to her, and Mary waved her hand. "I'm an eighty-year-old woman, baby. Don't you worry."

The women walked toward the stairs where Don and Nellie stood. Bobby Duff was standing close behind them.

"What about my dad?" he asked Mary. "Did you know Duff?"

"Sure, honey. But that was between him and Gus. Personal, you know. Gus just liked doing that finger thing, like it made him a gangster or something. Go figure."

Jane watched Bobby watch Mary move slowly and deliberately down the stairs. She accepted Oh's arm and now leaned a bit more heavily on her cane. Jane smiled. She didn't believe for a minute that Mary needed the cane any more than she had before; she was just practicing her eighty-year-old-lady act for Munson.

Jane knew she'd have to tell Bobby what she had found out by reading the letters Lilly found: his mother and Gus. Looking at Bobby, she saw it. The eyes. The shape of his head. Gus Duncan and Louella. What had Duff done when he'd found out? Poor Lilly, facing this alone in Gus Duncan's basement.

Tim was watching the clock downstairs. They were twenty minutes away from the arrival of the first bus with the visitors to the McFlea. Oh had planned on driving Mary Bateman to Munson, but Munson had come to them. Thank god he hadn't shown up in a black-and-white. He drove up in a subtle sedan and strolled into the McFlea just like any other paying guest—except for the paying part. Tim was relieved that Jane had worked it out with Mary and Susan on the second floor. They had alternative plans. They had hung all the old photographs, waiting for something to trigger a reaction, a conversation. Nice that it could work in isolation, and Tim could keep the party going in the basement. The student volunteers had arrived, and Tim had set up two at the front door to take tickets. Tim sent two others to sit at the kitchen door and direct any strays to the front. All would enter through the front.

Betsy, the pretty senior, came back to Tim immediately. "What about the guy in the pantry?" she whispered.

"What guy?" Tim whispered back.

"The one with the spray paint. Is he just finishing up before everybody gets here?"

Tim raced to the pantry, but he was too late. Jane's wallpaper and shelf paper was nearly covered with red spray paint. The sprayer was trying to finish the last shelf when Tim knocked the can out of his hand.

Nellie had come in behind Tim and yelled, "Punch him in the stomach. He'll fold like a house of cards."

"No, please," Stuart said, covering his midsection.

Munson was right behind Nellie. He came in and cuffed the man, picked up the can of paint, and led him out to the car. Oh had promised him an arrest, but he didn't think the timing would be that smooth.

Jane and Charley came in to check out the noise, and Jane felt her heart sink as she looked at her handiwork destroyed. Oh joined them, shaking his head sympathetically.

"Two former Chicago judges had connections to Bateman and Duncan. One was a prosecutor on Bateman's case. His office had lost the files when the appeal came up. He died last year. The other one had been an alderman, and he had a stroke six months ago. His family was quite protective of his privacy, didn't want him bothered while he recovered. Seems he's been quite happy at the Grand Heritage, keeping company with Mary Bateman. Stuart, the spray painter here, is her friend Leonard's nephew.

"Look," Oh said, pointing out the window.

Mary, standing by Munson's car, was patting Stuart on the cheek with one hand and putting a Tums in his mouth with the other.

"Susan didn't have anything to do with this, did she?" Jane asked.

"I don't think so. I don't think Mary told her anything about the past. Mary is very loyal and knows how to keep secrets. Dot and Ollie drove her down to see Gus. Wanted to ask him about his records, she said. Wanted him to get rid of everything if he had anything. Said she was doing it for Susan and as a favor to Leonard. Claims Gus was alive when they left."

"These weren't Duncan's accounts, though," said Jane, studying the wall to see if anything readable remained. "It was just some beautiful old handwriting. And spelling tests."

"Elmira's stuff?" Charley asked.

Jane nodded, touched that Charley remembered the little girl's name. She hadn't thought he had seemed that interested when she first brought it home.

"All of this over records that we don't even know are for real."

Tim yelled to them that the bus was coming. They tidied up the pantry as quickly and as best they could. Jane went over to the window to see if she could open it and diffuse the paint fumes. If she couldn't get the paint smell out, Tim's pie baking was going to be wasted.

The partially used punchboards were still lined up on the windowsill. Jane grabbed them, stacked them, and opened the window. A rush of air came in and began the cleansing. Jane picked up a yellow-and-blue Cigarette Stakes board and held it to the light, looking at the punched-out holes.

"Funny, it almost looks like . . . ," Jane said aloud, then, "Detective Oh, Tim, Mom, Dad, Charley, come here."

"Jane, the guests are arriving," said Tim, shushing her as he came in.

She held up the board. "What do you see?"

"Is this like one of those tests to see if you're color blind?" Tim asked.

"The punched-out holes are all surrounded by non-punched holes, and it makes a pattern," said Oh.

"More than a pattern," said Jane, handing off that board and picking up another one. "Look."

This one was unmistakable. Held up to the window, the light shining through the punched-out holes, it was clear that the open pattern formed the letters EZ.

PINK, DUFF, they were all spelled out, each in a separate punchboard. The pieces of paper rolled up and inserted into the board were small, but not too tiny for Duncan's meticulous printing. Jane used one of the keys that had been Scotch taped to the back of the board that said EZ and pushed out a few of the tightly rolled pieces of thin paper measuring two inches long, three-quarters of an inch wide. "You love Chinese food," read the fortune. On the back, in his tiny printing, Gus had written:

"Remember somebody named Teetch, Dad?" Jane asked.

"I think there was a cop named Teetch, an old-timer," Don said. He picked up one of the boards and held it up to the window. "Duncan sure as hell was more ambitious and creative than I ever thought he was."

"So that's what the son-of-a-bitch did all day," said Nellie.

The McFlea was a huge success.

The buses dropped off thirty to forty people every hour, and they were wowed by the creativity and innovation of Tim's brainchild. He had three offers to buy the Gerber place, which prompted him to think about getting a real estate license.

"Yeah, you can be a florist, antique dealer, appraiser, realtor. Your business card will be five by seven," Jane said.

She and Charley had adjourned to the back porch, where there was a glider and two lounge chairs that Jane was sure she remembered from the days Eddie Gerber had lived in the Gerber house. Jane was studying one of the punchboards coded with the word JUG which surely meant Hunter's bar, the Brown Jug. She wasn't really seeing the punches, though, she was thinking about Charley, next to her on the glider, his long legs thrust out in front and his arms draped across the oilcloth-covered back cushions. The sun was low in the afternoon sky, and Charley had closed his eyes as the beams fell across his face.

What had been different about Charley when he'd walked into the McFlea? What had given her that rush of feeling, that involuntary lightness that used to pick her up whenever he walked into a room? It had almost faded away in the last year, now here it was, making her as warm and itchy as would a full box of vintage Bakelite priced as old plastic junk.

Same khaki pants, same blue shirt, same brown hair and eyes, same weathered skin, same gorgeous hands, large and strong. His inventory was the same. What about hers? Same jeans and T-shirt, same plaid shirt worn over, a Charley reject as a matter of fact, same short, dark hair, same deep worried eyes, and same . . . no, different . . . smile. She hadn't smiled like this for so long: content, satisfied, happy. She was just purely happy, sitting on this thirties glider with a good, handsome man on a late September day in Kankakee, Illinois.

"I solved another crime, Charley," she said. "Sort of."

"Yes."

"I have two job offers."

"Impressive."

"We're taking Nick back to our house," Nellie said, poking her head out the kitchen door. "He's bored as hell."

Jane gave Nellie the punchboard she had been holding and asked her to give it to Hunter if he was still in the basement. All the saloon keepers would be leaving with a party favor, their customized gambling payoff/bribery history, hand printed and fetchingly presented on a vintage punchboard, courtesy of the late Gus Duncan. Out in the yard, on two wooden Adirondack Chairs, Bobby Duff was sitting with Mary Bateman's granddaughter, Susan. The two orphans had found each other. They were talking intensely, Bobby holding the punchboard that spelled out DUFF, Susan looking like she was hanging on for dear life to the straps of her purse.

Jane knew she owed Susan an apology for accusing her upstairs, for scaring her. She decided to wait a few days. Susan would be in no hurry to speak to Jane, let alone listen to her rehash what she had heard from her grandmother. Jane owed Bobby an explanation, too. Tomorrow. His parents' secrets had been buried for a lot of years; they could wait a few more days.

"Those two could talk forever and never run out of stories," said Jane.

"Or questions," added Charley.

Bruce Oh had accompanied Mary Bateman when she left with Dot and Ollie to give their statements. Jane tried to picture them that night, the three women reminiscing with Gus, talking about bowling tournaments, basketball games. It was after dinner, he was probably half smashed. Mary took his hand, for old time's sake, and stuck him. Loaded him up with him some potassium from the medical supplies she had so carefully stored in her basement. Jane had asked if Mary needed a lawyer.

"Possibly. But as she says, she's eighty years old. She hasn't admitted anything. No murder weapon has been found. There's no record of any of those medical supplies because Mary begged them from Susan for the church. The potassium and syringes were never in Mary's possession because they were allegedly destroyed after they were no longer needed by Susan's patients. They didn't exist," Oh had said.

"They waited for him to crumple, then Mary took a knife off the counter and wrapped Gus's hand around it and sawed at the finger where she'd injected him," Jane said. "Eighty-year-old Mary almost sawed the damn thing off thinking about what he had done to Bateman."

"Revenge can make you strong," Oh said.

"She waited a long time. If she hadn't been worried that there might be something in all that Shangri-La stuff I bought, none of this might have happened. She probably felt safe with everything in the basement, everything all packaged up. Losing control of that and seeing Leonard again after all those years . . ." Jane shook her head.

"If you're worried, Mrs. Wheel, you needn't be. I suspect that, just as she said, Mary will be back playing card games with Leonard at the Grand Heritage in record time," said Oh. He promised to call her when they finished at the police station.

Jane stretched her own legs out and relaxed against Charley's arm.

"I might become a dealer with Tim," Jane said to Charley.

Charley kept his eyes closed and nodded.

"Or a detective with Bruce Oh," she said.

How did Charley manage to raise his eyebrows while keeping his eyes closed, Jane wondered?

"What do you think?"

"I think the rest of your life is full of possibilities," Charley said.

Jane thought that sounded like something she might read in a fortune cookie. *Just the same,* she wondered, *did it make it any less true?* Was there any reason she should make a smart aleck remark to Charley about it and send him reeling to the other side of this vintage glider? Was there any reason to argue about the wonderful possibilities that loomed large? Continuing as a picker for Miriam, becoming a dealer with Tim, or working as a private investigator with Bruce Oh? Or all three? And how about the wonderful immediate possibility—going home with her husband and son?

Never allow perfect to be the enemy of good.

"Me, too, Charley," Jane said.

The Wrong STUFF

A Jane Wheel Mystery

SHARON FIFFER

When a school permission slip gets lost among the towering boxes in antique picker Jane Wheel's kitchen, causing her son Nick to miss a field trip with his friends, Jane vows to get rid of it all and hopes to organize her house and her life in the process. She's entertaining two offers of employment, as an associate at her friend Tim Lowry's antiques dealership and as a consultant at a private investigations firm with former police detective Bruce Oh. Unable to decide between the two, Jane decides to take a crack at splitting her time between the two pursuits. Before she even gets settled in, Jane finds herself smack in the middle of a case that will draw on both of her new jobs. An antiques dealer has been accused of murder. Jane can hardly wait to investigate, that is, until she learns the identity of the accused: it's Claire Oh, wife of her new partner Bruce . . .

"Clever . . . Pack rats and fans of lighter mystery fare should be perfectly satisfied."

—*Publishers Weekly* on *Dead Guy's Stuff*

"Sharon Fiffer's first mystery is a must-have . . . This one's a keeper."

—*Chicago Tribune* on *Killer Stuff*

**AVAILABLE WHEREVER BOOKS ARE SOLD
FROM ST. MARTIN'S PAPERBACKS**